Wing Span

Elizabeth Munro

Blue Swell Books
Nanaimo, B.C.
Canada

First Print Edition: April 2013
ISBN: 978-0-9879724-4-6

www.elizabethmunro.ca

"…kings of the land and the sky we are; proud gryphons."

Stalker stands, the epitome of pride. Naked and muscular, his wings widen and his feet dig in as if he alone restrains the Earth and supports the heavens, keeping the two ever separate.

"But you aren't yet a master of the sky. Your body is still that of a human as is Feather's. You will get on your hands and knees and ask the Earth to shape her ruby.

"Only when the stone has been reshaped may you return home. When Feather forgives your theft she will accept it and in that moment she will have the stamina to fly true distances and I will be proud to call you gryphon."

Talon remains on the riverbed as Stalker turns and within a few strides is airborne; great wings take him away from his son. As Talon gets to his feet he suppresses the urge to call out in spite of his terror which is worse than his sudden loneliness. He's beyond lost in the wilderness the humans call Ontario.

ELIZABETH MUNRO

Prologue

Jenn's motorcycle jacket is a little tight. The zipper comes down, letting her breathe and setting off a round of laughter from Terry.

"Easy on the zipper, Sis."

She scowls and swings her boot nearly as hard as she can, catching Terry's ankle. His boots are sturdy and no harm's done but the message is clear. Comments on her weight are off limits even from her twin brother.

The wind catches his unruly blonde hair; a complete contrast to his sister's tame brown braid. The usual joke that whoever mom was must have had herself a busy night because they can only have different fathers is understood. He's big and loud where she's petite and excruciatingly shy. Jenn has picked him up in the morning from the police station more times than she can count and he drops her off at her steady job as a bank teller before sleeping it off at her Parksville apartment or his. Terry is her best friend, father figure, confidant and conscience all rolled into one.

He's also her only living family.

"Maybe I shoulda bought you a man's jacket."

This time it's an elbow to the ribs. He only wears a t-shirt and grunts from more than just his sister's displeasure. It's only a few hours since he went to bed after a late one.

"If a man's jacket is too good for you then it's too good for me, Terry."

"Touché," he laughs but keeps his arm down in case she decides to strike again. The jacket is the last birthday present he'll ever give her and his suggestion she get one for a man earned him the finger at the motorcycle shop. She'll be damned if she'll ever dress like a man just to get a jacket done up. The sleeves would be too long anyway since the five foot mark on the bank door is at eye level. She's never been flashy so it's plain and black but it's also clear she has all the right curves.

Jenn puts her hands on her hips and purses her lips, daring him to speak.

"You're pretty, Shadow," Nuke interrupts. His eyes rake down her body. The compliment is only tame because her brother is listening. Terry's forbidden him to speak her name so he calls Jenn after her ride, a 750. The handle stuck so long ago that at least half of today's group doesn't know her real name. Everyone calls him Nuke because there's a good chance his engine will do just that before the dozen riders get halfway to Tofino.

Terry punches Nuke's body armoured shoulder harder than necessary and knocks him off the cement barrier he sits on. Nuke's a big mouth on a small body and he doesn't land too hard.

"Fuck you," Nuke spits.

"You're still not my type," Terry lights a cigarette. "But keep asking. You got nothin' to lose."

Jenn shrivels at Nuke's attention, leaning behind her brother and tugging her jacket closed. Nuke thinks it's a game, hitting on her to make her 'pretend' she's not interested but she just feels dirty. Whether she ignores him or not it only escalates when her brother isn't there to shut him down. Terry's fingers are under her chin and he pulls it toward the sun.

Hold your head high, his big eyes smile.

Nuke walks away kicking dirt and holding his tongue. He

knows when his bike dies he'll be riding Jenn's Shadow since none of the guys will give him a double and Jenn will spend the rest of the trip hugging Terry from behind. Terry's boot scrapes his smoke into the gravel and he takes Jenn's hand, tugging her to their rides and signaling to the rest that it's time to go.

"So where's mine?" He reaches for her saddle bag. A week earlier Terry bid on a baseball and he's still steamed about losing in the final minutes to someone else. He doesn't know he lost to his own sister who spent her vacation savings winning it for his birthday.

"You'll get it later!" Jenn pushes his hand away so he hugs her like it's what he meant to do all along.

Port Alberni is nice but it's thirty-five Celsius and she's sweaty in her jacket. A swim in the ocean is the only incentive to get back on the hot highway. Unlike her reckless t-shirt and shorts wearing brother, Jenn prefers to be protected if she takes a spill.

Terry pulls out first. Jenn is close behind and takes some satisfaction in cutting off Nuke. The roar of engines behind them is nearly deafening as they stick together as best they can through the traffic and lights and make their way out of the city.

Everything is drier this side of Vancouver Island. The cool rainforest they passed through before Port Alberni is gone and the road gets twisty. Terry pushes the group faster, speeding up and leaning over as far as they dare in the turns. Another group of riders comes the other way and he gets a hand out to wave then turns to Jenn, grinning from under his beanie. He loves this: speed, heat. Showing off. It's a good day. There's a place by the river they'll go when they get back to Parksville: drinking, camping, and the sounds of sex from the other tents.

Jenn winces at a small explosion and checks her mirrors. Nuke isn't losing any speed but there's a vicious dark grey cloud for the riders behind him. Someone's bitch seat girl mouths him off, her voice lost in the wind.

Jenn sets up for the next turn by moving to the center of

the lane so she's clear of anyone coming wide the other way and gravel near the shoulder but there's a pickup skidding out of control into their lane.

Terry doesn't stand a chance.

His brakes don't light up though his bike wobbles as some part of him starts to react. Jenn has a little more time and manages to lose some speed. Her heart sticks in her throat as her brother makes a Terry sized dent in the truck's front fender. His arms and legs beat the roof and Jenn catches the rear of his bike. He's already out of reach when she tries to grab him and as she tumbles he lands behind the truck.

It stops half in the ditch.

There's no pain so Jenn thinks she's unhurt and when she looks for Terry she sees Nuke. He doesn't even look at her brother and comes to her.

"Jenn, Jenn," he cries. "Shit, Jenn."

"Terry," Jenn moans. *Why don't you help my brother, asshole?*

Nobody helps Terry. There's a lump under her shoulder so she reaches to pull it free but it's a boot and it won't move. Nuke takes her hand and holds it still as he looks at the wreck.

The driver gets out, unhurt. His passenger won't stop screaming.

"Don't look," Nuke says but she has to. Through her deeply scarred visor she sees the big logo on the back of Terry's shirt. The small one in front is out of sight. He faces her: jaw slack and eyes half open. It doesn't make sense that he could have put it on backwards without her noticing.

The air ripples and takes shape above Terry; half again taller than a man and gracefully tapered at the top. The mirage folds in the middle before straightening again and collapsing.

"Thank you," Jenn sighs to the shirtless man approaching her brother. The hot breeze moves his long black hair as he touches Terry's shoulder but only for a moment before he stands. The air around the man changes, thickening and spreading like wings slowly folding and unfolding. The angel's wings darken then disappear as he walks away.

The police arrive before the ambulance and Nuke leaves

Jenn's side only long enough to throw up. The beautiful angel is gone. The knowledge he came for Terry is small comfort as she watches the police cover her brother with a yellow sheet and weigh it down with parts from his bike.

Chapter One

Jenn's motorcycle jacket is a little loose.

Two years of choking grief will do that to a girl. She's been sober for a week to make sure it isn't the booze and pills that make her feel so desperately alone.

It isn't.

Nuke came to see her once in the hospital after they repaired her femur with a gross amount of titanium. It had been broken in two places and bent beneath her in the crash. When he asked if she needed anything she asked for a gun to kill herself.

He didn't come back.

Six months of surgeries and rehab get her back to work. Sleeping pills and alcohol take the memories away, at least for a while.

Insurance paid out Jenn's Shadow and a nice smelling man Terry knew brought her papers to sign until his apartment belongs to her. At first she's surprised her shoot first brother had life insurance but he always shot first when it came to his sister. Dollars don't make up for being alone. They shared a soul and Terry took it with him.

The used 600cc sport bike Jenn rides is the fastest thing she's ever taken down the highway. The last owner put a lot of money into it before he knocked up his girlfriend and had to sell. It's black and orange and covered in flames and sexier than anything Jenn would ever dare show on the outside.

Today it carries her south to a liquor store she frequents; out of town enough that anyone local won't see her stocking up.

Jenn rides free of the last knot of cars and finds a lone semi-trailer truck slowing for the lights at Northwest Bay Road south of Parksville. The speed limit drops to sixty as the highway descends in both directions toward the intersection. It usually fills with cars like a giant bowl but today it's just her and the truck. A gas station covered with a big red roof is on her left but all her attention is on the rig. It gears down noisily on the hill and she has to do the same to avoid nailing it from behind.

The number on the trailer gets Jenn's attention, prompting her not to run the light. It has a T and a K. Terry Klein. And an eight and a two, the age they were when he died. Not eighty-two; they were twenty-eight. The trailer itself is dirty. Even its plates attached high above haven't escaped the brown layer of filth brought up by its wheels.

Jenn glances at the stop line as she pulls up next to the cab, getting the toes of her boots on the pavement. Her mirrors say nobody is set to plow into her from behind as lemony diesel exhaust makes her nose wrinkle. The summer smells great; other vehicles at the red light, not so much.

"Nice bike," comes from up and to the right.

Inside she cringes. Nobody is supposed to talk to her today. It's her day off and she'd planned a quiet drunk; the only regular companionship she has left outside of work. Interaction on the liquor store trip makes Jenn's drinking problem more real than she's prepared for.

The driver should be watching for the green light and thinking about where he's taking the dirty trailer or if he'll need the restroom in Nanaimo or if he can wait for Duncan. Maybe the air conditioning isn't working and he misses the wife and kids; bills and the dog.

Jenn pushes her visor up out of the way and turns, drawing

her eyes up the clean black door and past a pair of painted on gold wings to find a muscular arm bound in a tightly sleeved black t-shirt.

"Nice truck," Jenn echoes. It's one thing to keep her eyes down and her mouth shut out of shyness. It's quite another to be rude and not answer. She hopes the lame reply is enough to end the conversation and presses her lips together, making her eyes wrinkle and giving the illusion she's smiling inside her helmet.

His big ringless left hand closes around on the metal bar holding the mirror. He strokes it, first away then toward the body of the truck. Jenn feels her mouth open, tongue just touching the tips of her front teeth and his bicep flexes, pulling his short sleeve tighter. It slides again over the smooth chrome before closing completely and her heart stutters as her gaze reaches his smile; warm and genuine even though she can't see his eyes through his dark lenses.

"Yeah?" he leans closer. Curly shoulder length dark hair perfectly frames his jaw and Jenn leans in response, her right foot flat on the ground as the motorcycle tilts between her thighs.

As her pulse gets going again Jenn inhales his male scent and her skin prickles under the heavy leather jacket like sweat breaking out only her skin stays dry. It's a little painful and feels so, so good. He smells of straw and sun but underneath there's something raw and dangerous; a far greater lure than the quick buzz and blackout she still half looks forward to. It's the scent of rebellion and she sets her jaw against the challenge. More than anything she's overwhelmed with the urge to crush it.

"Bet it's nice inside," she ventures with a glance at the traffic lights. The cars turning left from Northwest Bay Road don't have an amber yet.

The trucker looks her over and it's not the degrading leer Nuke used to get away with. This guy seems to size her up more as an adversary and less like a piece of meat as he pushes the sunglasses onto his forehead.

Why can't he be imperfect? Jenn wonders. *Or less gorgeous? And what in hell are you doing flirting at a red light? You're a bank teller, idiot. Nice bank tellers don't flirt!*

Eyes so brown she can't make out the pupils bore into hers and she stands a little taller, holding her head high and doing her best to look confident and tough. For a moment his expression is a mix of power and fear, mirroring the adrenaline and shaky nerves dueling inside Jenn then the warm smile returns.

"You want to see," he states and calls out a couple of street names north of Duncan.

"One o'clock."

A horn honks. Jenn startles as she feels her motorcycle roll backwards. She crushes the handbrake with her right and she continues to roll as his rich laughter fills her ears. It's the illusion of reverse caused by his truck pulling ahead for the green. The horn blares again as the motorcycle stalls and Jenn gets her trembling thumb on the starter. If he hadn't stopped her heart already she's sure the horn would have.

Jenn gets her motorcycle going, revving the motor too high as she mistimes the clutch and throttle for the shift to second. She's going well over a hundred before she's out of the sixty kilometer an hour zone, focusing only on getting some distance between herself and whatever the hell she's set up with the handsome stranger.

The next few kilometers are a blur and she pulls into a Nanaimo mall, stationing herself at the far side of the parking lot. The kickstand is barely down when she drops to the grass and rips her helmet off, venting the laughter that's turned her knees to rubber.

Two years ago Terry would have pulled up between her and the truck and given the guy a 'hey buddy.' The only men he approved of came figuratively pre-neutered or he offered to do it for them. It made dating hard but he'd headed off a lot of trouble. In spite of the predictably nice men who passed his inspection, the one relationship lasting more than a couple of months had failed miserably.

Jenn watches the highway until the black truck with the dirty white trailer passes by then looks at the nearby coffee shop. She and Terry used to sit at one of the tables out front for hours at a time. Jenn stuffs her helmet over one of the mirrors and buys a coffee before taking a seat at their table. Terry's seat is empty so she closes her eyes and imagines him there.

She senses his hand on her back, nudging her forward, rather than the more familiar protective brother vibe.

The coffee smells good so she wraps her hands around the paper cup and blows on the surface.

"I don't know," she whispers as she puts the cup down. "He's not like anyone you've ever wanted around me."

The breeze cools her skin and she realizes she's crying. Maybe it's simply the movement of tears running past her cheeks but she imagines her brother's fingers under her chin.

Hold your head high.

Chapter Two

Mark Williams watches the unusual female pull away. Between gear changes he puts the window up halfway and pushes his hair behind his ears. It's early enough the morning sun shines straight in, glaring off the dash and warming his skin.

He doesn't doubt she's interested in him. Her nervousness is obvious and he suspects her age is partly to blame.

Yeah, but you're still a kid, he laughs at himself. *Not even a hundred.*

The fact that she's on her own could also explain her caution. Females rarely travel alone away from their eyrie and though she returned his advances he suspects she's in a hurry to catch up to her father or brother; the only males who should be with her.

A nervous glance at the empty sky reassures Mark that a rough encounter with them isn't in his very near future at least. With his training he's sure he could beat them both to pieces but honour requires he take his licks if they don't like him. As he pushes the heavily laden rig through another gear he realizes she's been away from her eyrie for a while if she's learned to ride a motorcycle.

She could be a true rogue, abandoning eyrie life for the

human world like he had years before. Many find satisfaction in service to the Sire and Dame, the hereditary royalty, but not Mark. As Talon, the gryphon male in his spirit, he trained for decades to be ranger. A proud place in the elite royal guard was the only service he felt worthy of him but seeing bigger less talented males selected time and time again put him off.

Instead he indulged in a female who appreciated him and his fighter spirit. She was a larger western gryphon, nearly his height, but she was flighty and prone to wandering for months at a time with his own sister. They had all come to prefer the wind under their wings to the stone Jasper cavern they called home.

Talon managed to abandon courtship as well by never offering Swift his bite though there seemed no shortage to the tears she would offer, shedding them his way every time things seemed serious. Swift accused him of having commitment issues but in his heart he needed someone who saw him as more than an intimidating male to show off to her friends or escort her through some human shopping mall while she picked out something shiny.

But this little female is different. A demanding vulnerability in her scent commands him to win her; a line he'd never even wanted to cross with another. Her size could be driving him to be protective. Gryphons from this side of the continent are decidedly larger than those further east where he was reared but she's truly tiny, her scent so exotic he can't begin to guess where she's from.

He never thought he'd find vulnerability sexy but in *his* little female it's searing hot. Maybe he'll find her motorcycle ahead, her scent and clothing leading him through the forest as he undresses and takes wing, becoming Talon and knowing she's high above stalking him already. Their magic would hide them from human eyes as he finds a clearing and enough space to spread his wings and take off.

Talon's strength and size would overpower her and he'd revel in her submission before letting her go, anticipating his own terror as her speed and agility let her get her claws to his exposed throat...

He hasn't hunted like that with a female in years. The chance she'll show up is slim. The chance she'll stay interested long enough to hunt is even slimmer. In spite of the weak prospects, he's excited with the possibility.

You're in way over your head with this one, Talon, his human voice warns the unfamiliar gryphon need for a mate. *One shot. You screw this up you won't get another chance with her.*

As he enters Nanaimo her scent grows strong and he leans toward the window, inhaling deeply. Mark groans with need, sweeter than when they first spoke. Light brown eyes, he recalls, and her long hair tied back. As he remembers the shape of her ass straddling the seat her scent disappears and he casts his eyes wildly about for any hint of her.

"Damn it," he mutters, nearly tearing the wheel free in frustration.

It's past one-thirty when Mark finally reaches the short strip mall and gas station. Even though he has half a mind to press on to Victoria to wait for his next load he's still hopeful she's waiting for him.

That's just your arrogant gryphon pride talking, Talon, he grumbles, though his human half hasn't given up either. *If she's here it's all about her and how she wants it and you know it.*

As he pulls in he catches the smallest hint of her on the air. If she was here she's probably gone but her scent gets stronger as he reaches the end near the pumps. Just past them he spots the front end of her motorcycle on the other side of an SUV. His pulse shoots up as he looks skyward hoping for a glimpse.

Instead she's curled up on the grass behind her motorcycle. The helmet is perched on the handlebars and her jacket is balled up under her head.

She's even more exquisite with the gear off.

A small strip of ivory skin fills the gap between the rise of her denim covered hip and the hem of her white tank top. As he kills the engine his eyes partially shift, improving his vision. He picks out a slim line of blue over her shoulder where the top slid toward her neck. Then there's the thick brown hair piled loose behind her.

Mark checks the contents of the grocery bag at his feet: condoms, jerky and canned fish. The bottled water is already in the small fridge behind the passenger seat.

It's clear she wants a human encounter and he's glad he thought to run to the pharmacy for the condoms. He'll be surprised if she's not likewise prepared but he's expected to show courtesy and bring some too.

The conception of a child in human form would be catastrophic for both of them. If by some miracle she survived and carried it to term the child would be human and abandoned. It would be a devastating loss for its dame though these days it was the human adoption system that took responsibility. A century ago its sire would fly as far from the eyrie as he could, leaving the child to the elements and scavengers.

He pops the door, steps down the first rungs and jumps the last, his worn cowboy boots striking the pavement at the same time.

Easy, he warns himself. Females are sensitive to moods even in their human form and if he charges in ready for sex she's sure to change her mind. One step at a time and let her lead is the only advice he ever received from older males and he prays it's worth the hundreds of rounds he's bought over the years to get it.

She sits and her sudden inhalation tells Mark he's startled her but she doesn't turn his way just yet. Come to think of it, all those older males were unmated. Damn, it was the only advice he had.

"Hey," she calls; the tiniest tremor in her voice.

"Hey yourself," he steps onto the grass only a half dozen paces away. The young woman modestly tugs her top before she turns to face him.

"Sorry I'm late," Mark tries to take her all in without clawing her up with his eyes. She's perfectly proportioned, breasts slightly high and arms toned and a face he'd never tire of looking at. In spite of his efforts not to stare he catches her looking him over and tries not to smile as her cheeks turn pink.

Mark knows what he looks like: six foot two and nearly all muscle. He takes a seat behind her in the hopes of looking less intimidating. There's grass in her hair and he starts taking the little bits out one at a time. Her gentle musk is intoxicating as it mingles with the smell of summer from her hair. After a minute Mark trails his fingers down her back and she cautiously reaches behind to slide a hand under his knee. As he leans forward to taste her skin she moves her head to the side. It isn't the symbolic submission of exposing her neck he expects but it's enough to invite him in.

"Shadow?" a man calls from the parking lot. Mark is too focused on his dark haired beauty and curses himself for not keeping an eye out for competition; both gryphon and human. "Damn, Shadow. I thought it was you."

Shadow looks up. Her hand grips Mark's leg and tugs him closer. She's uncomfortable as hell with the little man and pulls her knees together, arching into Mark. He reaches around, putting his hand over her womb in a display of possession usually reserved for mated pairs but Mark is dead set on making his claim public even though the interloper is human.

"Hi, Nuke," she says. Nuke waves with two fingertips as he palms his pop. His other hand is jammed down the side of his female companion's shorts. Mark stifles a snort. Nuke's woman is six inches taller and a hundred and eighty degrees prettier. Judging by the big diamond on her left hand the reason for her attraction to him is clear. It doesn't keep Nuke's eyes from wandering.

"You keeping busy?" Shadow asks.

Nuke shrugs and Shadow crosses her arms as Nuke's eyes drop and linger. He appears to hear Mark's low warning growl and remembers his manners.

"My uncle got me a good logging gig up island," Nuke

says. "This is Bunny. We got ourselves set up with a nice apartment."

Nuke makes eye contact with Mark expecting an introduction.

"Talon," Mark says before Shadow is caught not knowing his name. He can't decide which one of them is the predator. Nuke thinks he is, judging by how he looks at Shadow but Bunny with the prey name has her attention on a nearby Lexus that smells of the two of them.

Prey indeed.

Shadow drops her eyes with what Mark first takes to be submission to the little shit then he scents deep pain in her, somehow associated with the man. He must be meant for Shadow if simply being near attunes him to her moods. He was always fucking things up with Swift when he guessed wrong but he's already clear about Shadow. The old rogues never mentioned that and it explains why they were drinking alone at Cooper's, the Calgary rogue favoured bar. A small layer of golden brown feathers bristles beneath his shirt and he quickly squashes the idea of squashing Nuke, letting them fade. Taking wing with his shirt on is something a child would do.

"Well... ah," Nuke says with a sideways look at Bunny. She appears bored; rolling her eyes under thick fake lashes. "Good to see you doing better—"

"Yeah, bye Nuke," Shadow cuts him off.

Mark wonders, better than what? She's far more distraught inside than she lets on and he rubs her shoulder with his free hand. Shadow deflates as Nuke and Bunny walk away.

"Hi, Talon," she says as the mismatched human pair drives off.

"Hello, Shadow," he answers. He knows her gryphon name: subtle and secretive. Calming. It's an appropriate name for this female who appeared out of nowhere and into his life.

His female. Talon is going to make sure of it. No man like Nuke is ever going to upset her again. He's surprised with himself. He'd always thought taking a mate was about genes and temperament. A male wanted a healthy mate to be a compassionate and patient dame to his children but right now children are the last thing on his mind.

All he wants is compassion for Shadow; not to posses but to be proud that she chose him.

As she straightens up he takes his hand from her stomach.

"There's no, um, story to Nuke," Shadow says like she knows the idea of the two of them together makes Talon's skin crawl. "Nothing."

When she turns to him she tucks her feet in and holds her head high before flashing him a brilliant smile. Damn, she takes his breath away. The top is cut low and the sight of her skin and exposed neck makes him want her even more. Whatever the story is with Nuke it's not sexual.

Then her hands are on his legs and she's only a dozen inches away, studying him like he's a puzzle. Below her furrowed brows her eyes watch as she feels the muscle in his arms. Shadow's delicate and persistent touch works its way up over his shoulder.

"You're big," she winces. "Sorry, that sounded stupid."

But he doesn't let her pull away. He takes her wrist and puts her hand right back where it was.

"Where I call home, I'm not considered all that big."

"I find that hard to believe."

Talon turns his head to the side, blocking access to his neck. As bad as he wants her, he's not going there just yet. When he turns she's even closer and he lets her touch his cheek as her mouth opens. The mere wisp of her lips over his is torment and he tears up a handful of grass she can't see.

Before he can come up with any plan to figure out how he's blown it, her lips seal over his and he gives in as her fingers slide over his carotid. The vibration of her nails on his half-days stubble rams straight into his groin.

I'm yours, Talon surrenders as her tongue tries his lips and he opens to meet her hot prying challenge with his own.

Shadow straddles his thighs and he takes her hips but her hand tightens on his throat as she takes control, remaining in the dominant position above. Talon stops pulling and instead slips a hand under her snug tank, palm over her flat bare stomach, to show the distance between them is his choice, not hers.

She seals the kiss around his tongue and yelps at the sound of metal crashing to the pavement. In what seems like an eternity he's pinned her protectively to the grass, already certain it was an aluminum boat falling off a camper and not her sire come to kick his ass.

"Talon!"

Shadow's hands fist his shirt and she has to be aware of his erection and every other part of his body holding her down. Her pounding heart and wide eyes say she was completely in to him when the boat fell.

Then she laughs as Talon lets his head fall to hers, close to the warmth of fading fright on her cheeks.

"I planned that," he jokes. "To get you in my arms."

"You didn't have to," Shadow says.

Chapter Three

Shadow looks up at the driver's seat high above. After Talon hinted at the forest she reminded him he promised a look in the truck. So be it. Other than the old guys never having felt a female's moods following her lead seems to be working.

"Climb up," he urges and she grabs the handle inside the door. Talon takes advantage of the moment to watch the shape of her ass. She favours her left leg but has no trouble getting into his seat. She sticks her feet out, coming far short of reaching the pedals as she runs her hands over the big wheel.

"I can't see a thing," she cranes her neck up.

"Watch your toes." Talon shuts the door and lets himself in the passenger side. She's already found the handle to release the driver's seat and swung it around to face the sleeper cab.

"You live in here?"

"On longer trips."

He's only on the seat for a moment before dropping to his knees and mirroring her approach to him. With his hands on her knees he watches her reaction. Her body language says she's committed in contrast to her scent which betrays caution. Damned if she hasn't changed both every couple of minutes. No wonder females are such a mystery. They're impossible to figure out. Just when you think...

But his train of thought is interrupted as she moves to the edge of the seat and slides her knees around him. This time her arms come over his shoulders as he claims her mouth, letting out a soft rumble from deep inside. The breeze can no longer carry her scent away and Talon can't resist. As her head falls back he slides one hand up over her breast, noting the feel of her heavy lace bra through the thin knit of her shirt. He finally has access to her exposed throat, dragging his teeth over it as he accepts her display of surrender.

"Come," Talon says, startled by the thickness of his voice. She stands but as he backs up to the bed she stops, feet rooted to the floor. She's afraid. It's fight or flight for his little gryphon. She's going to bolt but first she'll say something; a little gem of advice to explain how things went so horribly wrong.

"Everything about you feels like danger," Shadow eyes the door.

That's what I am.

"Look," he keeps his hands at his sides to look as non-threatening as possible. "If this isn't what you want, if you don't feel comfortable with me, it's okay. I understand."

"That's not it," she says.

Talon's eyes snap up and he realizes he's been looking at the floor pretending she's already gone so his disappointment isn't so painful.

"I just…" she sighs. Her brow furrows like when she felt foolish for calling him big. "Promise you'll get between me and anything that comes in the door."

Jesus.

He's completely misread her. Even scenting her feelings he has no shortage of ways to mess things up. He won't let it happen again, deciding to act on his own instincts and stop worrying about what she means.

"*Arlette*," he whispers. *Baby eagle.* "I promise."

This time she accepts when he pulls her further into the sleeper.

Her body carries traces of the rich leather she wore and

the heavy leather belt holding up her jeans keeps its cloy close to her skin. She watches; her hair falls past her flawless shoulders as he opens the buckle then pushes her shirt up enough to feel the warmth of her skin. If he could sink into her now he would but he wants to unwrap her and make sure he doesn't miss a thing. Instinct says take your time, Talon.

He grabs the waist of her jeans and reaches up her pant leg for the zipper on her boot. It seems to go up forever, nearly to her knee and he wishes he could get the pants off and keep the boots on. Shadow complies, lifting one foot then the other as he puts the boots and socks aside.

Then she turns her back to him.

On the wing it would trigger his hunt response and as a human it does something similar. Aggression drives him closer than ever to taking her. He slides forward, her calf between his thighs and as she pivots it grinds into his hardening cock. Then she turns the other way, rubbing it again. Bad girl, when the time comes she's going to get it.

Talon pops the button on her jeans before sliding the zipper down then he tugs exposing more of the blue he saw when he first pulled up.

"My Shadow," he sighs and presses his lips to the small of her back. The pants come down and she steps out. As his hand runs down her thigh she moans at his touch. The panties are the same heavy lace he felt on her bra, cut high and exposing so much skin he may not need to take them off.

"God Damn, Shadow," he breathes. "Damn hot."

"Just a small town bank teller with a two hundred dollar underwear habit."

Her hips move in time with his caress, over the rounds of her ass and slipping beneath the blue lace.

"I'm just a prairie trucker and I've never seen two hundred dollar underwear," he admits. Never thought he'd dig a human encounter with a gryphon so much he believes he'd miss out if they'd taken wing together.

But her response to his touch is undeniable and keeping her back to him is such a brazen tease. Talon reaches between his legs and adjusts his cock, letting his hand linger in time with her. It's more than he can stand. If he waits too long it's just going to be sex and too late to offer his bite. The exchange has to be done before they both finish. Then she'll make her offer of tears and he'll decide if he'll change both their lives forever and accept them.

His teeth ache as they shift to unnaturally sharp points and he pulls one side of the lace down. With a quick prayer, he bites. His saliva enters the cut, burning her, as the ritual of exchange begins.

Shadow's response is instant. She yells as her body tenses and he laves the wound, soothing it with his tongue as her fist comes down toward him.

"Fuck!" Jenn yells, nearly drowning in the useless thoughts bubbling up and hitting her all at once. It isn't just surprise that paralyzes her. Why didn't she ignore him at the light? Why did she even show up? And why the hell didn't she get back on her motorcycle and ride off when he gave her an out?

He's twice her size and she's not getting away without disabling him but she's too panicked to remember anything her brother taught her about putting a man down with pain.

As she takes a swing at him she goes weak with the sudden rush of heat deep in her belly. Talon's tongue caresses the bite as sweetly as if it were between her legs.

At first she's intent on clawing out an eye but by the time her fist is on him she's clinging to his hair and holding him fast to the wound.

"Oh, man," she moans as her sex tightens with Talon's mouth on her hip. Jenn's not even sure if he really bit her or if he's just found some pleasure zone she never knew she had but it sure as hell is the best thing she's ever felt.

"Talon," she gasps as he takes the inside of her thigh in one hand, his other arm around her waist keeping her on her feet. She's helpless, rocking with his mouth, seeking more and more friction with his tongue.

Talon's knee moves, forcing her legs further apart as he takes the string back of her panties and runs a finger down beneath it. His warm fingers pull the blue elastic free of her folds then he cautiously seeks through the slick heat between her legs.

Jenn shudders as his finger enters her, gently swirling around her entrance before pushing deeper. He adds a second and Jenn squeezes with pleasure, hoping to hold him there.

Jenn sets the rhythm, easing her rough hold on his hair once she's sure he has it just right. Even with her legs braced against his she'd topple over if he didn't have an arm around her. Her orgasm already close, Jenn opens her eyes and stares out at the wall of trees in front of the rig, hoping to enjoy this a little longer. A black shirt, she remembers. He's wearing a black shirt. Her stranger is about to get her off and she doesn't even remember what colour his damn jeans are.

"Talon, I'm…" she warns, deciding she wants it with him covering her up completely like when the boat fell; sweet pressure all over and the heavy erection she felt driving her past the point of no return. Talon's tongue runs over the swollen ridges marking where each tooth broke her skin.

"I know," he pauses to speak.

So cocky, Jenn thinks as her whole stomach tightens and her toes curl up on the industrial carpet in appreciation of his boldness. *On my own too long. I need this, just for now. Terry and grief and drunken Jenn can damn well wait outside. In here it's Shadow and Talon looking after her.*

"But," she protests.

"You will."

Shadow obliges, letting her head fall back so she can feel the tips of her long hair tickle her ass and create the spark she needs. It only takes her a second to ignite for him. Grabbing hold of his arm she cries out as the first waves of climax shatter through her limbs before crashing down deep inside her belly and everywhere Talon touches her.

He softens his pace, pushing her along until she's nearly spent. Her knees finally go and she falls in his arms.

"Beautiful," he whispers as he places her on the narrow bed. "I could watch you do that all day long."

She unfolds as a final shudder passes. Talon centers himself over her, knees between hers, and seizes one breast in his hand. She shivers as his thumb and finger come together, gently squeezing her already swollen nipple through her clothes.

Talon digs his knees into the mattress and gets his hand between them to open his belt. When Shadow looks down she can see the heavy square buckle. Jagged mountain peaks stand out in relief on its shiny gold surface. She gets her hands between them to help, tugging the t-shirt up and free.

Shadow doesn't hesitate. As he leans over the side of the bed and rustles about she pushes his jeans down past his hips and takes hold. Shy Jenn would wait but in here she's Shadow and Shadow doesn't wait.

"Not all that big my ass," Shadow breathes. Talon's laugh is cut off by a low moan. She pulls; both hands moving together as he tears off a condom. Her grip tightens as she pushes his chin out of the way to nibble at his neck. Then he kneels, watching her and absently stroking himself with his left like he had the mirror. His eyes do the real dirty work.

"Off," he says as his other hand squeezes the wrapped condom.

"What?" She still has three things on.

"Shirt," he swallows. "Off."

But he hasn't removed a single stitch or even his boots and his buckle is cold against the inside of her thigh. He's had his way with Shadow and now it's her turn. Her Talon is confident to a fault and she has the feeling he doesn't want to be with a pushover in the sack.

She's right.

"Do it," he says, his voice sinking deeper. Shadow looks up bravely like at the traffic light and clamps her thighs around his for support. She crosses her arms and slowly pulls the top up, wriggling from side to side as she exposes her stomach then the lacy blue bra. He's forgotten about her defiant stare when it clears her head sending her long hair everywhere.

"Bra."

Jesus, he loves this. Shadow is too though there is no denying it's a slow torture. Like a voyeur to her own liaison she watches him get more and more keyed up the longer it takes.

She hesitates just a little too long and he *growls* like a big cat so she tightens her legs around him hard and quick to get his attention before pulling one strap off her shoulder. Two hundred dollars gets pretty, not sturdy, and Shadow is grateful she doesn't hear threads pop as she works her arm clear.

Talon drops the condom on her stomach and reaches. Her breast is still hidden in the cup.

"Stop," she orders, putting a hand up to block him before taking it out.

Half a nipple, that's all I'm giving, she thinks. Now it's time to see what he'll take.

Shadow drops to her elbows to ease the ache in her stomach as she watches him lick his generous lips and slip a finger inside the cup. Talon drags it along between her skin and the lace without exposing any more.

"Other side, just like that," he says but the need in his voice is nearly more than she can take. Sex for her used to be lots of stimulation and a mercy orgasm to end it. This gets better the *less* he touches her and she's sure when he finally does it will be explosive.

Shadow frees her other breast just like the first and as soon as she's half uncovered Talon pushes his knees apart. He takes both her hands in one of his and holds them loosely in the small space between her head and the cab wall. His other is busy with the condom and his tongue slips into the cup teasing her eager nipple free of the lace.

Then a hand under her ass drags her into the center of the bed as he plants his elbow by her ear. His knuckles then the head of his cock sweeps over her from end to end as her knees come up, urging him in. When he does she wraps an arm around his bicep and quiets an embarrassing squeal in the soft knit of his T.

Talon keeps his fist at her entry as if to hold himself back from taking too much too quickly. The pressure startles her at first but she wants to feel the whole thing at once and bucks up underneath demanding it.

"Easy," he whispers, clearly enjoying her impatience. He draws away before claiming more making Shadow squeak again and he rumbles in reply. Desperately, she wants to taste his skin, to find out how salty he'll get, to see how it changes but the damn shirt is in the way so she pushes the sleeve up over his shoulder and scrapes her teeth over his muscle before licking at the scratch.

"Yes… more," he whispers as he gets the traitorous hand out of the way and sinks in all the way finally giving her what she wants. And damned if a single slow thrust later she's apologizing.

"This is going to be so, so quick," she gasps around his arm as the bite on her low back heats with friction against the rough blanket but he doesn't answer, instead he presses her head to his arm. Shadow is ruled by the erotic connection between his cock, his bite and her mouth and feels an ache in her teeth to complete the circle with a mark of her own.

Talon's shout is deafening as she grabs a mouthful of his shoulder before releasing both her bite and her second orgasm. She feels it in her tongue as she laps at his wound and in every pulse deep inside. Talon hooks his elbow under her knee, spreading her wider, and she sucks at his arm as her mark swells. Only moments later he comes on the tail end of her orgasm, grunting loudly in her ear with each solid thrust.

Then he clamps the base of the condom as he indulges her in one final push, using all his weight to hold her down. Shadow lets her lungs empty. She's completely exhausted and when he moves to her side she can barely breathe.

"Oh, I'm sorry," she bursts out with her first breath. He's bled down to the elbow and when she touches her chin her fingers come away red.

"That's not me," he explains, his voice filled with tenderness for her. "Here."

He dabs a wet-wipe along her chin and all the way to her ear before grabbing another for his arm.

"It's okay," he rolls her to the side and cleans her hip with a third.

"No, I bit my tongue," she feels a slice in the edge of it. The condom is gone and his pants are back up so she frowns though his apparent modesty is endearing. Shadow covers her mouth with both hands as she yawns and Talon chuckles. A handful of plastic wrapped jerky appears before her and she yawns again before making a face. He doesn't seem to notice as he tears one open and half of it disappears.

"Um, no thanks."

He stops chewing. If she was standing she'd collapse. At first she thought it was her orgasms making her tingly but it's plain old fashioned fatigue.

Then he pulls out a can and offers it to her. Fish by the looks of it and he seems pleased to have a back-up snack to offer, weird as it is. Shadow shakes her head.

"Sex doesn't make you want meat?"

"No."

Yawn. If she wasn't half asleep his assumption would border on bizarre.

"Even really good sex?"

"Even the best. I'm a vegetarian," she explains and grabs his elbow in alarm as he coughs like he's choking.

"Seriously?"

"Uh huh," she mumbles, losing the ability to speak.

"You have to go anywhere?"

Shadow thinks about drunken Jenn waiting by the motorcycle to buy a bottle of vodka. How long was it? It couldn't have been any more than half an hour. Half an hour of intense reconnection with another human being and every destination she had ahead of her has disappeared. A new direction waits to greet her at Terry's apartment. It's too much to step from her black hole of despair and she's grateful for her savior.

"Nowhere."

"Then stay here, *Arlette*," he whispers. "You're not riding off like this."

Shadow doesn't know what an 'Arlette' is but the soft accent he slips into when he says it is intriguing. When she gets home she'll look it up to see where his parents are from, guessing it's what his father called his mother. He says it like a man would say 'lover.'

"I don't have to be anywhere until eight tonight," he reaches around behind her and unhooks the bra. She stays sitting but only because he holds her.

"Who hurt you," Talon asks and Shadow opens her eyes to see he's looking at her damaged leg. She doesn't want him feeling sorry for her or asking too many questions.

"Please tell me," he tries again. She can't feel his fingers run down the long dead scar left when they opened her leg up to bolt the bone back together.

"I took a tumble on my bike," she admits, leaving out everything she'd left outside; everything he promised to protect her from and had.

"I got back on," she finishes as proudly as she can and for a moment she sees her pain echoed in his eyes.

"You're stronger now because of it," he insists. "It doesn't always feel that way. But you're stronger."

He believes it.

"Stronger," he whispers again.

"Yes," Shadow agrees, feeling strength blossom inside.

She sniffs then pulls her lips tight across her teeth as she sobs, crying for the second time today. Talon lifts her, kicking the blankets clear and lowers her to the pillow as he watches her eyes wet. His fingers hold her cheeks as he kisses her eyes; kissing her tears away with his lips, his tongue. Talon takes every last one as she gives in to the deepest exhaustion.

Chapter Four

Talon watches his mate sleep.

His little rogue hasn't moved in hours since she has no choice but to sleep it off. Food would have restored the energy mating took but she seemed content in his arms as he accepted her offering of tears.

Shadow's deep slumber is a good thing. What started as a flash headache that blinded him with pain every few minutes spread over the next two hours until he spent half of every two minutes in agony. She breathed softly at his side, peacefully riding it out, as he bucked and moaned. Within another hour the sensation lessened, feeling more like breaking bones than crushing, until he only feels it every five minutes and more like the end of a day of combat training in Master Sky's gym.

He feels good during the breaks in the pain. Sated and relaxed, he checks her face for stray hair and even though he doesn't see any he goes through the motions of pushing them away. There's time to think between episodes albeit briefly.

It's not the exchange of saliva which has him twisted in knots or she'd feel it too. The only other thing they shared were her tears but then why doesn't she hurt?

Her tears are already inside her, smart guy.

Yeah, that would be it.

Talon stretches through the next round of aching and

sighs. It feels good now, no arguing that. She stirs at his side and he watches eagerly for her to wake. He'd hoped to talk: to find out where she lived, when he can see her again, when she expected to be in season but there's been nothing except pain and sleep. When her season comes she'll track him down anyway. If she made an eyrie her home he'd pay her a visit but she's a rogue with a job and a very human life like he has. Setting up house would be a screwy thing to do right away. They don't know each other at all though there is time to become close; centuries in fact.

A patch of tiny white feathers grows like a flush between her breasts. Talon's breath catches as it spreads south, narrowing to a fine line before becoming coarse white hairs just below her navel and mixing with the short brown tuft peeking out from under the tiny piece of blue lace. They fade to tiny red bumps on her skin and are gone in seconds.

White? Every gryphon he's ever seen is some flavour of brown.

Her small hand strokes his cheek and he looks into her pale brown eyes. She's caught him looking so he rewards her with a soft kiss.

"Thirsty," she whispers. Her throat sounds dry and for good reason. Even though he spent a few minutes turning his rig around to keep the sun out and the windows are open it's warm. He could have run the engine and the air conditioning but the heat inside eased his own aching so he didn't. She doesn't seem to mind waking up uncovered.

"Got it," he clambers over her to the fridge and cracks open a bottle. She drinks greedily and it spills from the corners of her mouth and down her chin making her shiver. He has another ready when the first is finished.

"Better?"

Shadow nods as she returns the second empty to him.

"Thank you," she tells him. "Not just for the water."

Her head is high. She sits cross-legged on his bed wearing nothing but the little blue panties she never took off. He feels her pride. The pain she felt earlier has ebbed.

"Ouch," she reaches around to feel his mark like she's surprised it's there. Then she pushes up his sleeve to see hers. It's red and swollen. Over the next few weeks it will heal to an unobtrusive rough circle of white scars. The lasting marks from the ritual of exchange will only swell and become sensitive again when they're on the wing. For now, the bites are the only human sign they're mated.

Shadow puts her fingers under his chin and this time he doesn't move to stop her. She's claimed him and it's her right to praise him whenever she damn well feels. Talon stays still as a weak echo of the ache in his bones passes. As she pushes his chin higher her lips find a place on his throat and his pride is nearly overwhelming; pride in her and in himself. Them.

"I don't have the words to explain what today has done for me," she whispers as she nips her way higher. Then with the most devious look in her eye she moves to her mark and licks.

Talon groans, damn near instantly hard again. His little female, naked before him *demanding* another round.

What's a gryphon to do when she asks so nicely? Talon shoves her to the mattress, burying himself in her delighted laughter.

Terry's sofa used to be comfortable or at least Jenn thinks it's the real reason she spends every night on it. It's more comfortable in fact than his ten thousand dollar king sized bed which sits as he left it two years before. For the past hour she's tossed and turned, watching the reflection of the setting sun in the dark screen of his big TV.

After their hurried parting Jenn rode north. She wanted to linger but Talon had just enough time to check his rig over and pick up a load in Victoria before catching the last ferry to the mainland. No exchange of phone numbers or real names. Jenn still feels too messed inside to take a chance on any more than what she and Talon shared through the afternoon. Now she's jacked up with restless energy from their second encounter, a total opposite to the exhausted sleep following the first one.

"Damn," she mutters as she tosses the light blanket aside. "No more putting it off, Jenn."

There's no answer from the empty room.

The small kitchen on her right is opposite the cabinet that holds Terry's treasures. Front and center is the 1951 World Series baseball signed by DiMaggio himself. She never got a chance to give it to Terry and it survived the wreck quite intact. She knows the story behind every piece on display.

The one bedroom apartment was her haven before he died and she spent more time there than her own cramped quarters; the place she felt his protective presence even when she was there alone. She'd given up on that feeling ever coming back and its absence tonight is no different.

It's hers and he's gone.

The dryer goes silent so she opens the accordion door in the hall and gets folding but quickly closes it, determined not to let excuses keep her from moving forward. Talon's emotional gift got her started but he's not with her and the next step is hers alone.

The vacuum marks stop just past the bathroom door. Terry's footprints leading to his bedroom are the only thing which has disturbed the thick pile. She feels strange approaching his room wearing nothing but a t-shirt and panties. Out of habit she makes a quick courtesy knock on his door like she used to, warning him to cover up because she's coming in. There's no grunted greeting so she opens the door all the way.

The light switch is up but the room is dark. He'd left it on and it took nearly six months for the eco bulb to finally burn out. The emotional impact of losing Terry's light was nearly her last day on Earth. The tailspin it put her in found her on the floor two days later covered in vomit and half digested pills. She has no recollection of the light going out, but its absence as she recovered alone from her overdose was the only thing which would have pushed her so far.

Jenn walks around the foot of the bed and past the window to turn on his lamp. No surprises in here. The bed is as she remembered from the last morning. His crookedly capped deodorant is tossed in the center with half a dozen others. Terry was somewhat obsessed with how he smelled and Jenn laughs, remembering his care in his appearance didn't extend to regular brushings of his wild blonde hair. The accidental dredlocks were nearly comical and she'd corner him in front of the TV with a hockey game like a little kid and his cartoons to brush them out.

The memories don't hurt as much as she expects though they are far from painless.

Other things mixed up in the mess of blankets are the books he was reading, a dead iPad he used instead of a computer, a couple of girly magazines and an old shirt Jenn outgrew when they were twelve. The floor is clear and the clothes in his dresser are neat but what she joked was his 'nest' is as messy as his hair.

Even in the lamplight she can make out the layer of dust on everything so she opens the window wide to the outside before she disturbs it. It doesn't take long to pick up the things that don't belong on the bed and strip it. His full laundry basket and bedding are piled in the hall since it's too late to run the washer without bothering the neighbours.

It's well past midnight when everything is dusted and the bed is made with the stale spare sheets from the bathroom cupboard.

Jenn Klein falls asleep like a queen in the big bed that's now hers. She can allow herself that at least.

Chapter Five

Jenn's trucker probably isn't real.

In her fantasies they make love, usually in his truck but sometimes in the apartment she still thinks of as Terry's.

In her dreams they fuck. There's no polite soft euphemism to describe the chase and struggle for dominance and submission. If by some miracle she sleeps through them pounding against each other in hot sand or up against frozen rock then they lie together under the bright sun or icy stars. It's a complete contrast to the two-way hunt and bloodlust leading up to their powerful moment of connection.

The deep wound left by Terry's passing heals a little more.

Parksville winter has set in and the small town is overwhelmed by wind and rain. The lights flicker in the bank lobby as Jenn waits for the machine to spit out a little cash. She crosses her fingers, hoping it stays on long enough to get home and cook.

"Oh dear God, I wish I was forty years younger," Delilah gasps. Delilah claims her ancestors founded Parksville and she runs the bank including the young MBA recently installed as manager.

The rest of the ladies laugh with her. They finished cashing out early and huddle together inside waiting for their rides or a brief enough break in the downpour to run for their cars. The thick mat under Jenn's feet squishes with the day's rainwater as she shifts her weight toward the ATM.

"If you were forty years younger, Delilah, you still wouldn't do any more than gawk at him out the window."

The machine grumbles to life as the gears chew out a small pile of twenties.

"But his coat isn't even on!" Delilah protests, her voice rising to a squeak. "Look at the size of those arms! And do you think he'd keep the boots on or take them off?"

Another wave of laughter fills the small tiled room as the door opens, letting in a cold wet blast of air to try and stifle their levity. Jenn absently raises a hand to wave at whoever left as she gets her wallet just so in the bottom of her purse.

"On, definitely on…"

"With the hat…"

"Mm…"

Jenn's eyes are on the dark cloudy sky as she reaches around Delilah and pulls their shoulders together, lightly rubbing the older woman's arm.

"Have a nice night girls," she murmurs, gripping the broad door handle. The rain blows sideways so she grabs an elastic from her pocket and tips her head forward to put her hair up. It'll be easier to let it dry later than replace her umbrella.

Wet drops cling to her ankles as she steps out. There's no avoiding the rain for the three block walk home. Jenn gets ready to jump over the deep channel of water running along the sidewalk but stops when she sees cowboy boots. A gold plated belt buckle she remembers crowns the man's thick thighs and low jeans. His thumb is hooked into his pocket, fingers resting near the zipper tempt her not to look any higher.

"Talon," Jenn breathes as she stumbles to a stop. Delilah oofs as she bumps into Jenn, nearly knocking her from the curb.

The rain soaked front of his grey t-shirt clings so the muscles running down his abs are easily seen. Talon raises a hand to tip his worn cowboy hat and nods. There's a quiet scuffle behind Jenn as the lobby empties around her.

It only takes one more bump from behind and Jenn jumps over the stream to get to him. She's quickly drenched and Talon gently brushes the rain from her eyes.

"Jenn has a man?"

"She doesn't…"

"She'd have said something…"

The speculation behind her continues as Talon's cold fingers tug her chin higher and his lips come close, kissing one corner of her mouth then the other.

"I started to think I imagined you," she whispers, reaching her arms high around his shoulders.

"No, *Arlette*."

"Your baby eagle," Jenn answers.

"My *Arlette*," he corrects and she giggles, pressing her face into his chest.

"Jenn?"

It's Delilah, her voice as nervous as a kid's.

"Mark Williams," Talon whispers in Jenn's ear as she turns, clutching him around the waist. The weight of his arm over her shoulder seems enough to keep the rain at bay.

"Delilah, this is Mark Williams," Jenn says, hoping it doesn't sound like she's saying his name for the first time.

"H… Hello," Delilah stammers, setting off laughter behind her. Talon smiles at Delilah like she's the most beautiful woman in the world. No wonder her tongue is tied.

"I know what this is!" Delilah takes some control of herself. The other ladies jump expectantly before setting their eyes on Mark.

"It's that Julia Roberts movie where the billionaire comes and takes her away! I *need* you tomorrow, Jenn Klein. Christmas is a week away and I need you rocking the business wicket!"

Rocking? Did sixty-four year old Delilah Amelia Dunmore really use the word rocking?

"Miss Delilah," Mark drawls, playing right along with the headstrong old woman. It's a sexy accompaniment to the hat, boots and gold buckle and Jenn turns, tucking a knee behind his. "I promise Miss Klein will be at work tomorrow and I will of course keep my hat on."

With that he takes it off and bows to Delilah, making her squeal with laughter. Before he puts it on he kisses Jenn like they have all the time in the world and the last five months apart haven't been any more than five minutes.

Then the hat is on and Jenn stands with her mouth open as Mark turns her toward a black pickup.

"Night, Jenn!" Delilah calls. Her husband has pulled up and she's getting in. At some point during the kiss Jenn realized the pilot light never really went out and he feels it too.

"Up you get," Mark says and she has to pull her skinny skirt up to get a foot on the running bar to step in. A blast of cold suggests the tops of her stockings might be uncovered then the wind and driving rain are gone as Mark closes his door behind him.

"You look good, Jenn."

"I think I prefer Shadow," she says. It's not that she doesn't like Jenn but Shadow was the brave woman who'd been with him.

"So do I," he laughs. "Come here."

Shadow slides over to the center seat as Talon puts the big truck in reverse. It has to be twenty-five years old, judging by the sparse instruments and fake chrome on the vinyl dash but it's immaculate and still smells a little new. She wraps her arm around his elbow and holds on.

"How did you find me?" For some reason Talon waiting outside her place of work at closing time should feel a little unnerving but it doesn't.

Talon clears his throat like he's going to say something ungentlemanly and puts the truck into park. He's only backed up to the other side of the lot so they're out of the mall's lights.

"You said small town bank teller so I started where we parked and went north looking in the window of every bank I passed until I got here and saw you about four-thirty."

Shadow doesn't know what to say.

"Then I went and checked in to a hotel and came back for closing. That's not pathetic is it?"

"But what if I left?" she demands, her voice flush with irrational anger but he smiles as her panic settles. "Sorry, but what if?"

"I'd have been waiting here for you in the morning."

He puts the wet cowboy hat on the dash and she finally gets a good look at him. His hair doesn't seem any longer but his dark brown eyes shine for her. Shadow drops her hand between his knees and feels the firm muscle of his thigh as she remembers what attracted her to him: his confidence and how comfortable he is with her. How exactly did she do without his touch for so long? A small river of water escapes from her hair and runs straight down her back, perking her nipples and setting off a shiver.

"I haven't had anyone, um, special to shop for at Christmas in a long time and I wanted to see you again," Talon's hand slides into hers and he deposits a heavy chain in her palm.

"Talon?" she asks as she holds it up to look. Even in the dark and the parking lot lights the bracelet glows with pure white fire from end to end. It's a complete circle of diamonds of a half carat or more each. And good quality; her part-time jewelry store job through college taught her that.

He looks expectantly at Shadow as she touches it like it might disappear if she doesn't do it just right.

"It's ridiculously expensive and far too generous a gift for a second date. I admit," he says as if he can read her mind. "I'm not expecting anything in return. I know I'm taking a risk by springing it on you. If you wish to do something equally generous for me then please accept it as simply something beautiful I want you to have."

If you're sure, she thinks. It must have cost him thousands. And thousands.

"I'm certain," he says. "I figure you like to hide being pretty and I think you deserve a little flash on the outside, okay? You don't have to tell anyone where you got it but I guess I just want everyone to know someone believes you deserve it."

"Talon, I'm proud to accept it," she offers her wrist and as the wind batters everything outside his sure fingers fasten the clasp.

"Thank you, Shadow," his confidence failed and returned at nearly the same time.

Whatever the meaning of the gift is to him, her taking it is more than she can understand.

Shadow turns to him as much as the seatbelt and their legs beneath the wheel will allow as he kisses her again. She untucks the side of his shirt to get a hand on his wet skin. Without hesitation his tongue pushes its way in and she pushes back, creating instant heat. Grabbing his belt she tries to pull him down on her in the front seat but her hand slips up his obliques.

"Unh," he mutters as he tries to get his shoulder on his hip to protect himself.

"Are you ticklish?" Shadow asks. Her hand is frozen to his side as she tries to hide how pleased she is; her big grown man with a little kid soft spot and her warm hand resting right on it.

"I'm… ticklish," he mutters pausing where a 'not' would fit.

"Are you sure?"

He doesn't answer. Instead he opens both seatbelts and pushes her over. Shadow moves closer to the passenger seat and gets a knee up letting him settle completely between her thighs.

"Changing the subject?" she tries.

"Yes…" Talon's teeth grind together and Shadow feels the vibration in his whole body as he tries to hold the word back. Then he grabs her leg and works his way up her black stocking before feeling around for the clip attaching it to her garter.

"I thought that's what I saw," he says hotly in her ear.

Subject changed.

She opens her eyes and watches him above, careful to not move a finger and cause him to change the subject again.

"Panties?" he asks.

"Minimal."

"Colour?"

"Seasonal," she replies. The set is bright green with a little bell between her breasts. It would make noise if she didn't have a snug green cami muffling it.

"Shit," he mutters as he sits, leaving Shadow overheated and confused.

"What's wrong?"

He runs his hands over his face and pushes his hair back into position. She's barely upright when the engine starts and he pulls out. With one hand he buckles up and Shadow squishes over, fumbling for the lap belt.

"I have plans for us tonight. Is there a place a dripping wet trucker can take his equally soaked bank teller for vegetarian food and a steak?"

"You want to take me out?"

"Absolutely," his big hand swallows hers as they stop at the exit to the main road. "First I'll take you to your place."

Shadow gestures left as they pull out.

"Run in and pack a bag. We'll spend the night at my hotel so your dad doesn't catch us and run me off."

Shadow laughs at the ridiculous statement. She and Terry grew up in several foster homes, taking the last name of the Klein's, their first foster parents. They didn't keep in touch with any of the families they grew up with.

"If you think I'm kidding then humor me."

"Then what?"

"We stop at my room so I can change and then I'm buying you dinner."

Shadow points at a small apartment building on the opposite side of the street and Talon expertly turns the truck around so she doesn't have so far to walk.

"Overnight bag," he reminds her. "I'll get you back here before work."

"Then what?" she asks his empty seat as the door closes and he runs around to open hers.

"I have a few days. If you want we can do it again tomorrow."

Talon takes her elbow as she slides out and dashes to the front door.

"Shadow?"

If he dried at all he's soaked again already, standing there oblivious to the West Coast winter. His shoulders broaden in challenge to the weather.

"Ditch the panties."

The memory of Talon's sire's large calloused hand on his shoulder tells him he's finally fallen asleep. He knows he's dreaming and reliving a possible solution to his puzzle.

He can't lie to Shadow.

Not even to uselessly deny something which is plainly true. *I'm not ticklish.*

Easy to think, easy to say as long as it's not to her. The only answer is magic and it has to be his. No eyrie would ever let a royal female, a descendent of a very magical matriarchal bloodline, run loose as a rogue. Shadow's birth would have been as common as his.

The only real magic they possess binds them as mates. Talon can call on a small amount of magic, a symbiotic male way of shaping the magic in the Earth, but it's in no way his. The Earth can choose him and he can have a say in what it does but without its power he has as much magic as a human.

The Earth is a serious ally and she always demands something in return.

Like honesty.

His sire's phantom hand won't relent to let him doze in peace.

"Talon," Stalker says. "Get up, child."

Sire's pinfeathers, Talon silently curses. He's seventeen and still called 'child.' Talon's twin Feather had become an adult gryphon three years earlier. After Feather's first season she attended a ceremony where the females prepared the spirit of a dead old rogue for the hereafter. The rite of passage meant she was a *gryphon* and no longer a child like him. All Talon knows is becoming an adult male would wait for his sire to have time.

He holds back his excitement that the time may have come and slips from the mat he shares with his sister. The first indication his sire was in the den was usually the quiet 'inside-voice' coupling of his parents in the other room but the sound of his dame's snore suggests his sire has come only for him.

"You will need your pouch and your dagger, child."

During his sire's last visit Talon had been given the items and forbidden to touch them. Feather received a raw ruby in a pouch like his and she never complained about the lump it made under her side of their mat.

"Steal your sister's ruby."

Talon freezes. Is this the test? Is he willing to break one of the cardinal rules of the eyrie? Or does committing the crime mean he'll wait months for his sire to give him another chance and the test is of his willingness to disobey Stalker?

His sire nods sternly toward Feather.

Talon doesn't hesitate again. She stirs but does not wake and he bounds silently after Stalker taking position at his left wing, the position of protection. Only a gryphon sworn to protect Stalker with his life would stand at his right. He follows with his leather sheathed dagger in one hand and the pouches in the other and soon they climb toward the eyrie entrance. Stalker's heavy armour and proudly positioned wings remind Talon how very far he has to go before he's an adult.

The distance from Feather worries him but he holds his head high as they pass other gryphons up tending to things in the night. Talon slows as he's struck with the sudden urge to run for his den and replace the stone. The guilt he feels for his crime is overwhelming. When she wakes to find him gone and her ruby missing his betrayal will devastate her.

Stalker turns and grabs Talon's elbows, pulling him so they stand chest to chest. They're the same height, Talon nearly as broad, but his muscles seem soft and his limbs ungainly in comparison to his sire's powerful presence. The big rogue doesn't speak; instead puts his fingers under Talon's chin and pushes it up in praise.

"Yes, sire," Talon says, feeling stronger inside. Self-doubt will only work against whatever Stalker has planned.

As they near the entrance Stalker directs him into one of the many rooms that lead off the entry corridor.

"Undress," Stalker orders as he removes his own armour.

Talon's heart-rate picks up. Are they leaving the eyrie? As a child he's never been allowed to leave the mountain. There are several caverns large enough to learn the basics of flight and he only saw outside when he snuck to the hole in the stone to do it. All he wears is a pair of child's trousers, not even a gap in the rear for a tail, and he folds them neatly beside his sire's armour.

"Take wing, Talon."

Stalker waits as his son imagines heavy muscle and bone tearing free. In seconds Talon's body responds: first a mouthwatering tingle in his skin as his knees lock to bear the extra weight then light headedness threatens as the frames of his wings extend nearly nine feet in each direction. It hurts but not so bad that he might spoil the moment with a shameful whimper. Finally long golden brown flight feathers form from the air. The rest of his body remains bare.

Stalker assesses his son, walking around behind before grabbing hold of his wings. Talon hisses in response. No gryphon, child or otherwise, ever wants to be disadvantaged by an adversary in the rear.

"Silence," his sire whispers and Talon snaps his mouth shut though he keeps a sharp eye behind him. "Tail."

"Sire," Talon acknowledges and imagines his spine getting longer as his back straightens. He quickly feels the coarse hair of his own tail brushing his calves. He's never been permitted a tail and marvels at the sensation of being completely winged as Stalker expertly binds the dagger to Talon's upper left arm and ties the pouches around his waist.

"Follow," he orders and together they approach the entrance. On the wing, Talon doesn't mind the cold even though he's naked but for the feathers and hair on his wings and tail. His sire points to the opening. It's night and Talon's shifted eyes make out the terrain in the distance.

Before Talon can think Stalker's foot is on his ass, pushing him into blackness.

"Fly!"

Talon tumbles through a second of forever before he catches the air and coasts, reveling in the swell of his wings. He beats, climbing higher, and hurries to join his sire. What the hell are they doing? He's stolen and now he's running away.

At dawn they follow a large river north over snow covered forest.

"The humans call all this land Ontario," his sire says but before Talon can try the strange word on his lips Stalker dives and Talon tucks his wings in to go after him. By the time he reaches the ground his sire has shifted further. Stalker's clawed hands and sharp teeth have a deer by the throat.

Talon watches every move his sire makes, sure it's important.

"Quickly, your dagger," Stalker points. "Here. Drink."

Talon bares the blade for the first time, slicing into the deep artery then covering it with his mouth. He swallows again and again; a primal growl in his chest as he gulps air as greedily as blood. Talon's wings beat against his sire's, their nearness with the deer between them is undeniably intimate considering it's two big males with food.

Mine, get away, he thinks before he remembers the kill is Stalker's. As Talon pulls away to share his head is pushed roughly back into the wound.

"Your kill has bonded you to your blade, son," Stalker whispers in his ear.

Pride fills him at being called anything other than child. He can hear it in his sire's voice. It is only then Stalker releases Talon. The deer is butchered and they eat, the taste of fresh warm venison is nothing Talon ever dreamed of and he feels his strength return from taking wing and the flight.

They fly for days, killing and sleeping, Stalker teaching his son the pleasure of the hunt.

Late in the day Talon feels drawn to a spot below.

"Sire?" he points and they descend, landing on a bend in a cold river.

"What do you feel, son?"

Talon's nostrils flare with the scent.

Gold.

"The Earth chooses who finds her treasures," Stalker explains. "I scent nothing here. If you do then she wants you to have it. She will exact a price, however."

His sire pushes him to his knees and places his hands in the gravel. Talon hides his apprehension. Being on all fours before anyone is a punishment which can go on for days or weeks. He'd rather receive a few licks to the butt as the price than assume the position of apology.

A gryphon never apologizes. To do so shows weakness.

"She is your first lover, son, and you must be close to her. You will not eat or sleep until the gold rises," Stalker says in the old language. "You may speak to her but in the old words. When she feels you have suffered enough, you will receive what she has offered."

With that Stalker flies off, leaving Talon alone.

On his hands and knees the weight of his wings quickly becomes unbearable. He's built to be suspended beneath them, not hold them up like this, and even after days of flying and hunting building lean muscle and strength nothing could prepare him. Though his aching body begs for relief or even a small break, Talon whispers to the Earth praising her with thanks for bearing his weight and feeding his body, for sustaining the deer that will fortify him for his journey home and for sheltering his sister in the warm stone of their mountain.

As darkness falls the sound of wings announces his sire's return. Stalker consumes fresh venison before him, making Talon's mouth water and stomach ache. Talon is still weakened from the afternoon's travel and keeps his mind busy thanking the Earth for the deer and the trees which shelter Stalker's sleeping form.

Morning finds Talon muttering endlessly on the ground.

Stalker speaks, gnawing on half frozen venison. To Talon the distraction seems an act of pity and at first he tunes him out, refusing sympathy and struggling through his agony on his own but eventually he falls into the old words. He learns how to bond with a mate, the ritual of exchange, and that he may only share the ways of harvesting the Earth's treasure with his own son.

Unnourished far too long, Talon shivers in the cold. Even moving his wings no longer makes heat in his muscles or releases his pain. He refuses to give up even when the shakes blur into violent shudders that chafe and cut his already bruised knees on the rock.

Then something subtle changes beneath him; the gravel bed vibrates in his hands and even tilts. Stalker squats expectantly nearby.

A new pain fills Talon, blinding him. He forgets about the ache in his back and shoulders. He's aware of Stalker's roaring laughter as the rogue falls over holding his full belly.

Talon blinks furiously and as his sight returns he can see a nugget of gold an inch and a half across covered in his dripping blood. Several smaller chunks pop to the surface nearby but none with the vigor of the big one which has given him a deep cut and black eye.

"Well done, Talon," Stalker pushes himself upright. "Although I should have warned you to turn away."

Sitting upright is agony but Talon allows himself a grin at his amused sire.

"Wash, eat," Stalker orders as he tosses the deer's back end to his son and Talon's stiff fingers remove the leather pouches and his dagger. The freezing river bites as he scrubs the dirt and blood away and the swift current kneads the feeling into his limbs. He washes the blood from the big piece of gold and puts it with the others.

Stalker regards his son as he eats the rest of the deer. Talon knows he's completed some task and in his heart he's sad this time alone with his sire could be coming to an end.

"Do you know how long we've been away, Talon?"

Talon fractures one of the long bones, twisting it in his strong hands so he can get a finger in the channel and scoop out some marrow. Then he shakes his head, annoyed with himself for missing something as fundamental as time.

"The full moon has come and gone twice," Stalker continues, still in the old words. "It has been a long time since you stole the ruby."

Talon's thoughts turn to his sister. Would her anger at him be tempered with worry? He pushes the last of the deer aside.

"It is time we part, my son," Stalker stands. "You will gather from the Earth until your pouch is full then fly west, following the sun. When the Earth calls again you will enter her and find the place she's chosen for you. She will protect your hoard."

"Sire," Talon nods, understanding why he must go on alone. The location of a male's treasure is something only he will ever know.

"Once inside you will take out Feather's ruby. Kings of the land and the sky we are; proud gryphons."

Stalker stands, the epitome of pride. Naked and muscular, his wings widen and his feet dig in as if he alone restrains the Earth and supports the heavens, keeping the two ever separate.

"But you aren't yet a master of the sky. Your body is still that of a human as is Feather's. You will get on your hands and knees and ask the Earth to shape her ruby. Ask her to use Feather's forgiveness to make your bodies those of true gryphons. Feather must also offer something for you both to gain. And she can never know.

"Only when the stone has been reshaped may you return home. When Feather forgives your theft she will accept it and in that moment she will have the stamina to fly true distances and I will be proud to call you *gryphon*."

Talon remains on the ground as Stalker turns and within a

few strides is airborne, his great wings taking him away from his son. As Talon gets on his feet he suppresses his urge to call out in spite of his terror which is worse than his sudden loneliness. He's beyond lost in the wilderness the humans call Ontario.

Chapter Six

Soft steps a dozen feet above wake Talon. He doesn't twitch or hold his breath. His heart stays steady; nothing to give away his awareness of the visitor on top of the hotel. He chose the third floor room so he could hear any nosy gryphon on the roof and so they could take flight right off the deck without a run up.

Instantly alert, he assesses the situation: he and Shadow are naked and his only weapon is in the end pocket of his bag. Shadow's breathing doesn't change. It's not training which has kept her from reacting. She's out cold.

He moves only enough to touch the diamond bracelet on her wrist. Its magic has been spent like when his sister forgave him and accepted the ruby. It was spring when Talon finally filled his pouch. More animal than anything else, it wasn't until he saw his own reflection in a still lake that he remembered his sire's instructions. At first he thought the rough terrifying male was his sire and he stood, turning wildly in search of him. Then he remembered Stalker's words and flew west.

Feather's shaped ruby was a perfect circle surrounded by some of his gold into a strong armband; a perfect fit just below her elbow. Talon's crime cost him a month on his hands and knees in the largest cavern in the eyrie.

It was fall when his sister forgave him.

The feet above are bare and the drag of one feathered

wing tip on the upward slope of the roof says it's not human. It's an invitation. To Talon, most likely but if it's to his mate then it will go through him. At the edge of the roof the sound of the footsteps disappears as his visitor glides away.

Untangling from Shadow is simple, only her diamond covered arm is across his chest though he aches from the loss of contact. Talon can't resist, he places his tongue in the fold just under her breast and wets it as he brushes his nose over her nipple. The room smells so strongly of them and sex he nearly forgets the gryphon waiting outside and stops himself before he can wake her.

Once on his feet he edges his way toward their heaped clothes and pulls his jeans on commando style then his nearly dry t-shirt. He slides his telescopic baton into one pocket then the card key for the room into the other.

"Talon?" She's barely awake.

Don't ask, he silently pleads.

The bargain with the Earth was simple though he'd been on hands and knees for three full days; Shadow wouldn't accept the diamond bracelet until she loved him and all he asked is that he knows if she's in trouble. A give and take like with the ruby but it appears the Earth had other plans. Maybe love wasn't a big enough trade for what he wanted and the price included truth as well.

She took it. She loves him. Though neither has spoken the words Talon is certain beyond a doubt he feels the same way.

"Running down to get some water or something," he manages as he decides to do just that when he's out. Boil water signs all over the place in all the God forsaken rain don't make much sense but neither do a lot of things these days.

Boots on, wallet in rear pocket, jacket on. He's really fucking stupid not being a little more prepared and misses his crossbow and his blade. Just because she's his secret doesn't mean there aren't other gryphons around, particularly so close to the Vancouver Island Eyrie.

"Can I have something sweet?"

"Sure."

But she's asleep before he's finished answering.

Once outside he hangs the bulky coat on the doorknob then scans for humans both by sight and smell before taking his shirt off and tucking it in the waistband of his pants. The rain has stopped but its wetness still soaks the air. Surefooted, he steps onto the railing overlooking the parking lot and with a flex of his shoulders he takes wing. First he feels the weight of the extra muscle and bone required to support them then from the very air his deep golden brown feathers appear, extending down several feet from his wings' structure. Smaller feathers cover his back, meeting at his spine and another patch replaces the short dark curls on his chest. They form a line down the center of his stomach then turn to lighter golden hair and disappear into his low waistband.

Talon steps from the ledge. His massive eighteen foot wing span bears him to the center of the parking lot below. He waits, wings extended, for the other to make the next move.

"I'm hurt," a pouty female voice reaches him after only a few moments.

Feather.

Pleased as he is to see his sister, Talon groans on the inside. She rarely displays an understanding of privacy.

It's been nearly a year since he's seen his eighty-year-old twin and she hasn't changed much since their physical aging slowed around twenty-five. They both look about thirty in human years. All she wears is jeans, leaving little to the imagination. Her ruby is displayed proudly on her left arm and several dozen long gold chains adorn her neck. Though he smiles in greeting, Talon shakes his head. Don't unmated females get it? Any gryphon would be intimidated by the display. Even though her gold is of the human variety a male would worry his adornment, the physical manifestation of his hoard appearing on his female after consummating a bond on the wing, would be sadly lacking. Any gryphon who claims he doesn't care is a liar.

At least her long brown hair covers her bare breasts. Good thing. If there was another male around Talon would have to waste time kicking his ass for looking.

"Why are you hurt?" Talon asks as he takes her hands and kisses her forehead. As annoying as sisters are he'd do anything for this one.

She pulls her hands back like he should know.

"You've taken a mate and didn't invite me!"

Feather glances at Shadow's bite. It's as red now as when it was a few hours old. Her arms cross.

"I didn't know you developed a taste for watching."

"I haven't and you know it," she pretends she's offended but at least she doesn't look so pissed. Then she bounces on her toes. "I meant to make sure I was at the eyrie when you brought her! Which eyrie is she from? What's her name? Oh my God, how does her adornment look?"

Damn, she's going to wake Shadow up if she keeps going at full volume.

"I could smell the two of you going at it from blocks away!"

"Feather," Talon rolls his eyes. "When did my sex life become our sex life?"

She grins at him, trying to look sheepish.

"It isn't," but she's noticed his change of mood and smacks his arm. "You're always so serious, Talon. Mark isn't as unbearably stuck up. You get your tail shoved up your ass?"

"Not recently," he claims setting off peals of laughter from her. A car carrying an older couple pulls through the middle of the parking lot and Talon takes his sister's hand and drags her clear. They carry on without noticing the winged creatures they nearly ran over.

"Her name is Shadow and I don't know which eyrie she's from. She works in town here."

"A rogue?" Feather gasps, nearly swallowing her fruity gum. Talon knows exactly what she's thinking. He's thought the same thing. Something terrible must have driven Shadow from her eyrie.

"She hasn't spoken of her eyrie or even about being a gryphon," Talon explains as he glances up to their room.

"There's a deep pain in her, Feather. And she's so young. I'm not even bringing it up. She'll talk when she's ready."

Feather looks sad for him and turns her attention to the third floor.

"You have a good spirit, Talon," she places a palm over his clutch of short golden chest feathers. "I hope she sees it."

"She does," he says, thinking of her accepting the bracelet. "Anyway, what are you doing on the Island?"

"Shopping!" she exclaims then she takes a step away, pushes her wings up high and wiggles her butt. The jeans are skin tight. Talon vows to see her more to keep the males under control.

"Aren't they cute?" she finishes her circle. "There are a couple of local jewelers in the area so I picked up something for me and Swift."

Talon growls. Yeah, it's really great his ex and his sister are like *this*.

"She's back in Jasper," Feather waves dismissively like Swift and her murderous feelings toward him are no big deal. "I flew here in an airplane! Isn't that hilarious! Anyway I *fly* out of Vancouver first thing tomorrow so I need to get back across the Strait to check out and check my luggage."

She steps close, demanding contact from him and he obliges, working his fingers around and into the back of her neck making her purr contentedly.

"I'll be around more. I promise."

"You'd better, family man," Feather whispers as she praises him by pushing his chin high.

"Feather, have you ever seen a white gryphon?"

"White?" she pauses her take off run long enough to answer. "No such thing."

Then she's gone into the low clouds and heading east to Vancouver. Talon gets the t-shirt over his head as his wings fade and his heart pounds momentarily as his body adjusts to the increased blood volume; fluids his wings were using. He runs to the convenience store down the block for water and a bag of fancy jelly beans for Shadow.

Chapter Seven

Shadow's apartment is quiet when she lets them in. Silence is good. If her alarm is sounding it means she's late. Talon let her sleep while he showered and she figures she's got a little extra time to get ready for work. As she gets the lights on and tosses her coat and bag on the couch Talon puts their coffees on the table in front of the big TV. They'd each put down a couple of cream cheese filled bagels but she's still hungry.

"Wow, you're into this stuff?" Talon's nose is against the glass of Terry's cabinet. "DiMaggio?"

"Every piece has a story," Shadow turns her back because she doesn't want to see him look. It's already too much to hear Terry's voice in her head as she talks about the baseball he'd wanted so much. "1951. Yankees took it in six. It was DiMaggio's last World Series."

"Neat," Talon says as her alarm sounds from the bedroom.

"Shit!" she grabs an apple to eat in the shower. "I'm late!"

"It just went off."

"To tell me I'm late," Shadow pulls her clothes off and tosses them aside. At least Talon's lost interest in the cabinet.

She finishes stripping on her way down the hall and disappears into the bathroom certain he watched the whole thing. As the shower warms she gets a brush through her hair then stops to stare at the mirror. She barely recognizes the woman in the glass.

When was the last time she remembers actually looking? She still pictures herself thirty pounds overweight and covered in baby fat. Now all that roundness is gone, replaced with strong lean muscle. Who'd have thought a really great body was under all that? And Talon? He was solid as a fucking rock once she got his clothes off him. Now that she's covered in nothing more than the bracelet she's aware that Jenn's body image was far from reality. She's seen what she looks like but after spending the night appreciating how Talon sees her she accepts it.

The hot water feels good even though it feels like sacrilege to wash Talon from her skin. As she pauses for another bite of the apple she lets the last of the conditioner wash away before she hisses at the sting of the needle-like drops on her tender nipples.

As long as we stay out of the shower I'll survive another night with him, she laughs but she's also sure she doesn't want to ride a bicycle anytime soon either.

A day of mashing twenties through the bill counter is going to feel like forever with Talon to look forward to. Maybe the next night as well.

Are you sure you're ready for love? It's the shy Jenn voice inside. *How are you going to feel when he leaves? You don't do so well alone.*

Shadow scowls at her reflection, seeing the overweight naïve girl from the past for a moment before she looks away.

"Nobody said anything about love or alone," she mutters as she clicks on the hairdryer but the idea lingers. If she's attached then it's going to hurt when he goes. What if he doesn't feel the same way and it's easy for him to get in his truck and drive off?

Her hair is mostly dry when she gets out of the bathroom. "Jenn?"

"Talon?" she answers. He's in her kitchen, white lace bra and panties on the counter in front of him.

"Jenn."

"Mark?" she tries again. The realization that Jenn and Mark are complete strangers hits her hard.

Talon and Shadow are gone. Mark is wrapped in a wall of stone and Jenn is wrapped in a towel.

He chews at his bottom lip to contain a minute tremble and even in the poor light from the living room his eyes are red.

I broke his heart? Jenn's stomach rolls. *How did I break his heart?*

"I'm sorry," he starts. Just a brief look at her before he drops his eyes. His long fingers caress the lace bra, smoothing it out and fussing to make it into something else. "I wanted to pick out something for you to wear today; watch you put it on. Our secret. Maybe order in tonight and expose it together. Later we'd talk.

"Probably about nothing other than how great it is to knock boots but eventually I'd tell you I think about you all the time and I can't leave without knowing when I'm going to see you again."

He puts his hand between the bra cups, where her heart would be if she had it on then he makes a fist, balling the lace up and dropping it on the panties.

Jenn sags, her shoulder hits the wall and she grabs at it trying to stay up. Fuck, she knows exactly how she broke his heart. As she starts to slide backwards Mark takes her elbows and lowers her to the ground before drawing back like she burned him.

"Your top drawer," he crouches before her. "That's where women keep that stuff right? I was just going to go in your top drawer but it's full of men's socks. Boxers in the next one.

"I kept going. I'm so…"

Tell him, Shadow demands but Jenn can't. She never started to get on with it. She moved in to Terry's room and shares his closet and pretends she doesn't need a drink and all of that to keep her brother's loss away. Shadow isn't real and even if she was Talon isn't here to listen and Mark is shutting down before her very eyes because Jenn is a fucking coward. Her mouth is so dry she'd never pry her tongue from the roof to speak.

"There's nothing of yours in the dresser," he whispers like he doesn't trust his voice. She's killed him inside and she disgusts herself, still trying to feel nothing to keep the grief away. Nothing for Talon, nothing for Terry. It never left; only waited. Mark looks at the bracelet and Jenn is sure he's going to want it back but instead he stands up and turns away.

"Your underwear is in a plastic tote box in the coat closet. The freezer is full of meat," Mark walks toward the door. "You don't eat meat."

Jenn crumples sideways to the floor as the door quietly snaps shut behind him.

The street in front of Jenn's apartment is empty except for a lone male gryphon standing on the solid yellow line. Talon pretends not to notice since no human eyes will see his silent observer. Three floors above him Jenn starts crying; a strangled lonely wail that makes him feel like a justified jerk. He's an idiot thinking that mating and love are the same thing. She loves him, he's sure, but he's not the only one and she didn't bother to hide it.

If she's half as broken hearted as he is she deserves every empty sob.

Doesn't matter how genuinely happy she was to see him again. The apartment belongs to a male. Talon's eyes still burn from the male's scent but of course he had to stick his nose in the closet for a good whiff either to be certain or to rub it in his own stupid face. He's not sure which.

Yeah, that's why they were watering and explains your hitching lungs too.

Screw off.

The driver of a speeding car doesn't slow his vehicle as he passes, oblivious to the fully shifted gryphon in the middle of the road. Its wake stirs fallen rain into his long black hair and heavy dark brown wings. Soar's tail is held perfectly to say he means no threat.

Soar, grandson of Master Sky and as much a recluse as Lev, the Royal Sire of the Vancouver Island Eyrie, since he was recruited as Master of Sire Lev's personal guard squares off with Talon. Jenn's apartment didn't smell of Soar so he's not the other male in her life. Soar wouldn't share a female anyway. Soar wouldn't mate with a stranger. Soar wouldn't let his dick talk him into bonding with the most precious female he'd ever met.

Sure Soar would. He's as open to a broken heart as the next gryph.

He's here for something though. Maybe to tell Talon he's being watched and she's not as alone as he thinks. Or to give Shadow his best shot, unaware she's committed to another.

"She's mine, old friend," Talon says softly into the breeze, well aware Soar's hearing clearly catches each word. "Do fifty years of friendship count for nothing?"

Soar mirrors Talon's impassive expression. If this was about friendship Soar would be straight with him. His silence says he's under orders to be quiet and the only one who'd give him those orders is the gryph's Sire, Lev.

Soar is shirtless, wearing only the rough linen trousers of the eyrie so he's not dressed for battle yet he doesn't approach or speak. A screech from above reaches them and Soar's head snaps up, centering on Shadow deep inside the building. He turns and in a few running steps is airborne. His powerful wings drive him deep into the low cloud.

Chapter Eight

"Dis da las' one, miss?" Ambrose asks.

Jenn's fingers smooth and reroll her list of M. Williams.

"Yes," she sighs. "If this isn't it I guess I'm going to see Winnipeg for the first time."

Ambrose' heavy French-Canadian accent talks about his Maude as the second to last Saskatoon address disappears behind them. The taxi is warm and Jenn's eyes close, picturing his wife of forty years as young and beautiful. The old man's reverence for her is overwhelming. Maude is eighteen and pregnant, running off with him to Niagara to elope. Ambrose is much younger, whispering dirty things to her as the Falls thunder in the distance.

Mark whispered to her like that. Minutes pass as her breathing slows and the dark taxi hides the heat in her cheeks. Pain in her hips and bad leg from days seated on buses and in taxis makes sex unthinkable anyway.

Don't get your hopes up, Jenn. If he wants to see you then take it slow.

The old cab driver laughs. Steadily thickening snow completely covers the road.

"Why you look for dis trucker?"

"We had a misunderstanding," Jenn explains. The radio squawks and she pauses. "I was too upset about something else to clear it up and he walked out."

"So you ride da bus to Calgary an Edmonton an Regina an Saskatoon an go to every 'ouse wit 'is name jus' to 'pologize? Could phone, eh?"

"It was a bad misunderstanding. He deserves better than a phone call."

Ambrose stretches as they wait for the green light; thick fingers and thin thighs from years of working in a seat. He wears a tie and Jenn figures he's one of the hardest working men she's ever met. Two blocks later he turns the cab right onto a nearly invisible side street. Even during the day with a flashing street sign she would have missed it.

"Dis use to be good neighbour'ood," he nods. "When I bring my family out 'ere was bad. Workin' girl an drug dealer, eh. Dey pay, dey ride."

He takes his hands from the wheel to shrug; shoulders high, palms up. In the past few hours Jenn's learned the gesture simply means 'it is what it is.'

"Now even dey move on. Da city even forget dees street."

This late in the day the good neighbourhoods look the same as the bad as long as you don't look too closely. The street Ambrose turns left on doesn't even have a sign. His cab lights illuminate a boarded-up house, its porch sagging under the weight of years of abandonment as they wheel around the corner.

"If dis not it my beautiful wife fix you dinner an' tuck you in. Take you to da bus tomorrow."

"That sounds fine," Jenn agrees.

"Dis your trucker?"

The old guy's eyes are good. Under a single streetlight three blocks away are two vehicles: one big, the other bigger. Jenn's eyes strain to see through the snow and she makes out Mark's rig and in front of it his truck. As they get closer the hood shines like a black eye where latent heat refuses to let the new snow stick.

"Damn," Jenn sighs and her heart sinks. The trucks face the taxi up against an empty lot. Only a couple of old leafless trees are visible past the fallen down fence.

"'dere Miss," Ambrose points to the other side of the street. "Dat da one."

Jenn turns just in time to see the curtains fall shut, making the house look as empty as the others. A narrow covered porch crosses the front, windows on either side of the old door. When Ambrose picked her up his practiced mind calculated the best route and he'd only been off by a few dollars so she offers him another twenty.

"Ah, keep it Miss," Ambrose passes Jenn his card. As she reaches for it he bends his elbow, snapping it away. "Deal 'ere dis. Don' work out you call an' ask for Ambrose, eh? You don' call den I tell your love story to every fare dat listen. Secon' bes' to me an Maude but still good, eh?"

Jenn glances at Mark's door and imagines the story of the crazy Parksville girl he'll tell if she doesn't phone.

"Deal, Ambrose," she agrees. "And it's not a love story."

He shrugs again and before he gets his arms down Jenn hugs him. It is what it is.

"Is cold, Miss," he says as her door pops open. "Don' stan' out long if 'e won' listen."

One last wave at Ambrose and Jenn stands alone, her bag over her shoulder. The cold instantly pulls the moisture from her skin, tightening it over her nose and stiffening her fingers before she gets her hat down a little lower and tries to warm them in her pockets.

As Ambrose backs up Jenn faces what she hopes is Mark's door. The cab turns around at the first cross street and sits, its red tail lights looking out for her.

Maybe Mark has another woman or he'll hear her out and say good-bye. It's more likely Jenn will choke up like in her apartment and she'll spend the night with Ambrose and Maude. After she's come all this way to apologize to Mark it'll be disappointing if it's just a repeat of the scene in the hall.

Stiffness in her bad leg sets in after only a few steps. The insufferable prairie winter goes right through her flesh and into the metal that holds her up more than her own bone. After she takes another painful step Mark comes out, glowing in a grease-stained high-vis parka.

He stops and stares so Jenn pulls off her toque letting her long dark hair fall around her shoulders.

"Jenn?"

"Hi, Mark," bravery makes her voice a little too loud and Jenn glances at the neighbour's house certain she's been heard but it's black inside and doesn't have a door. A trail of exhaled air follows him down three stairs and along his shoveled walk, heavy work boots leave a trail of fresh prints. His attention is on the waiting taxi and he doesn't face Jenn until he's a few feet away.

"Do you have a few minutes?" Jenn starts, still brave inside. "I mean, if it's a bad time I can come back or something."

"You want to come in?"

Jenn peers past her freezing lashes to make sure Ambrose is still there. Waiting in the cold for him to come back looks more and more unappealing.

"No, I just need a minute if it's okay," she resists palming her eyes as the wetness eases the discomfort. The speech she'd run through is ready but stage fright is already taking the words away.

Mark nods and she starts with a deep breath, hoping it will give the first hard words the momentum she needs to finish. After that, she thinks, the rest will be easy.

"My brother Terry died," she chokes, hands hiding her face and pressing back tears until she gets control again. "Two and a half years ago. I haven't even said his name since that morning."

When her hands come down Mark is closer, eyebrows pressed together and his head tips with concern.

"He left me everything. His apartment, his sports stuff. It still doesn't feel like my place. He loved those things so I did but they were his love, not mine. When you noticed it wasn't my apartment I was overwhelmed with everything I'd buried coming to the surface and I thought if I talked it would wash me away.

"I know what it looked like," she goes on, picking a smudge on his coat to stare at in case he shows pity on his face. Even in the cold the smell of heavy grease settles around them. "Like I brought you to another man's home. In your place I'd have felt cheated, used. I'd have been angry and I wouldn't have held my tongue like you did. I appreciated that."

Mark nods.

"After you left I started boxing Terry's things up. I'm getting my stuff out of storage and when it's ready to go I'll rent something and put his life away… get mine back."

"I didn't think my problems would hurt anyone and I'm so, so sorry."

"Jenn…" he says.

"Anyway," she looks left, seeking the shelter of her waiting cab. "You deserved to hear a real apology."

She's barely a step closer to Ambrose when the reverse lights come on.

"Wait, Jenn."

The taxi keeps coming as Mark tries again.

"Please," he says as he takes her elbow then she's folded up in his big coat. Inside it's dark and warm. Outside they glow in Ambrose' white lights shining out danger like a yellow-jacket. Mark smells clean of deodorant soap and fabric softener and his lips rest in her hair. The big muscles squeeze and Jenn's neck tingles, loving it and forcing out any fear she had that Mark would send her away. "Stay here tonight. Tell your ride you're staying."

Unable to get her hands from her pockets she surrenders in his arms.

"Please," he says. "No expectations."

"Okay, Mark," she says as he lets her go. What Jenn really wants is a shower and some sleep but first she has to face the chill outside his coat and thank Ambrose. The crunch of snow under tires stops.

Ambrose leans over, looking up at her when she opens the passenger door.

"Thanks for waiting. I don't need a ride."

Ambrose laughs, shaking his cell phone in his big fist.

"I call Maude first, tell 'er 'bout you!" he proclaims. "'bout you an da love story!"

Jenn shakes her head to protest but then shrugs like he does. It is what it is. She blows the old man a kiss and he holds his hand over his heart before he waves. The door closes and he pulls away, purposefully this time.

Mark holds the rolled up paper. It's frozen and the snow slides off and falls to the ground.

"You went to all these addresses?" He sees them there, sorted by city. Every one is crossed off the list except his and Winnipeg. "You could have tried the phone."

Mark leads her to the house and brushes the snowflakes from her shoulders before they stomp their boots clean. The echoes fall flat in the snowy air. Her coat disappears into the closet with his and their boots sit together on a rubber mat. Jenn stands uselessly by the front door rubbing at her eyes. The deep itch is all her exhausted numb body feels.

"I just got in," Mark explains as she tries not to yawn loudly. When her eyes unblur the list of addresses is gone.

Behind him the hallway stretches down to a pair of doors, another to his left. To his right the hall opens up into his living room lit only by a fireplace and a flat screen TV. Mark's Xbox is on. Through the far end is a kitchen, a couple of red lights on the stove. Jenn isn't surprised the place is as clean as he keeps his truck and himself. The whole house isn't much bigger than the apartment.

"I don't want to put you out," Jenn mumbles but her forehead is suddenly so heavy she might pass out and block his front door.

"Shower and sleep?" he offers and points down the hall. "It's the door on the right."

When she doesn't move he picks up her bag and walks her there. Clean towels are on the counter and it's still a little steamy. Mark pulls open a small closet behind the bathroom door revealing the stacking washer and dryer.

"Toss anything you want washed in here," he offers.

"Can I borrow something to sleep in? Everything is dirty." It has to be; she's wearing her last clean pair of panties.

When she gets out there's a clean t-shirt on the counter. Jenn pulls it on, amused that the sleeves hang down past her elbows.

She finds Mark on his sofa; two plates in front of him. His is empty. Hers has a baked potato and some salad, generous since he wasn't expecting a vegetarian. A glass of wine. He barely looks away from the mayhem on the screen as the headset comes off.

"It's game night," he explains. "I only miss if I'm on the road."

Jenn yawns and sips at the wine, simply relieved to have found him. Her plate is almost empty when she curls up against the arm of the couch. Mark tosses a blanket over and grabs her ankles, stretching her legs out over his.

Chapter Nine

Mark signs off the Xbox when most of his friends decide to call it a night. Tomorrow is a work day it seems for everyone but him. His exhausted mate murmurs his gryphon name and sighs.

Impossibly, her small frame sinks further into his sturdy couch and he scents a little more peace in her. The pain she carries nearly overwhelmed him when she arrived and it's still strong.

Reluctant to leave her side, Mark slips out from under her legs and turns down the TV before kneeling near her head.

"*Arlette*," he whispers. "I'm ashamed."

You can be a selfish asshole, Talon, he curses himself. *Running out on her when she needed you so much. The wound you opened must have been brutal.*

It's easy to put his feelings into words when he's been human so long. His eyes close and he rests his head near her stomach, startling when she cups his rough cheek in her palm.

"It was a really good day," she whispers. "We were headed across the Island to Tofino for a swim in the big waves. Terry loved the heat of summer and the wind on his skin. We turned twenty-eight that day."

Mark's eyes close as she shares her feelings: their joy and closeness. He knows that bond since he shares the same with

Feather.

"I was riding behind him when a truck came out of nowhere, out of control and Terry broadsided it. I hit them from behind."

His lungs empty with a rough hiss and he brings his head up, close to hers.

"I tried to hold on to him," her voice breaks, tearing at his heart. "I tried so hard."

He'd do anything to spare her.

"Nuke was behind me."

Now he knows why the little human made her feel so terrible. Shit.

"Don't push it, Jenn," he whispers. "I should have stuck around for you."

She shrugs like she did to the cabbie.

"After you left I got ready for work," she says, leaving out the tears he heard that morning. "I walked all the way to your hotel and banged on your door but you were gone.

"I got in to work late. Delilah was covering my wicket and as soon as she saw me she hauled me down to the coffee room. I couldn't sit up I got so dizzy I fell and they got an ambulance."

"Jesus," Mark mutters.

"Vertigo but they couldn't find anything wrong. I got to talking to the nurse about Terry and all the bad things I did to try and cope—"

"What bad things?" he's glad to be sitting down.

"Drinking, sleeping pills," she explains. Mark wants to throw up. "I told her the hurt was still as bad as the day he died so they sent in a shrink. They put me on stress leave… post traumatic stress they call it. My insurance pays for a nice counselor. She comes to the apartment and we talk about Terry and she helps me pack."

'The' apartment, he notes, not 'my.'

"Post traumatic stress," Jenn sighs. "But I know what it really was."

"Yeah?" God, he's trying to be cool for her but all he

wants to do is go fuck something up.

Like that would make it all better.

"I tried so hard to hold on to the man I couldn't have that I almost gave up the one right in front of me."

Mark watches, washed in her emotions. She seems peaceful then the pulse in her neck picks up and it's like she explodes inside, then complete despondence…

"You meant it," she says, now filled with unshakable resolve. "What you said. You wanted to see me again."

"Yes," he whispers. God yes, he thought about her as he drove away leaving her crying on the floor. *Asshole*. But he takes her hand, kissing her wrist around the bracelet as if to say the words neither one of them has spoken.

"Shadow—"

"Mark," she interrupts. "I think for now Jenn and Mark. They talk and they feel and all Talon and Shadow are going to do is make it alright in bed when maybe it's not the right thing to do now."

"I want you close," he says as he helps her sit up. "My bed, no making it alright. I promise."

"That bus ride was three days with the stops," Jenn rubs her leg. "It's bad tonight. I'm not so sure I'll get back to sleep."

"What do you need? I don't keep anything around for pain but I'll run out."

"My bag."

"I'll get it."

First in his room he pulls back the blankets for her then grabs the bag and while she digs around he gets her some water.

"I don't like taking them," she admits. "Oxycontin makes me feel really strange for a while."

"Were they what you had a problem with?" he kicks himself for asking but he still has the urge to take the bottle away and dump them down the toilet. "Shit, I didn't mean for it to come out like that."

"Once, I think," she won't look at him. "I overdosed. I don't remember what I took but there was a bunch of stuff missing when I woke up two days later. Careful with them ever since; try to stick with the over-the-counter meds now."

You're being too hard on her. And on yourself.

Of course he is. Survival rate is only half for gryphons who lose their sibling when they're so young. She made it this far. He should be grateful and he is; proud of her too.

"Where are your parents, *Arlette?*" he asks.

"Parents?" she laughs but she's shaking and Mark knows he should have kept his mouth shut. "Terry and I grew up in foster care. All we had was each other."

Mark has to grab her before she falls over. Something is terribly screwed up for her if they were abandoned. Terribly, terribly screwed up.

"Enough," he insists, scooping her up in his arms and carrying her down the hall. She seems to weigh nothing and feels smaller and smaller with each step. Dear Lord, he's not asking her another thing unless she brings it up.

Jenn won't lie down. Instead she curls into a ball against the headboard, barely allowing him to get a pillow behind her. He wraps himself around her, keeping everything away.

Chapter Ten

By the time their dishes are put away the dryer is done. Mark folds her clothes, leaving them on the counter and is hanging her underwear over the shower rod when he's interrupted by a loud thump on his roof.

Why can't gryphons knock on the damn door like everyone else?

As he checks on Jenn the footsteps make their way in the other direction to the street out front. She's lying down at least though it was a struggle. All he can see is her brown hair sticking out from under the blankets.

A quick look past the living room curtains tells him his night isn't about to get better.

Torrent, royal heir to Talon's adopted home eyrie in Jasper, stands in the street. With his wings extended he tries to exude every bit of intimidation his station lends him. Unfortunately the warrior in Torrent has never truly been tested; something about not embarrassing him or some other brilliant bullshit though Talon would love to forget that simple rule if only for a minute.

Three hundred years of being a prick has left Torrent with little in the way of personality. His long black hair is loose and he wears nothing more than jeans.

Talon pulls his boots on, already pissed. If he has to take

wing he'll have to tear off one of his favourite shirts to do it. Halfway down his stairs he's distracted that Shadow is so far away even though the distance grants him some perspective on her feelings.

As Talon steps onto the street Torrent spreads his wings further and beats them down, blowing up a cloud of fresh snow. It's fucking cold enough for Talon already with his coat off and now even more snow clings to his skin.

"Torrent," Talon drops to one knee.

"Cut the shit, Talon. You don't mean it."

Talon shrugs, getting on his feet and jamming his cold hands in his pockets. Disrespect it is.

"I guess if I hadn't nailed your sister we could be friends," Torrent goads.

Talon's reply is an insincere nod. He doesn't understand what Feather saw in Torrent and why she made him swear to stay out of it.

"Well, perhaps I can change that."

Not likely. The only things which keep Talon from running him off are his royal status and Feather's wish he let their 'thing' go. He'd like nothing more than to tie Torrent's wings in a bow and drop him from a building.

"I'm listening, Torrent," Talon grudgingly remembers his manners. "I should offer you the hospitality of my home."

"Indeed," Torrent smirks. "I'll keep it out here. You look cold."

A winged gryphon can survive any climate given sufficient protein and at the moment Talon isn't winged. He's relieved, however that Torrent isn't getting near his mate.

"My sire's guard is aging, Talon," he starts. "His right wing is retiring as are several others. Sire Sher extends his invitation to you to return to Jasper for consideration as a replacement."

Talon doesn't do a very good job hiding his surprise and suspicion. Sher has led the Jasper Eyrie for several hundred years and his guard is known for their size. Torrent has four inches on Talon and wouldn't make the height requirement himself. Also an invitation to serve would come from the Sire himself, not his son. And why now? Sher's guard isn't as old as Torrent makes it sound.

"*LIAR!*"

Talon flinches at Shadow's volume. His hope of avoiding an altercation with Torrent is fading.

"You're *not* taking him!" she bellows. She stomps toward them barefoot in nothing but his t-shirt.

"Human entertainment?" Torrent laughs. "That's plain sad."

"It's okay Shadow, go in."

"It's not okay!" she cries.

Torrent's laugh is cut short. His nostrils flare as he figures out she's not human and she speeds up, not feeling the cold or the pain in her leg.

"You're *not* taking him," she sobs. "Son of a bitch! You took my brother and you're not taking Talon!"

"*This* little thing is Shadow?" Torrent growls with more than just offense at the insult. "You'll pay for her big mouth."

Crap. Feather must have said something.

Shadow breaks into a run, fists swinging wildly at her side and before Talon can get his arms around her she takes a swing at Torrent, her right opened up and partially shifted into a claw. Her long nails rake across his chest as he steps back in surprise that she'd actually try it. Talon pulls her off as she gets her clawed feet up, just missing in her attempt to disembowel Torrent.

"Bastard!" she screeches. "Lying bastard!"

I'm screwed, Talon thinks as he pulls her away. Nobody touches royalty or questions a royal's integrity.

Ever.

Blood runs down Torrent's chest and stains his pants black in the streetlight. Talon groans, pushing away the pressure to take wing and fight. He has Shadow to protect and for the moment that need is stronger than his reaction to aggression and blood.

Torrent's hand is over his wound and he charges. As Talon stumbles with Shadow up the slippery sidewalk she casts a hand toward the house.

"You won't enter here!"

A flash of heat sears him, fading as quickly as it hit and Talon looks down to see a line of scorched grass at his feet.

Jesus, she's stoned.

Shadow's pupils are blown wide open and she sobs, completely hysterical. Like comforting his sister, Talon cups the back of her neck in his big hand and squeezes only much more firmly. When done gently it soothes a female but enough pressure will put her under.

"Hold on," he whispers and tightens his grip even more. Shadow goes limp as Torrent comes to a sudden stop only a few feet away on the other side of the burnt line in the frozen grass.

Talon backs into his door and assesses Torrent's threat to Shadow. The bigger gryphon is on his ass in the snow, nose bloodied from an injury Talon didn't see him receive. Torrent gets on his feet and with a roar charges before he's fully upright.

And bounces off an invisible wall where the smoking grass is. Blood ruptures from Torrent's forehead where he must have struck it, adding to the mess from his nose and chest. Talon watches, fascinated, as he cradles Shadow closer.

Torrent staggers up, this time probing the invisible barrier with his toe then he disappears into the night.

"Who are you?" Talon asks as he gets Shadow on the sofa and covers her up. Another piece of wood on the fire should help warm her. He takes her bottle of pills from her bag and reads the label. One it says and he's certain he saw two in her hand, maybe even three now that he thinks about it.

And sure as shit it was her magic that banned Torrent from his house.

Shadow is no common gryphon. She has to be pure royalty to pull that off but a royal abandoned to live the life of a human?

It doesn't make any sense at all.

"Mark?"

Jenn tries to focus through the pills that still rage through her system. If she's awake it means her messed up metabolism is burning off the narcotics and it shouldn't be long before she's mostly alert and free of the hallucinations they cause her. An undocumented side-effect, her doctor said, and added more pills to her regimen to compensate. She doesn't take them since they do nothing for her.

Blinking doesn't help with the blackness and she remembers being carried down the hall to his bedroom before the usual nightmare about Terry became really weird.

"Here, Jenn," Mark moves and she realizes he's completely wrapped up around her. The little hairs poking out past his top button tickle and she runs her lips over to try and make them lay flat. "You're okay."

Ouch, maybe the tickle isn't too unbearable. Jenn's throat hurts and the movement makes her neck ache.

"Where are you from?" Mark asks.

"Parksville," she gets on her back and pulls the pillow out from under her head hoping to straighten the kink in her neck.

"And before that?"

"Terry and I grew up in Victoria. He supported me through university and we moved to Parksville when I got my BA. We lived there ever since. He always talked about moving further up Island but we never did."

Mark slides down under the blankets so she stays covered up and Jenn realizes why she thought she was alone in the bed. He's fully dressed so he felt like more blankets. She laughs as Mark pushes up her shirt and gets his mouth on her belly just above her panties. Jenn imagines he sleeps with his clothes on as some sort of protection thing so he's ready for anything. Okay, that's romantic. The canned fish was strange. She pulls her fingers through his soft hair as she feels more like herself.

"Bad dream," she apologizes. "Did I wake you?"

"No," he mumbles into her skin. "Fuck that smells good."

"Are you wearing boots?"

Jenn pulls her legs up, trying to catch his head between her thighs but he laughs and blocks her.

"What about your dream?"

Though Mark doesn't stop lapping at her tummy, Jenn feels her libido shrink as her thoughts turn to the accident.

"The engine on Terry's Harley is somehow still running. It's in pieces but the tank and engine are together so it rumble, rumble, rumbles and I can feel it in the ground underneath me," she says and is rewarded with a nip from Mark. The hint of their first day together keeps her away from the cave-in that usually takes her when she thinks about the accident. "Nuke's there, holding my hand and telling me not to look but I can't help it. Terry's too still and there's a woman screaming behind him.

"So strange, seems to come from his open mouth but I know he's gone already. Then the angel comes."

"Angel?" Mark asks.

"Yeah, his wings were never solid but I could see their shape; each was longer than he was tall and he shaded Terry for a moment before he walked away but instead of waking up tonight there was a bad angel, not like the good one who took my brother to heaven."

Mark kisses his way along her hip, bringing her back into the moment. He seems to know when she's too into the dream so he can bring her out of it, gently encouraging her to talk more.

"Then it's you in the middle of the road instead and a bad angel is there," she remembers the bad angel, his wings black against the street lit snow. "I wasn't too late to save you. He acted like he was there to take you somewhere good but he was lying.

"I fought him and chased him away," she feels so damned proud. Mark crawls up above her, settling between her legs. Jenn's aware she should be hot like crazy for him but she isn't. She's still soaked in disappointment she couldn't save both

Mark and Terry. "What smells good?"

Mark looks straight down into her eyes and puts a small amount of space between them; enough for him to put a hand low on her stomach.

"You, fertility," he whispers. "I want permission to break my 'no expectations' promise."

"Hey!" she half-shouts, pushing herself out from under Mark. Jenn knows exactly which day of her cycle it is and even with a condom she's hesitant. And how the hell can he tell that anyway? Maybe he's just guessing. "We are so far away from thinking like that."

"How far?" Mark demands, pulling at her panties. "Months? A year? More?"

"Jesus, never!"

"What the hell?" he withdraws before she can push his hands away and Jenn can hear the confusion in his voice.

"It's our second night together and you want to try for children?"

"You know better than that," he scolds. "And it's been six months and of course I don't mean like this."

"Hey," she tries, aware the pills and all the talk of Terry have made her irrational. "I'm thinking like a single girl when I don't feel that way with you."

Use your words, Jenn, she thinks; the mantra the counselor gave her. You can always apologize for the bad ones but if you never try to say what's on your mind then your feelings will never come out.

"I'm living so much in the past right now; clinging to it even though I know there's a lot I need to let go of. I feel like tonight I took a step into the present with you and I was scared beyond belief even though I knew I couldn't make things any worse between us by sharing Terry.

"I want to be in the present more, Mark. I'm not ready for the future. I'm sorry for barking at you," Jenn apologizes, holding her hands to him. Mark accepts, taking the same position as before and stroking her cheek as he kisses her eyes.

"You challenge me like nobody ever has," he says as Jenn

reaches for his heavy buckle.

"Mark?" She pauses, fingers down in the waistband of his pants. His knees come up driving hers apart and giving her some room to work. "Thank you for not sending me away."

"I shouldn't have walked out," Mark's hungry kiss drives to her throat and all Jenn can think is she'll never want another man as long as she has this one. She deserved the wake up call back at the apartment and should be thanking him for it. Satisfied with the open buckle she tackles the buttons on his shirt. "I meant what I said. I want this; with you. It's long distance, I know but if you want to make it work as much as I do we can pull it off."

Mark pulls her big t-shirt up and skin on skin they connect sharing something as intense as their encounter in his truck. His acceptance moves her more than anything else. Disconnection and emptiness are all she's known for too long, the past six months interrupted by dreams and the hope she'll dream again.

"I've made some bad choices," she admits. "With men and other things. I can't help thinking you deserve better."

"Do you think I'm a bad choice?" Mark rolls away, landing beside her. The temperature drops considerably as air fills the space between them. It's twice in as many minutes that something's come out all wrong.

"Not you, Mark," she gets on her elbows beside him. "I came here prepared for you to send me away and here I am in your bed wearing your clothes. I've done so many stupid things I feel like I don't deserve your forgiveness. Maybe I'm having a hard time accepting it."

His eyes are closed and his breathing slows as she waits for him to say something. Anything. She gives up and rolls over.

"Jenn is so incapable," she says to herself. Her embarrassment for the admission is tempered by a new feeling of protective distance; protective of both Jenn and her utter and complete weakness. It's like she has to push Jenn away for her own good and it's just as bad as locking away her grief instead of dealing with it. But it could also be the only way she'll ever hold on to anyone like Mark. The angrier she gets about it the more she realizes it's something she might never be free of.

Mark startles as she slaps her pillow.

"I just wish she could be okay with things," she blurts out. "You know I can only do so much. I can put her aside and I can shelter her but all the time she's telling me—"

"Ah, crap," Shadow finishes. Now she sounds more messed up than she really is; talking about herself in the third person like her problems are so far away she can only face them if she pretends to be someone else. But that's how she sees them when she's strong with Talon. Reintegrating even the smallest piece of Jenn's pain with Shadow's strength feels like bailing out a sinking ship with nothing but her bare hands.

"Shadow," Talon says. Even his scent has changed to match her change in perspective.

I really am off the deep end tonight; thinking we're both two people.

"Is it too soon to say how attached I am?"

"Really?" Inside, Jenn takes a deep breath. It's what she's wanted to hear for a very long time. And coming from Talon she's able to hold herself together enough to experiment with her feelings. With two tugs on her hip he rolls her over, making her head spin as they meet nose to nose in the center of his big bed.

"Really."

Shadow grabs at the muscle of his arm as he pulls her flat against him. They kiss, bumping noses in the dark then he pulls his head back, letting her lick at his neck and inhale him until her lungs are full.

"I know you feel complicated right now," he whispers as his thumb hooks the top of her panties. "I appreciate every piece you show me, Shadow. Inside and out.

"And yes, I know I sound too good to be true but I really am that good."

"Wow," she giggles. The statement is as full of himself as she's come to expect from Talon. Secure and self assured in every way she's experienced him. Except when she blew it at

Terry's apartment but he was Mark then, not Talon. She gets her hand over his and pushes her panties down. "You really are."

"I'm going to bribe you," he continues as she lifts her hip and lets him pull them down even further. Talon gets his hand up in her shirt, cupping a breast then nibbling at it through the fabric. "Because even though I promised I can't help myself."

"Okay," she agrees although he doesn't need to. She's on the verge of climbing up and proving just how okay she can be.

"Tomorrow we're going to talk like I wanted to at your place," he insists.

"Yes," Shadow kicks clear of her underwear, shoving them deep under the blankets. She wants to be naked, unhidden, to show Talon she feels safe when she's exposed with him.

"You'll rest up for a few days and I'll drive you home."

"No!"

"Yes," his hand slides between her thighs and she opens for him. "But not until we've decided where we want things to go.

"And you'll promise to keep being yourself with me," he whispers, starting with a teasing stroke between her legs before he reaches for the shirt.

Chapter Eleven

"Please go get her," a woman's voice begs from the front of the house. "Please?"

"She's still asleep," Mark answers. "As long as you keep your voice down."

"Awe," she whines.

Jenn rolls over and reaches for Mark, hoping to ground herself in him until the voice goes away but the other side of the bed is empty. Only his scent is near and it's not enough.

"Please?" another woman snorts. "He smells more of her than he does of himself. Isn't that all you need to know?"

"Be nice, Swift."

Cutlery rattles in a can as the voices get lower and Jenn slides out of bed. The room is cold and she takes a step sideways onto the soft rug and off the frigid hardwood. Across the hall she can see her folded clothes on the bathroom counter so she hurries inside without looking toward the front of the house.

Mark had put her expensive underwear on the counter with her clothes so she pulls on the black set, jeans and a dark blue t-shirt before brushing her teeth without running the water, hoping to remain unnoticed.

When she opens the door again the second voice croons seductively and Jenn boils over. She's pushed by a need to display possession more than hide so she sets her shoulders and walks out into the living room.

Mark faces two women: the one with long brown hair has a shoulder between him and a red-faced blonde; her short spiky hair makes her look even taller than she is. The two wear huge amounts of gold, jeans, and what appear to be bathing suit tops. The blonde is more than six feet tall, the brunette several inches under but it's the blonde Jenn sizes up as an adversary.

Blondie glares at Mark then her eyes flash to Jenn. The blonde is jealous and stinks of arousal, grabbing a can of salmon from the kitchen counter and jamming a fork full into her mouth.

"*This* is the royal?" she demands around the mouthful of fish.

Jenn's nose wrinkles as Mark pulls her in tight, getting his big arm around and tucking her in under his shoulder.

"We saw the scorched circle around your house, Talon," the brunette says. "You can't keep denying it."

"No wonder Torrent is so pissed," Blondie laughs and lowers her eyes on Mark as she fingers a heavy gold chain.

Jesus, she's eying his gear right in front of me, Jenn thinks but she's so weirded out by the scene before her she doesn't do any more than grab Mark around the middle and hold on.

"Hi, Shadow," the brunette waves. "I'm Feather, Talon is my brother."

"Hi," Jenn answers, her voice no more than a rush of air from her lungs. Now she's certain the women have seen her and she slips free of Mark to duck behind him. She holds on to his shirt and buries her face between his shoulders.

"Maybe she'll come out for treats?" Blondie laughs and Jenn can hear the fork rattle in the big empty can. "I think I deserve an introduction."

Mark's hand finds Jenn's lower back and rubs so Jenn peeks out to see the blonde still failing at eye contact.

"Hey, Blondie," Jenn growls, finding her voice and confidence now she's hidden behind Mark. Using her words.

She holds a hand up at eye level, reminding herself very much of Terry keeping Nuke in line. "Eyes at least this high, bitch."

Jenn's never called anyone a bitch and is horrified by the choice of words but damn it, Blondie's ogling her man and deserves a reminder the view isn't free.

"Not in my house, Swift," Mark yells as he pushes Jenn back toward the hall.

The can drops to the floor as Blondie gets her arms out but then Jenn sees they're not her arms; Blondie's arms end in *claws* and the other limbs appear to fill out with brown feathers and take up the whole kitchen. Canisters and drying dishes go flying everywhere.

"Bad angel!" Jenn gasps as Feather grabs Blondie by the wrists and pushes her toward the back door.

"Not in my house!" Mark shouts and Blondie stops struggling with his sister though she looks just as angry. He has Jenn sandwiched between his chest and the wall and she struggles to see as Blondie's shrieks and *holy shit* her wings disappear outside.

Feather closes the door and for nearly a minute there's nothing but heavy breathing, Blondie's fading cries and the smell of canned salmon.

"Talon?" Feather approaches cautiously.

Jenn looks up and her heart pounds even harder when she sees his eyes have gone completely black. She's unable to retreat further into the wall so she lets her knees go, hoping to find escape below but he takes her elbows and holds her up before resting his lips on her forehead.

"Talon?"

He takes a deep breath and blinks. Jenn watches in a mix of relief and horror as the whites return to his eyes.

"Talon, you need to take her before Arden," Feather says. She rests her hand on Mark's shoulder and his muscles relax as she gets his attention. Whatever is coming from Feather isn't the same rancid and desperate arousal that came from Blondie. It's much more intimate and much less threatening. Jenn wishes Feather would touch her like that; reassure her that this is just another Oxycontin induced nightmare.

"Arden," Feather repeats. "Before Torrent gets you both before Sher."

"You shouldn't be in the middle, Feather," Mark takes a hand off Jenn to hold Feather by the back of the neck and she seems to calm down like he did at her touch. Jenn on the other hand feels more and more confused.

"I won't be," Feather smiles. "I promise."

Then she brushes her fingers under Mark's chin, pushing it up like Terry used to, and dashes out the door.

"Are you alright?" Mark asks.

Jenn can only nod. Three Oxy's was a really bad idea but at the time the pain was too much.

"Where's your phone?"

Mark thrusts her bag at her then gathers up the empty cans, filling them with water in the sink. No sooner does she have the phone out than he takes it and dials making his own phone ring. After a few seconds he ends the call.

"Am I in trouble?"

Mark glances at her. "Yes."

"Why?"

"You attacked Torrent on the street last night... the bad angel."

"I imagined that."

He doesn't answer. Instead he grabs his wallet and keys from the counter and stuffs them in his pockets.

"I need some things for the trip," Mark gives her a stiff hug. "Do *not* leave the house and call me if anyone comes here. You're safe inside."

It takes nearly five minutes for him to warm up the pickup and drive away but Jenn already has her bag packed. She's in trouble for sure if she's seeing angels even when she's awake.

After double checking she has everything she calls the cab company and asks for Ambrose.

"Jenn?" Mark yells inside his empty house. "Shadow?"
Fuck.

The small set of human prints on the walk tell him she's gone but he still hopes. If she walked away then it wasn't with Torrent. A prisoner her size would have been carried off. He'd only been gone ninety minutes for supplies and now he has to find her before anyone else does.

Mark weighs his options.

A call to the bus depot tells him he's missed her by only half an hour. He could outrun the bus and catch her in Edmonton but if she's gone to the airport she could be a long way away.

It's clear there's a gap in Jenn's knowledge of what she is though it's hard for Talon to believe. Talon first took wing around seven years old. How could she be thirty and not know what a gryphon looks like? Even if they grew up alone, it would have been difficult to ignore sprouting wings.

If Torrent brings her before Sire Sher and Jenn can't prove her royal blood her punishment will be severe. A month on hands and knees is nothing.

Torrent can ask for her throat.

Jenn's phone goes right to voicemail so Mark plays the hunch she's taken the bus and it's off to preserve the battery for the long trip to Vancouver Island.

Of course she'd answer. She'd never turn it off to ignore you.
It's all he's got.

Mark packs and transfers the supplies from the pickup to the rig as it warms up. The clutter of food, water and survival gear for two gnaws at the last of his patience as he pulls out but he doesn't have another minute to waste satisfying his gryphon need for order.

He's got six hours to try and put the pieces of Jenn's life together; to try and find some way to explain it to her.

Last night it became clear her gryphon and human identities are far from connected. Shadow's strength is balanced with Jenn's ability to feel weakness like the balance between Talon and Mark. It's like she's belatedly going through gryphon puberty; erratic behavior, emotional withdrawal and one side of her personality in denial of the other. Like Jenn's denial of Shadow even though when Shadow is dominant she sees Jenn for what she is like a loving parent and an immature child.

But this, running off at the sight of a gryphon and calling her an angel, tells Talon it's more than denial of her real self. He doesn't know anything about the pills she took and can only guess what combination of perceived hallucination and fear made her flee.

"I should have said 'I love you,'" he whispers as he pulls onto the Yellowhead Highway.

Shadow can only be descended from a magical royal blood line. It explained her ability to build a barrier to keep Torrent out.

Talon has never known true fear in his life until now and he's scared shitless.

You're going to need everything you've ever learned to get her out of this, his inner gryphon tells him. *She attacked a royal and has no way to get herself out of it.*

If he can't find Shadow, she's dead.

Chapter Twelve

The Jasper diner has a vegetarian section on the menu. Jenn learned on the trip to Mark that the further she got from Vancouver Island the harder it was to explain no meat on the burger. Or at least that's how it felt; more likely it was simple exhaustion making it harder to even picture what she wanted, much less put it into words.

Jasper, known for its ski resorts, is cosmopolitan enough that she could eat in the diner every night for a week without having the same meal twice and she can prove it. After abandoning the trip home she settled into a hotel unable to run any further from Mark or get any closer to where he was probably waiting for her in Parksville. Jasper seems closer to him anyway which doesn't really make much sense.

The ride to the bus a week earlier had been uneventful. Jenn enjoyed Ambrose's teasing and claimed it took so long to find Mark that she ran out of vacation. But as she waited, ticket in hand, her uneasiness grew. It's not just the angels she fled from. She has a sense she fits with him, disturbing hallucinations and all, and she's not sure she's ready for it. Or him, to be more precise.

As the driver opened the big bus door and started taking tickets, Jenn returned to the counter to get her money back and ask directions to a mall and a hotel. The next day she found four inches of new snow where Mark's rig had been so she took her disappointment to the bus depot and caught the twelve-thirty westbound.

In the diner her phone sits next to her placemat as it has at every meal, still off as she tries to get the nerve to call him. She decides to call Mark from her room and go wherever he is whether it's west to Parksville or east to Saskatoon.

Who are you kidding? You're too chicken to even power it up.

You bet I am.

"Shadow?"

Jenn ignores the woman's voice, dismissing it as the clutter of sound in the busy restaurant, and doesn't look up until she hears it again.

"Hey, remember me?" Blondie asks, grimacing like she's waiting for a loud noise. She chews her lip with discomfort as Jenn pushes her seat a little further away. "Damn, yeah."

"Hi," Jenn allows. The woman looks different. Dressed like any ski tourist she fits in better than Jenn in spite of the neon pink headband covering her ears. Jenn hasn't seen neon since she was little. The gold is visible inside the collar of her jacket.

"I was wondering… well, I understand if the answer is no and I'll beat it but I thought if maybe I picked up dinner we could, well, have some girl talk if it's okay," Blondie heaves in a lung full to recover from her rambling request.

"Sure," Jenn agrees. The woman is part of Mark's life after all and Jenn is starved for information though it feels more like high school gossip than anything else. Did you see what he was wearing? Did you see what I was…

"I'm Swift," Blondie offers her hand.

Jenn accepts it as Swift takes the seat across from her. The waitress moves in with a second menu as if she were waiting with it.

"Hold mine until my friend's is ready," Jenn asks the waitress and Swift seems to be a little more at ease. Swift barely glances at the menu before ordering a double burger with extra bacon and a glass of beer.

"The bracelet is pretty," Swift puts her hand out. "Mind?"

Jenn doesn't and offers her wrist to the tall woman. Swift inspects each diamond as she turns it around Jenn's arm.

"Talon?"

"Yes," Jenn admits. The silence that follows makes her wish she'd told Blondie to shove off.

"Look," Swift confides. "I just want you to know where I'm coming from. Talon was mine for a long time and it wasn't my call to end it. It was his. I didn't understand until he was with you that it was really over and I reacted badly. He's really gone from my life."

"I understand," Jenn offers because she does. "I lost my brother a couple of years ago and most days I'm stuck in the moments that followed."

"Oh no!"

"I guess that's why my trip home stalled out here in Jasper."

"Talon is worried sick about you," Swift says. "I don't know you, Shadow, but I know him. He's putting all he's got into finding you."

Jenn can only nod and looks at her phone; the life preserver she keeps pushing away. Nothing waits for her at the apartment other than missing Terry. She's just as silent to Mark now as she had been in the hallway and it was hurting him again.

"I guess I'm still protective of Talon," Swift explains, getting her cutlery out of the way for their plates as the waitress puts their food down. "No meat?"

"Don't eat it."

Swift raises an eyebrow and wipes ketchup from her chin with the back of her hand, leaving her paper napkin rolled around her cutlery. Are her nails longer than they were a minute ago?

"You need to call him," Swift insists. "He went through Banff looking for you and I took Jasper. Feather is waiting at his house."

"I guess you win," Jenn says. "You're right, Swift. I want

him to know I'm okay but I'm not sure I can talk just yet. I feel like such an ass for splitting."

"Idea?" Swift offers. "I'll call Talon and say I saw you going into a hotel. I know wherever he is he'll drop everything and come here. Go freshen up. When you get back he'll be on his way and we'll celebrate with desert."

Jenn looks down, surprised to see her plate empty. Swift's is as well so Jenn takes her purse and heads to the washroom. Jenn's embarrassment over hiding in the bathroom makes her even angrier with herself. Now she feels like she owes Blondie something.

Blondie who sprouted big brown wings and claws and it was only a surprise to Jenn. Damn, maybe it was the Oxycontin which made her see that too.

When she returns Swift waits with a banana split and two spoons.

"I kinda set you up," Swift admits. "But I want you to be in on it in case I made things worse."

"Uh, okay," Jenn accepts the spoon pushed her way.

"He's staying at the hotel you went to when he saw you last month in Parksville. Gonna take the next ferry to Vancouver and be here by morning. I told him we're meeting here for breakfast around eight but if you don't want me around in the morning that's fine."

God, it all sounds so reasonable. Blondie has to be on the level if she knows about the hotel.

"It'll give you the night to think about..." she rolls her eyes and takes another spoonful of the pineapple part. "Never mind me. Maybe I'm trying to make things right for me by making things right for you. I don't know."

"Swift?" Jenn waits until she looks up. "Thanks. I shouldn't have called you a bitch."

Blondie shrugs. "I was trying to piss you off."

"Fair enough."

It's uncomfortable again and Jenn puts her spoon down. Blondie takes the last strawberry for herself.

"I feel like I should invite you to my room, maybe do each

other's nails or something."

"Don't push it, Shadow," Swift's smile doesn't reach above her lips. She pulls out a couple of the new plastic twenties and tosses them on the table. "Don't assume I got involved for you."

In spite of the chill, Blondie gives Jenn a quick hug just outside the diner.

"I'm sorry," she says before she hurries down the block.

Talon's worry for Shadow wasn't weakened by four days sparring in both the sky above and lower reaches below the Jasper Eyrie. The time on the wing failed to even distract him from the human emotions he indulges in as Mark.

Giving up his search for her is unconscionable but leaving her for Torrent to find instead is worse. Talon couldn't risk being absent from the eyrie if he didn't get to her first. She hadn't been on the bus in Edmonton so he'd driven to Parksville. No sign of her there either. Her patio door had been unlocked so he'd let himself in but other than the smell of at least two unfamiliar gryphons there was no indication of trouble.

And nothing to suggest where she'd gone.

He drove to Jasper and left his rig at the transition house before making the two hour trip on the wing to the eyrie. The transition house is nothing more than a hotel owned by Royal Sire Sher, staffed by common gryphons and funded by legitimate human guests. Gryphons check in, leave their human vehicles behind and take wing on the roof to travel to the eyrie.

Word spread quickly that Talon was in the eyrie and the lower dens, usually sparsely populated by visiting rogues, were filling up with wandering males eager to prove themselves against him or at least watch him in action. And he was happy for the distraction. Anyone who'd trained under Master Sky for so many years had an obligation to teach and Talon had a knack for lessons, dragging out the inevitable defeat of his opponents.

A lesson learned in the sparring chamber could be a life saved in real combat. Alliances between eyries are fierce, divisions even fiercer.

Today Talon trained in the sky so he could keep an eye out for Shadow if she'd been caught.

The common baths are nearly deserted by the time he's taken dinner and made his way down to the pools of cold spring water. Every eyrie has one, even high in the Rocky Mountains where it was completely incongruous considering how much further it felt from the centre of the Earth. On the wing Talon doesn't mind the water's coolness anyway.

When he steps from the pool the water is cloudy with the chalk used in sparring. Much like paintball, he supposes. His hands were covered in chalk from the pouch he wore around his waist to mark where he'd struck his opponents. Many gryphons sparred only to mark. Talon made sure his marks stung.

Only a few steps from the baths the sound of two sets of barely stealthy feet reaches him from further along the tunnel that leads up to the common areas above. In the blackness his shifted eyes have no trouble seeing the pair as they round a bend ahead. Talon isn't in the mood to be invited back to the sparring chamber so he keeps his head high to warn them off.

"Talon," the larger of the two addresses him. Both males are in full armour and wear the mark of Sire Sher's Royal Guard burned into their upper left arms. Dame Arden's guard, many female, sticks mainly to the royal chambers in the upper reaches of the eyrie. The one who speaks also wears a black eye. He'd spent the afternoon monopolizing Talon's time, tumbling to the ground with him over and over breaking away in time to catch the air and avoid crashing into the glacier below.

"Gryphons," Talon offers a slight nod of acknowledgement.

"Sire Sher insists you voluntarily return to your den."

Talon rubs at his wrist as a small itch becomes an uncomfortable burn. There is only one reason he'd be confined.

"What is the accusation?" Talon has the right to ask and be advised of the charges.

"It is believed you witnessed an assault on the royal gryphon Torrent and offered haven to the traitor accused in the assault."

So that's how it's going to be. If Shadow is accused of treason it means Torrent seeks her death and by implicating Talon in the crime he could very well seek the same fate for him. The only good to come from their being charged together is they would both have the opportunity to speak. Had Shadow been charged alone it would be up to Torrent whether Talon would be heard.

"I shall of course comply," Talon holds his head high.

The smaller guardsman leads the way while the bigger bruised gryphon follows with Talon keeping a wary eye on him. Gryphons they pass pretend not to notice his escort but he's certain news of his custody is already spreading. By the time they reach Talon's den the burning in his wrist is nearly intolerable and it can only mean one thing.

Shadow is in trouble.

The wrist that burns is the same one on which she wears his bracelet.

In his den he finds the other males who shared it have moved out which suits him fine. Once the curtain falls shut Talon drops to his knees as the two guards take station outside. He closes his eyes, tuning out the noises of the eyrie and the burning in his wrist to focus on his mate, hoping that when she arrives her feelings will reach him even from the royal chambers far above.

Chapter Thirteen

Three loud thumps get Jenn's attention. She dreams Delilah is giving her a stuffed eagle at some strange home party. Its unusually long thin tail is stiff with wire and she bends it around to see if it can hold its new shape. The other ladies from the bank pick at cheese and crackers on the coffee table and look at other stuffed animals making their way from hand to hand. Empty wine bottles litter the floor and Delilah's husband is dressed in a tuxedo as he makes the rounds, topping up glasses in Terry's small living room.

"This fellow's name is Talon," Delilah explains, glaring at the noisy front door.

The ladies ooh and aah.

"Pass him along, Jenn. Only a couple more and then we'll get ordering and see what your hostess prize is."

But Jenn doesn't want to. The soft stuffed animal is hers and passing it along will take it closer to the door where another three loud thumps interrupt Delilah and shake Jenn awake.

In the blackness of her hotel room she sits and tries to remember where she is.

"Hotel security!" is followed by two more sharp raps on her door.

"Just a sec," Jenn calls. She wears nothing but the t-shirt

she'd worn at Mark's and doesn't remember packing it before she ran out. The hotel bathrobe is piled on the foot of the bed and she pulls it on as she goes to the door.

She peeks out the spy hole and sees two men dressed in matching dark blue clothes, some kind of badges over their pockets. Seriously? This place can't be big enough to have much more than the night clerk and maybe someone else to run extra pillows to the rooms.

Jenn leaves the chain secured and opens enough to see out. They look the same as they did through the peep hole except she has to blink in the blinding hall light.

"Ma'am," one of them says. They're both big and it seems fitting for security. "We need your assistance. There's been a break in down the hall and we believe the suspect is cornered on your balcony."

"I haven't unlocked it since I got here and checked it before I turned in," Jenn explains, anxious to be rid of them. She's not sure why they make her a little cautious, possibly Terry's numerous run-ins with the police are to blame which is silly but she's leery of them just the same. "Thank you but I'm safe."

She lets the door fall shut and the other security guard puts his hand out, stopping it from closing.

"We haven't been clear, Ma'am," he says as the first one glances down the hall and licks his lips. Nervous maybe? Jenn can't be certain but his uniform is newer so maybe he's still pretty green on the job. "We need to access your balcony to take him into custody."

"You have to come in?"

"That's what I just explained, Ma'am," he says. "We have him cornered and need to go through your room."

"Okay," she concedes. A lot of security to be sure if there are more on the balconies. The guard moves his hand so she can close the door and unhook the chain. As she does there's a soft thump on the glass behind her.

"I heard him!" she hisses, stepping aside to let them by. The newer one passes and as she turns to face the balcony the older one takes her elbows from behind.

"Wait here, Ma'am," he orders but Jenn doesn't understand why they don't let her wait in the hall. Shouldn't the senior guy help with the arrest or whatever they're going to do? New guy is almost at the sliding glass door.

As she tries to get away his grip tightens too much and Jenn's sure something is wrong. She pulls harder and takes a step onto his foot.

"Help me," the guard behind her says and she kicks him, surprised how quickly she's thinking. She has her feet and that's about it and as long as they think she's intent on struggling, the new guy won't suspect she's going to try and disable him. Unable to fight them both at once she's got to take out half her problem or it isn't even game on.

"What do you want me to do?" the new guy asks.

Jesus, Jenn is embarrassed for him. Terry taught her more about subduing someone than this guy appears to know. As he gets close Jenn's confidence spikes and she swings a foot up between his legs as hard as she can but the men stop acting like incompetent thugs. New guy grabs her by the throat as her shin smashes painfully into what feels like a steel cup between his legs. He doesn't even flinch as the man behind her replaces the hand with his bent arm and picks her up off her feet.

Jenn stops struggling as she grabs the arm to hold herself up and keep the pressure off her throat. One lame kick at the new guy only makes her neck hurt more.

"Let him in," the rough voice behind her orders.

She can't do any more than squeak for help as the door slides open and a massive shape enters, black wings silhouetted in the Jasper town lights.

"Shit, shit, shit," she breathes as the bad angel comes for her.

New guy steps away and Jenn renews her struggles, digging her fingers into the arm around her neck but then she's dropped to the floor. One of the guards turns on a lamp making the bad angel look even more terrifying. Four parallel slashes cross his bare chest and his forehead and nose are both heavily bruised. His wings are dark brown in the light. It's also clear he's furious and more than delighted. His wings spread, filling the room as Jenn's eyes widen to take him all in. As her lungs fill to scream he grabs the back of her neck to take complete control.

Docile is the word which comes to Jenn's short-circuiting mind. Her body is at least as it relaxes in response to the bad angel's pressure on her neck. Jenn's heart misses a beat as it slows.

"Shadow," the bad angel whispers in her ear. He kneels above her limp body. "Do you know who I am?"

Jenn shakes her head, willing the movement then as his thumb starts to slowly rub her head nods of its own accord.

"Torrent," she sighs.

He releases her but the happy numb feeling doesn't go away.

"I'm only going to say this once," Torrent tells her. "The rest of your life is mine."

He's not lying. Not like the week before when she's now sure she really saw him. She grunts as he drops her on the bed.

"Like she was never here," Torrent orders and one of the guards goes in the bathroom. The sound of her things being gathered up reaches her as her clothes are pulled from drawers. Everything is piled on the bed and Torrent goes through it all, stuffing it all but her razor in her pack.

Torrent pulls the collar away from her neck then lifts her shirt exposing her back.

"No," she whispers.

"Don't flatter yourself," he hisses as his fingers brush where Mark bit her months earlier. Jenn cries out in pain at the unwelcome touch. It never hurts when she or Mark touches it but Torrent's hands are an acidic assault worse than anything else she can imagine them doing to her.

"Sit," he orders.

Jenn complies. The weakness has worn off but she knows she needs to buy time.

Be good, Jenn thinks. *Submission until you figure out what kind of left turn your life is taking.*

There will be a chance to get away and stuck in her hotel room with her nightmare and his two big friends isn't it.

"Dress."

He's left out her jeans, boots and winter wear and she quickly puts them on then he bundles her in two spare blankets from the closet.

"Lock up behind me," Torrent says to the guards before he gathers her up in his arms. His wings fold up tightly behind him as he bounds out the sliding glass door and they dive off the balcony. Weightless, Jenn's shriek fills her ears until the rush of air over his wings is louder and she feels heavy in Torrent's arms as they climb.

"Silence," his hand crushes the back of her neck and there's nothing but blackness.

"I recommend you don't stray far."

Torrent is nearby. Jenn's bundled up on a hard surface in the dark. It feels like she's indoors and she hears voices in the distance, below she guesses. A rough oval of very weak light silhouettes his shape.

"Where am I?" Damn, even talking makes her neck hurt.

"You are in the Jasper Eyrie," his bored voice tells her. "I'm obliged to say you face charges of treason for an unwarranted attack on the integrity and person of the Sire's son."

"You're kidding, right?"

"That will be added to the list of charges, female."

Shit, he's nuts. This is all nuts.

"Where's Mark?"

Jenn jumps at a loud crack then a glow stick is shaken vigorously, glowing brighter for a few seconds before landing in her lap. The green light makes Torrent's skin look sickly when coupled with the bruising of his face. She doesn't know what caused the bruising but is certain she had something to do with the cuts.

"Don't stray far. Your chamber pot is to your left as is your bag. You will be fed this afternoon before you face judgment this evening. Outside your den is a ledge fifty feet from the floor of the cavern below. There is no way down without flight, prisoner. If you take wing you will be chained."

There's a hard lump in her throat that swallowing doesn't clear as Torrent stands, towering over her. He turns and walks out, disappearing past the limit of the glow stick when the sound of his steps stops and his wings rustle as he apparently drops from the ledge.

Treason?

It doesn't make any sense. Attack does if her recollection of that night at Mark's is even close to accurate. But that means Blondie has something to do with Torrent, doesn't it? She sprouted wings before Jenn's eyes and Torrent thinks Jenn can turn into an angel too.

Perhaps if she fell from the ledge she might.

And where is Mark? If what happened at his house was real then he was there and has to know what kind of bizarre trouble she's in. Doesn't he?

Her pack contains everything but the razor, as she remembers from her hotel room, including her wallet and her cell phone. It's still off from when she left Mark's so she turns it on, desperate to reach him. He's the only one who can explain what's going on. It obediently powers up but isn't able to connect to the cell service. She gives up after turning it off and on again, shutting it down one final time and putting it away.

The chamber pot is as advertised: a pot and a roll of toilet paper. In the glow stick's light she can't tell if it's dirty or stained and doesn't care to find out. The den, as Torrent called it, is a stone cave as big as the living room of Terry's apartment. The only notable feature is the door, a rough round opening about six feet high, and the space is furnished with a woven mat and the hotel blankets.

Jenn heeds Torrent's warning as she walks to the opening, holding the glow stick out. After a few paces she can make out a stone ledge about ten feet away. Jenn gets on her hands and knees and crawls closer until she can stick her nose over the edge. The void below is lit by tiny fires and after a moment she decides they're lamps, a lot closer than the camp fires she originally thought but still a long way down.

"Hello?" she calls down and there is silence below for a few breaths before the quiet chatter picks up again. "Can anyone help me?"

Jenn's voice breaks as she crawls into the den and away from the drop.

Chapter Fourteen

Jenn drank some of the water that accompanied the plate of meat she left uneaten before leaving it outside the den. The black hours pass slowly with the exception of a brief visit by a smaller female who collected the dishes.

The thought of the trial after the raw whatever it was she guesses was dinner looms as heavily on her as the idea of being trapped in an angel cave. She's come to understand she isn't just underground. She's deep underground which means these aren't good angels at all like the one who'd come for Terry.

And Torrent thinks she's one of them. Maybe her overdose had been intentional and this was the price; on her way to hell and away from Terry forever. And from Mark if she doesn't keep her head together and get back to the real world. She could just explain she didn't know about them and promise not to do whatever her crime was and they'll let her go but with what? Penance?

Did bad angels do penance? Were they even qualified to mete it out?

And she's sure the female she saw briefly in the green glow at her den opening had a tail. Bad for sure. Nothing that belongs above ground has wings and a long skinny tail.

Jenn sheds her coat and pulls off Mark's T replacing them with a bra and a shirt of her own. Her phone says it's well past seven in the evening and her stomach rumbles. There's half a box of chocolates left over from her sulky hotel night in Saskatoon so she takes a couple and puts the rest away for later.

I could really use a drink, Jenn thinks. *Or maybe three.*

But that won't do any good either. With the exception of the glass of wine at Mark's she hasn't touched the stuff since they met. The thought of liquor turns to fantasies of Talon and Shadow like some weird word association and from nowhere Shadow's inner strength props her up.

And she needs to be Shadow to get out of here. If Shadow fits with Talon and that's how the bad angels know him then Shadow it is.

The rustle of heavy wings outside the den gets Shadow's attention as she tries to pick a caramel covered almond from her teeth. The now familiar presence of Torrent stomps in unannounced. A quick move of his arm and she's hit by what feels like a pile of thick rough cloth. In the failing light of her glow stick she sees he only wears a pair of loose cropped pants; a twitching tail dangles between his calves. Its movement reminds her of a cat watching a bird out the window.

Definitely a bad angel.

"Change, prisoner."

Shadow realizes he tossed her clothes so she stands on stiff legs and unfolds them. The pants appear to be very much like his only much darker and the top is a simple pullover tunic with two slashes down the back closed with buttons at the hem. She supposes they're for the wings she doesn't have. Both pieces are far too big.

Torrent turns his back so she wastes no time pulling everything off and putting on the garments. The fabric is rougher on her skin than it felt in her hands and she squirms a little without improving the scratching.

"Remove your footwear," he orders when he turns so she does.

Torrent seizes her elbow and pushes her toward the ledge and she digs her feet into the cold gritty stone the whole way.

"Don't fight me or make a noise," Torrent's breath is hot in her ear. "I've been hunting you for a week and it wouldn't be unreasonable for me to drop you and say you struggled."

With that he grabs her and steps from the ledge. Like when they left the Jasper hotel they fall free for only a moment before they circle the upper reaches of the chamber, Shadow's heart in her throat as she waits for the floor to get closer. The lamps she saw earlier brighten until she can make out the ground. Several groups of winged angels have congregated beside what looks like a tunnel and it's near there Torrent lets her go.

Shadow stumbles, her feet sting slapping the stone and her bad bone complains. It's only from a couple of feet up but it's enough to remind her he's in charge. Torrent's big hand again finds the back of her neck and the firm pressure saps the last of her resistance. As he pushes her through the angels they part. Several hiss menacingly and Shadow is grateful when they are past.

The tunnel takes them up and the minimal light from the large chamber quickly dims to nothing. Circling to the right the entire way Shadow counts her steps hoping to build a mental picture of the caves. She lost track of her den above the big cavern during the descent and has no idea how many tunnels lead from it. There's no way to get up to the den anyway so if they take her back she'll have another chance for a look around.

Torrent pushes them along and Shadow trips several times, hands out in front as she runs to keep up. The echo of their footsteps changes just as Shadow starts breathing hard and Torrent slows, stepping proudly into another much smaller chamber. Two large statues are visible, crouching on either side of a pair of heavy chairs, their wings folded at their sides. Clawed front legs rest on the ground before them and their tails are curled up around their feet. Their enormous stone eagle heads end in deadly curved beaks and seem to stare Shadow down though it can't be more than an intimidating trick of their placement.

More lamps circle the room but they contain no flame. Instead they glow with a pearly shimmer like fire but cooler. The outline of several smaller openings is visible behind the statues but it's too dark to tell if they are tunnels or other rooms. Or even impressions in the uneven stone. On either side of the statues a pair of large angels rests on one knee, their attention completely on Shadow.

A dozen feet away Torrent pulls her to a stop and drops to one knee forcing Shadow down with him. Before she knows it she's on all fours, still panting from the uphill run.

"My Sire Sher, my Dame Arden," Torrent says loudly. "Before you is the traitor Shadow. I demand justice. The traitor called me a liar among other things and assaulted me. Her marks are plainly visible."

Sher and Arden? Get her before Arden before Torrent gets her before Sher, Feather said. But now it's both of them. And how can she plead to Arden and keep Talon's sister out of trouble?

And why am I more concerned about Feather than I am about myself?

Shadow watches the three openings behind the statues but nobody comes out.

"What justice do you seek, son?"

As Shadow focuses on the statue the voice came from the other starts to move. Both have very human heads as their beaks disappear and they straighten up.

"Oh, shit," she gasps as the last of her 'holding it together' fails. She crawls away from the changing statues and imagines the sound of grinding stone drowns out her own nonsense cries, the only real sounds in the room.

Her captor grabs for her neck again but Shadow turns on her back, reacting instinctively to his neck trick now that she knows what follows. She has to get away and can't when she's lying peacefully at his feet. Torrent drops a knee to her stomach and easily pins her hands above her head.

"The rogue is wild!" he exclaims. "Disrespectful. I demand she be tossed from the eyrie to the rocks below and denied the honours that would free her spirit."

"No!" Shadow screeches as she gets air in her lungs. Torrent flips her to her stomach and holds her down, forcing her face into the stone floor. Blinding lights flash inside her eyes matching the shooting pain in her shoulders. He doesn't use his hand to weaken her as if he needs her resistance to prove his point.

"The only remedy to my humiliation is to bring shame to her eyrie and her sire!"

"Please, Arden!" Shadow begs as Torrent forces air from her lungs again. "Help me, please!"

Shadow submits to Torrent's hold, exhausted and trembling on the ground, and strains to see the statues. Two angels stand before the chairs. Both look to be in their sixties and wear the same short trousers as Torrent. The female's shirt appears to be of pure gold. Sleeveless, it dangles down over the waist of her pants. She sparkles in the strange lamp light like it's laden with jewels.

"Please, please, please, Arden," Shadow begs, eyes stinging with tears that seem to have dried in place. "I'm not an angel and if you just tell me what I did wrong I swear I won't do it again."

"Silence!"

Shadow cries out as Torrent grinds his knee into her back.

"She's mated to the rogue who harboured her after her crime!"

"She's terrified and confused," Arden corrects and Shadow watches as she takes Sher's elbow. He looks as pissed as Torrent sounds but holds his tongue. "What exactly happened?"

"Sire," Torrent sounds like he's breathing hard to hold Shadow down but he shouldn't be. She's spent. "I was discussing a position in my guard with her mate when she burst from his home and accused me of lying. Before we knew it she slashed me and her mate hauled her away. I went after her but she cast a barrier, preventing me from entering."

"She what?" Sher can't hide his surprise. Shadow knows

part of Torrent's story is a lie like the night at Talon's but it's better to keep quiet. Calling him out is what got her in this mess in the first place.

"Magic," Arden breathes. "You know what this means, Torrent. She's royal."

"It's inexcusable!" he shouts and Sher hisses, silencing him.

In the quiet that follows, the frantic steps of another angel come rushing through the tunnel. Shadow twists as far as she can to see a young female with wild red hair pause, eyes locking with hers for only a moment before she takes a few steps away and drops to one knee facing Sher and Arden.

"Child, approach," Arden says about as softly as Sher's annoyed growl.

The girl stands with her head lowered and passes Arden a note. She scans it and shows it to Sher.

"We will see him immediately of course," Sher announces. "Escort him to this chamber, Cloud."

"Sire," the girl scuttles off, not taking her eyes from Shadow.

"Your matter will wait, Torrent. Sire Lev has urgent business."

Chapter Fifteen

"Child, come," Arden offers, her hand extended to Shadow.

Torrent's complaints are audible but he releases Shadow. Once at Arden's side the older angel takes her elbow.

"Bravery," Arden whispers and Shadow looks at her in surprise as her courage begins to return: only in bits and pieces but enough to hope. She's desperate to believe that not all angels are bad because she likes this one; the only one with wings who's treated her kindly. Feather said take her before Arden and it was Arden's calm head that prevented Torrent and Sher from tossing her straight out to the rocks below wherever the cave entrance is.

It seems Arden is in control of the so-called trial since Torrent and Sher have deferred to her and not with indulgence. It's with genuine respect and Shadow hopes that respect will see Arden's kindness prevail.

Torrent takes position with the two guards near Sher. His very presence is still frightening and Shadow steps into Arden, nearly pushing her over. She's as tall as Talon and pulls her wings closed about them, partially hiding Shadow from Torrent. Up close Arden's cool metal garment is as soft as silk. Shadow wants to imagine the scent of bird seed but Arden simply smells sweet, like walking through the cosmetics section of a giant department store.

The sound of approaching footsteps reaches them and Arden turns to face the tunnel. The girl Cloud rushes out and immediately kneels before Arden. No boys are allowed on this side of the room it seems and Shadow's mind races as it registers the guards on this side are female. Shadow watches the girl with interest, nervous that she's so close. She's a teen, maybe all of fifteen years old but she's much taller than Shadow. Her unruly hair reminds Shadow so much of her brother's. Cloud stares, just as open mouth curious of Shadow, until both realize they're doing the same thing and look away.

A bustle of activity at the tunnel opening gets Shadow's attention and she collapses weakly into Arden, her senses slammed by what she sees.

"Terry," Shadow whispers followed by an out of control "unh, unh, unh" as she tries to keep from deflating completely. Arden holds her up like she weighs nothing.

The big angel who strides in is the image of her dead brother armoured in a black leather vest, trousers, wrist bracers and gloves and the handles of a pair of crossed swords extend past his shoulders. Jesus, he still wears army boots. His enormous wings are held tight to his body like shields and his shoulder length blonde hair is just as she recalls when he remembered to take care of it. He doesn't glance at Shadow but she barely notices as her stomach goes cold at the sight of the angel with him. The good angel, the very same one who'd knelt by Terry's broken body on the hot worn pavement two and a half years earlier.

He does look at Shadow, long black hair draped past his shoulders. His armour is the same as Terry's with the exception of his choice in weapons; daggers at his waist and one bound to his upper arm.

"I'm dead," she states certain she must be. Terry and the good angel have come to bargain with the bad angels for Shadow.

"Sshhh," Arden whispers.

Shadow tries to take a step toward Terry but Arden's

embrace tightens.

"Sire Sher, Dame Arden," her brother says as he bows first to Sher then to Arden. The good angel to his right drops to one knee and rests his hands on the other. "My gratitude for your reception on such short notice."

"Sire Lev," is the response. "It is always an honour."

Lev? What the hell is going on? Shadow looks more closely at the big blonde angel. He appears to be a man in his mid forties, not the young twenty-eight-year-old she saw for the last time during the moments which changed her life forever. The good angel looks her way again and Shadow claims the bravery granted by Arden's touch and stares until he looks away.

"My eyrie has suffered a tragedy," Lev continues. "The events of that day led to a great deception in the face of my friends and further deep loss for my family. In the past two weeks the last of all I hold dear has disappeared. I have come to admit my deception and to take the difficult course of humbling myself before you by asking for your help."

"Lev," Arden speaks. "Any choice you have made to protect the remnants of your people requires no justification. You need only tell us what must be done for our friends and our action will not waver until it is finished."

"Indeed, my friend," Sher agrees and Lev bows again. "You have always done the same for us."

"Thirty years ago my eyrie was attacked by a band of rogues in strength and number never seen before. Dame Treasure was heavy with our children and her protective magic was weak. They gained entry and came for her first."

"My dear friend," Arden exclaims. "The extent of your loss was as terrible as we'd feared."

Lev continues, his voice thickening with grief; a sound Shadow knows all too well. She pictures the looseness in his throat and feels the shaking of his diaphragm which make him speak more slowly than necessary lest he give in to the tremors inside.

"Many gryphons died defending her as we made our escape," Lev pauses. Shadow looks at the wings and tails and knows these aren't angels at all. Impossibly scary as bad angels seem however she's hesitant to embrace imaginary beings. On some level she believes angels are real and is unwilling to think Terry didn't go to heaven so she dismisses the word.

"We took shelter in the forest miles from the eyrie. Treasure bore my young before she passed from her injuries. To protect them from further danger from the rogue army they were placed in the human foster care system and raised without knowledge of their past.

"When my son Condor turned six I introduced myself and began his education in the ways of the gryphon."

"And the sibling?" Sher asks.

"True to her mother's bloodline she shows no sign of taking wing these thirty years," Lev explains. "She does not know of us.

"Then three summers ago, Condor was killed in a very human accident."

Arden's arms tighten around Shadow. Lev's voice is too much and she turns to Arden, hiding in her shoulder. Again the room is quiet like there's nothing that can be said which is in any way sufficient.

"Last summer my daughter was seen in the company of a rogue," Lev looks harshly at the angel at his side. "The Master of my guard knows this rogue and felt him worthy of her and did not intervene. I have yet to decide if his actions warrant punishment or praise. It was believed they bonded and the rogue confirmed this a few weeks ago.

"Then she disappeared.

"The rogue is linked to your great eyrie and I hoped my search for answers could begin here."

So much of Lev's story tears at Shadow's heart. So much of it could be told about her own life.

"Without hesitation," Sher announces. "Point us in the right direction and we will begin now."

Shadow turns to Lev. She's completely drawn into his story and feels the urge to assist as well.

"Then, my friend," Lev holds a hand to Shadow,

acknowledging her for the first time. "You will explain how she comes to be in your chamber, dirty and battered, in the garb of a prisoner."

As Arden lets Shadow go all eyes turn in her direction. Her black clothes are covered in fine dust from the floor and she's embarrassed to be so dirty in front of everyone. She takes a step back to hide behind Arden but finds herself alone. Arden has moved to Sher's side leaving Shadow by herself and the focus of attention. Panicking, she tries to wipe the clothes clean.

He's telling the truth, Shadow knows this as sure as she knew Torrent was lying and takes a step to Lev. The big man smiles and nods in her direction.

Shadow moves closer, eyeing the dark haired angel and giving herself plenty of room around him. This is Terry's father. The fact rings so true. When she comes near him, Shadow stops. Her hands tremble as she pushes her hair clear and looks up at the huge whatever he is.

"My father?" she whispers.

"She is accused in the assault of my son, Torrent."

But Torrent has disappeared.

"Where did this occur?"

"The human dwelling of her bonded mate, I believe," Arden says.

"She is my blood and her dame's heir. For thirty years I have sat to the right of her empty chair. Torrent is her captor?"

"He is responsible for her state," Sher hisses, obviously displeased with the admission. "Her rule extends to the rogue's dwelling. Torrent did not know who she is nor that he breached protocol approaching her mate without first speaking with you or her. They have caused harm to each other.

"Then," Lev says loudly as he takes Shadow in his arms, his big fingers on the back of her neck calm her and she relaxes in his affection. It's nothing like the rough handling from Torrent. "I suggest a consensus. I will consider both matters clear and Torrent and my daughter free of their respective charges."

"Agreed my friend."

"There is still the matter of her mate, also charged with treason," Arden interjects from her chair. "As his accuser is not available I propose another option. He's also unaware he's mated to your heir. Should he refrain from deception during questioning I would suggest his selfless protection of Dame Shadow warrants his matter clear as well."

"Talon?" Shadow asks. "He's in trouble too? I didn't mean anything especially getting him in trouble."

"Send for Talon," Arden orders Cloud who again runs from the room.

Talon roars, smashing his hands against the rock and knocking dust from the walls. After he uselessly soaked in her quiet despondence, her feelings quite quickly turned to sheer terror and for the past hour he's raged in frustration. The guard outside his den grows with each outburst.

As long as they try and stop me in two's I can be past them in minutes.

But he does nothing. If he was beaten beyond repair he would be of no help to Shadow so has little choice but to take out his need for action on the stone walls.

Or a good fight, Talon thinks to himself. Anything to calm down so he can stop his embarrassing tantrum.

Then in minutes her fear turns to strength though her confusion doesn't fade. Now she's simply content and anxious with excitement. Talon doesn't know what to make of it; the only thing which will make it right is to be near her again.

Finally silent, Talon drops to his knees.

He hears a rush of light footstep then Cloud's voice. He'd been one of the first to witness the devastation of Cloud's home eyrie. The infant had been the only survivor of a terrible raid by a band of rogues he'd only ever heard rumours about. She was found clinging to the still wings of her dame and it was a miracle she survived. Cloud is a going concern for Tawny who won't give up on the task of instilling some sort of order in her life.

Talon, as part of the delegation from the Jasper Eyrie called upon to assist, arrived to find nothing in the caverns but death and spent weeks hunting with other males to sustain the females as they cared for the many dead.

The loss of Cloud's eyrie made her self-destructive and angry so the civil tone she takes with the guard is a surprise.

"Sire Sher wants Talon brought before him."

About time. Talon will make sure Sher and Arden knew exactly how special Shadow is; the royal gryphon who believes she's human. If Arden is there then her compassion should see Shadow as another unruly orphan needing only care and education.

Talon waits by the curtain, fisting his palm with urgency as black-eye draws it open.

"Gryphon, attend," he orders and holds the curtain clear.

When Talon steps out he is circled by six armoured gryphons. Talon takes his place in the center. The group is so tightly packed in the narrow corridor all Talon has to do is take one down and they'll all land in a heap impaled on each others' weapons.

The girl Cloud strides ahead, wings flared wide like she's cleaning the walls. Inappropriate arrogance, he thinks. Her display will bug the hell out of the guards but at least she's putting up a brisk pace. Cloud has always been a little off in the behaviour department. The first time Talon saw her she was three and slapped Torrent because he got too close to a human toy Tawny had given her.

Then she bit him.

Silence fills the main cavern where he's certain Shadow had been held. From the moment she was brought in and through the day he could close his eyes and 'see' precisely where she was. Even if she hadn't been moved, the sudden change in her mood would have told him her trial had started.

As they climb the circling passage, whispering starts in

their wake. Eyrie gryphons are never too proud to gossip. They find stability in uniformity of knowledge, safety in a shared opinion and strength in the common mood of the occupants. Talon knows his anger and frustration stand out and are disruptive and the residing gryphons, mostly female, are anxious for whatever path the trial takes so there will be consensus of emotion again.

The circle of guards around him tightens as they step from the tunnel and into the chamber. Talon is surprised by some of the occupants. He immediately recognizes Soar, his long time friend and Master of Sire Lev's guard. And Torrent is gone.

The big male to Soar's left turns and Talon sees Shadow in his arms. The smudges on her cheeks could be either dirt or bruises. Whatever it is doesn't matter. It's another reason to tune Torrent up when he finally gets his chance.

Talon's nostrils flare taking in a scent very much like the one from Shadow's closet. It comes from the male holding her. Talon's wings extend in aggression and the guards move in but she holds a hand up, plainly frightened of him.

"Talon," she breathes, her panic escalating. He's held back by the prospect of traumatizing her more than she already is.

The blonde can only be Lev if Soar is at his right wing. How the hell could Shadow be involved with Lev? Shadow's eyes drop to Talon's tail and she pulls in her trembling lip. Then she curls in closer to Lev just missing the sight of Talon drawing back his lips to expose his teeth. Lev however does not.

"You're an angel too," Shadow's muffled voice comes to him.

Damn, I guess I am.

"Talon," Arden speaks clearly and he remembers his place, dropping to one knee. "Assume the position of apology, prisoner."

"Dame Arden," he replies, stifling the urge to take Shadow and make for the exit. Instead he places his palms on the ground, taking the weight of his wings on his back.

"Your accuser is not present. You have been advised of

the charges?"

Talon acknowledges with a terse nod.

"You may speak."

"Dame Arden," Talon speaks quietly to the floor hoping his own low voice will keep him calm. Whatever is going on with Lev, Shadow is still his mate and it's his responsibility to protect her. "My mate knows nothing of what she is or what we are. She believes we are angels. A week ago she attacked Torrent in her belief he'd come to harm me. He was winged and she thought he'd come to take me to heaven. I pulled her into my home.

"She summoned a barrier and in that moment I knew her to be a royal. Only his cuts are from her, the bruises are from running into the barrier."

"I see," is the answer from Sher. "And would you flagrantly disregard your respected place in my eyrie again to help a criminal escape?"

"For her," Talon is certain he's doomed himself. "Without hesitation."

"We have a consensus on the disposition of the rogue?" Lev speaks.

"The rogue is cleared of the charges," Arden says. "Stand free, Talon, son of Stalker."

He gets to his feet at an utter loss to understand what transpired before he entered the chamber. What happened for him to be cleared so quickly? As the Dame approaches she blocks his view of Shadow without shielding him from her fear.

"Sire Lev has told us of the sad loss of his mate shortly after the birth of his children and how they were hidden in the human world. And of the death of his son Condor.

"Condor?" Talon asks. He remembers a Condor; a young gryphon he met once a decade earlier who looked very much like Lev.

"Sire Lev came to us today seeking his daughter and has found her here. Royal Dame Shadow is the heir to his mate's chair and the rule of his eyrie."

"Royal Dame?" he mumbles stupidly. Royal he knew but royalty?

Sire's pinfeathers, Talon, that's what Arden just said.

"Come, child," Arden leads Shadow away from Lev then takes a minute to whisper in her ear. "Cloud, fetch Tawny."

"Talon?" Shadow looks very lost among all the big gryphons. She seems to have pulled herself together. The storm of emotion around her now has a small but stable core though it flickers and he worries it won't last for long. As Arden shoos the extra guard from the chamber, Talon pulls his wings around his shoulders so the big hollow bones form a safe cocoon for her.

As human as Shadow thinks she is, she still reacts as he expects to the gesture by stepping in. Talon holds her in his arms, hidden until the trembling stops. Torrent couldn't have found her a rougher set of prison rags and Talon wants to rip them from her soft skin.

He can't hide his pride in her strength and pulls her chin up. She feels so small and cold yet his own emotional equilibrium returns simply from having her in his arms again. Thank God, he's going to need every ounce of his own strength to help her adjust. It's been one hell of an introduction.

"I want to go home, Mark," Shadow whispers, her eyes closed. "I don't want to see anymore angels or gryphons or whatever else is hiding in the rocks. I'm going to see my counselor and finish packing up Terry and we can talk on the phone so you can tell me all about what's going on here in your life and I don't have to be kidnapped or carried off or sentenced to death and I can hang up the phone and deal with it when I'm not here.

"I'm not moving an inch until you promise to take me home."

Damn, she can be demanding. And what's he going to tell Royal Dame Shadow of the Vancouver Island Eyrie? No? In front of everyone? He's going to have to.

"Talon," he says firmly as his thumbs brush her cheeks

and ease her lids up. "Here, I am Talon."

He glances behind her at Lev and Soar. They whisper inaudibly even for gryphon hearing and after a second Soar pushes a wing higher so Talon can't read Lev's lips. He has a good idea what Lev has planned and doesn't want to worry Shadow. What he said about her dad running him off is one of many unpleasant possibilities. While mating with Shadow is permanent Lev can make sure it won't be easy. Claiming the Royal Sire's heir without even a 'hey I'm in the neighbourhood' never goes over well and considering how he feels about Lev's absentee rearing Talon is quite certain he's not going to take it with his wings limp.

"Take me home," she hisses. Her fright and confusion focus on him; her one way out. If it has to be his fault her world has changed that's fine because he's the only person she trusts to fix it.

"I will take you home," Talon promises. A glance at Lev tells him the impatient Sire is done conferring with Soar. The pair waits at the tunnel leading down to the main chamber. Behind them he picks up Cloud's constant chatter in Tawny's ear as the girl fills the old gryphon in on her version of events featuring Cloud herself escorting the condemned to the royal chamber.

"But not tonight and probably not tomorrow."

Shadow purses her lips with displeasure. So fucking pretty. If they were both human or both gryphon his arousal would distract every gryphon around them. Fortunately they're one of each, feeling everything but sexual need for each other.

"I feel your moods, Shadow," Talon explains putting her hand on his chest. At first she draws back from the feel of the small feathers and he waits for her to give in before he continues. Her hand doesn't completely relax under his but it's as good as he's going to get.

"Sire Lev waits for me," he tilts his head. "Tawny will take care of you for a while."

"No!" she shouts, her panic escalating.

"I've shared your fear and confusion for hours. You feel

safe now but I know you're scattered inside."

Shadow nods and she distracts herself by curling her fingers, exploring his feathers with their tips. Then she notices her bite and looks at him in horror.

"It's not infected and it doesn't hurt. I'll explain later… tell you anything you want," then he tugs at her chin again.

"Tawny has a very beautiful and generous spirit. There are few I would leave you with besides her. I feel you from anywhere in the eyrie. If you worry at all I will tear my way through the stone walls to get to your side."

"Sire Lev, a pleasure!" Tawny announces herself without kneeling, bowing or even looking at him. Only the oldest living creature on the planet does whatever she damn well pleases. It's where Cloud gets the loose tongue Tawny tries so very hard to reign in. "And Master Soar I presume. You'll pardon if I don't kneel."

"Tawny," Lev says simply but she's already well past him.

Tawny is positively ancient. She wears traditional trousers and tunic and her thin white hair flows down her bone straight spine. Her wings are held just a little too high. If asked she claims it's arthritis that prevents her from moving them to any other position but Talon has seen her angry and she can use them to intimidate with the best of them. Behind her Cloud manages to get one knee nearly to the ground before dashing to Tawny's side.

Talon turns Shadow around and takes his place at her right, the position of her protector. He doesn't need to make any oath to proudly stand in her defense. Shadow tries to get closer to him, hesitant with the newcomers but a firm hand on her hip tells her to stay put. Then taking Tawny's hands he drops to his knees before her earning a suspicious eyebrow.

"Well, Talon," she mutters sternly. "What does all this sucking up mean? Nobody bows to old Tawny anymore."

"And you can be assured I won't," he bites out, only because she tires of rote respect and will appreciate some attitude from one of her favourites. "I present my mate, Royal Dame Shadow of the Vancouver Island Eyrie and daughter of

Sire Lev."

Tawny laughs, followed by a grunt as she leans heavily on Talon's hands to get to her knees. Cloud gets down as well.

"Dame Shadow," Tawny winces and looks suspiciously at Lev though the twinkle in her eye tells Talon she appreciates the surprise. "Lev?"

"Sire Lev," Talon tries to remind her.

"Talon," Shadow whispers as she takes Tawny's wrinkled hands and starts to help her up. "I can't believe you made her get on the ground for me!"

Cloud takes Tawny's elbow and between the two of them they get the old gryphon upright.

"Talon, attend," Lev calls.

Talon turns to say something to Shadow but her glare is enough to send any sensible gryphon running. She's stooped over brushing dirt from Tawny's knees.

"I am the oldest living thing on the planet Talon, son of Stalker, mate to Royal Dame Shadow of the Vancouver Island Eyrie! How dare you have the pinfeathers to put me on the floor!" Tawny calls using his full name. "I hope her good manners rub off on you!"

But Talon has already taken position at Soar's left wing as they stomp down the tunnel. Shadow is in good hands with Tawny. He's certain she's angry with him but faced with someone she perceives as more vulnerable her single minded focus is already healing the cracks in her shaken courage.

Chapter Sixteen

"Slow down, child," Tawny mutters though when Cloud does Shadow still has to work to keep up. The air grows humid and warm as they descend through the black tunnel. Shadow clings to Tawny's elbow hoping to keep her upright on the uneven surface but she's as steady as the stone on which Shadow stumbles.

"How do you see where we're going?" Shadow asks breathlessly.

"Our eyes have no trouble in the dark, child," is the curt answer. "And yours won't either when you take wing."

"Is it true she's never taken wing?" the young voice ahead of them asks.

"Manners, Cloud," Tawny answers. "She's right here."

"I'm not a…" Shadow starts unsure how to finish. Angel? Gryphon? Both work. Somebody has to come to their senses about what she is and she has the discomfiting suspicion it's going to be her.

"Is she crazy?"

"Cloud!"

"Yes, Tawny," Cloud answers with an appropriate amount of teenage tolerance. Shadow's not sure if the two of them are really arguing or if it's simply banter but it's probably better to let them have at it.

The tunnel takes a tight left and the welcome silvery glow of a lit room ahead gives Shadow reason to relax. Never a big fan of the dark, she's held her breath as much as she can and is nearly as winded from the descent as she was from the uphill run with Torrent. A shiver works its way down Shadow's spine as Arden's reassurance he'll stay clear gives her a little boost of bravery.

"Tawny, I'm sorry Talon made you kneel," Shadow exhales with her first full breath.

"A gryphon never apologizes, child," Tawny says firmly as she points to a pool on the far side of the room. There are several along the wall and Shadow notes a winged gryphon in one. Steam and the laughter of children rise from the splashing water. "You may acknowledge a poor choice but never apologize. This is the warmer bath used by children who have not yet taken wing. The others would be much too cold.

"Quickly, let's get you out of these horrible clothes," she whispers as they near the bath. "I don't want her to see you dressed in these."

Shadow hesitates. The fabric may be rough and dirty but its protection is as much emotional as physical. Heavy and black, they let her think she can fade into the dark.

"Come now, child," Tawny tries. "If you've got anything under there I haven't seen in all my years then you *must* show me."

Shadow drops the rough pants then pulls off the shirt before sitting on the cool stone to swing her legs over. The hot water stings her knees where the fabric chaffed. Shadow hisses as the heat sinks too deeply into the small of her back where Torrent pinned her down with his knee. As her bottom finds a natural shelf she notices the water moves past from one end of the bath to the other.

"Tahhneee!" a small voice bursts out and Shadow turns just in time to see a naked toddler shimmy from the other bath and take off toward them in an awkward run. He's wingless, little fists pumping at his sides.

"Echo," Tawny says calmly though she braces herself

against the edge of Shadow's bath. The boy speeds up, arms wide and with a bound more coordinated than expected for his age plants one foot on a stone and flies into the old woman's arms. Once caught, he squeals as Tawny spins twice before leaning again on the stone tub.

The woman wrapped herself and the other child in very human cotton towels before letting the little girl run to Tawny. Her towel is around her waist and her upper body is covered in a gold bikini-slash-halter-top. Its straps run over her shoulders merging to a single chain between her wings before splitting again and reconnecting just tight enough to keep the sparkling front in place.

"Echo," Tawny says again. "I introduce Royal Dame Shadow."

As quickly as he was in her arms, Echo is on one knee and tugging the little girl from the tip of Tawny's wing.

"Like this Mist," he says as he pushes down one of her knees and pulls up the other, which makes her the opposite of how he's doing it.

"But I don't see a shadow!" Mist complains as Tawny repeats her introduction to the woman. As she drops she places a firm hand on the shoulder of each of the children silencing their voices but barely stilling their squirming.

"Dame Shadow," she says. "Welcome to Jasper."

Mist breaks free and tackles Echo.

"It looks like you have your hands full," Shadow offers as the mother scoops them up and rattles her raised wings. Both settle down as drops of water fly from their dame's glossy feathers.

"They are as healthy and strong as their proud sire," she says, her chin rises and Shadow senses the woman's pride in them as well.

"They're beautiful," Shadow adds. They both have their mother's curly black hair and dark brown eyes and if they had little wings they'd look like chubby cherubs.

"I'm beautiful!" Mist squeaks as the woman stands, tickling them to stop the wrestling.

"We have interrupted the Dame enough," she tells the children and with a nod she takes her children aside to dress.

"Cloud, fetch my basket child," Tawny orders as the woman disappears. "I wasn't expecting anyone down here at this hour. Had she seen you dressed like a prisoner she wouldn't have stopped to listen and I'm not certain Cloud and I could have held her back."

"From what?" Shadow ducks her head under the water as Tawny holds out shampoo.

"Attacking you."

Shadow looks into the black tunnel to make sure the woman is gone.

"Dames are very protective of their young. She is the only gryphon in the eyrie who won't have heard your story but she is the first to meet you."

"How am I a dame? I don't have children." She looks to the side at Cloud. The girl stands with her arms crossed, putting on an air of boredom. In spite of finding the man she believes is her father this place isn't Shadow's life and she wants to go home, sure she can work something out with Terry's apartment that is still so heartbreakingly full of him.

"You are a capital D Dame," Tawny explains as she dumps a bucket of water from the upstream side of the pool over Shadow's head. She's rolled up her pants and sits on the edge with her feet in the water. "You are the hereditary leader of Lev's eyrie and figurative dame to all who live there or call it home. You sit higher than he does and when the time comes Talon will take Lev's place. I sat in the high seat here for many years until my mate passed. It would have been inappropriate for me to rule alone or with my daughter's mate at my side so I stepped down and passed rule to Sher and Arden. Their daughter would have eventually taken Arden's seat but she passed nearly a hundred years ago so the seat will go to Torrent's mate if the boy ever gets around to finding a royal to be his."

"Oh," another bucket knocks more questions loose than suds as Shadow's stomach rumbles, the sound bounces to their ears repeatedly even in the soft bubbling of moving water. Shadow can grasp the mutual misunderstanding which led to her captivity but even without being kidnapped by Torrent she feels there is something rough and cruel about him.

"Dinner last night," she mutters in answer to the sound of hunger. So much has changed since then, even more than the previous week where she'd seen a woman grow wings in Mark's kitchen just before she ran off to be captured by the gryphon she only imagined she'd hurt. *And when did I start thinking of them as gryphons?*

"Cloud?" Tawny calls. "Fetch Dame Shadow something to eat."

"I have studies," she replies like she's talking to herself and Shadow feels a scratch in her throat. The only thing that will clear it is to agree with her.

"Child," Tawny growls. "A meal for Dame Shadow, her belongings and some appropriate clothes. And since when are you interested in your studies?"

Shadow opens her mouth to say that her school is more important but Tawny places a hand over her lips and after a moment the strange throat scratching urge fades. Cloud rolls her eyes and starts to stomp toward the tunnel.

"Cloud," Shadow says, revolted at the thought of her last dinner. "No meat, please."

The girl stops, turning on her heel and addressing only Tawny.

"She's having fun with me!"

"Cloud," Tawny snaps, shaking wings flared wide as she pivots on her bottom and takes a few intimidating strides toward the teen. Shadow backs slowly to the far side of the pool where the current is a little faster and rests a hand on the ledge to keep from drifting sideways. "If Dame Shadow says no meat then no meat. You may use the internet if the task is beyond you but be certain I will check the logs!"

"Okay," Cloud exclaims and runs from the room, wings and red locks flying behind her.

"Might I—"

"Make an observation?" Tawny interrupts and offers Shadow a bath puff and some expensive body wash from the basket. "I'm certain it's nothing I'm unaware of."

"She's mouthy," Shadow says bluntly. If she's royalty then she's as entitled as Tawny to say what's on her mind.

"Indeed," Tawny laughs. "In a place so full of status it certainly sticks out. I'm twelve hundred years old... nearly... and I don't take shit from anyone; shit praise or shit shit. Cloud has seen fifteen summers and most gryphons attribute her attitude to spending too much time with old Tawny.

"Ouch, that bruise is nasty."

Shadow lets Tawny's soft hand guide her to sit on the edge.

"Nearly all gryphons here are common. No magic in their blood at all. Magic runs through some rare female bloodlines, royals, and a male is considered common or royal depending on the blood of his twin sister though you can be certain there is no magic in them. Sher is considered royal because his sister is but Sher has no magic. Talon is common because Feather is.

"The only royals present in the eyrie are you, me, Arden and Cloud."

Tawny places a palm on the bruise and Shadow pulls away.

"Easy, child. I suspect your magic is protective given what you did to Torrent. Arden can instill bravery and inner strength. My gift is healing. Don't move."

Neither of them does and after a moment Shadow takes a full breath without stiffness.

"Turn," Tawny lets her sink into the warmth of the pool before brushing her fingers along Shadow's cheek. "There, the bruising is nearly gone."

Shadow explores the sore spot on her back and looks at the old woman in surprise.

"You did that? Thank you."

"Bruises are easy," Tawny says dismissively but Shadow sees she's proud of herself. "I can heal most injuries but I can also make things worse when compassion demands it. I can't take a life but when the only path ahead is the last one I can hasten the journey. As long as there is a chance at life I can make things better.

"So to get back to your observation?" she suggests.

"Cloud is mouthy and royal?"

"And indeed," Tawny smiles. "You felt it when I silenced you. Her magic appears to be in persuasion. For the most part ineffective on me but works well on anyone who doesn't expect it and in particular males. She will make a challenging companion to some poor gryphon. She has a good sense of it and Arden, I and you, child, will keep quiet about it."

"Child," Shadow echoes thoughtfully.

"Yes."

"I'm thirty, not a child."

Tawny's laugh fills the chamber.

"From your scent you have been in season, as has Cloud but you have not yet shared in the blessing of the dead and until you have done that, you are a child."

Shadow doesn't feel enlightened.

"In human form you are in season every month but as a gryphon female you are fertile for a day or two every few years. You are mated to Talon. When you are in season you will only want him and he won't want children with another."

"How the hell did that happen?"

"He offered his bite," Tawny explains. "You returned it. Then you offered him your tears and he accepted them. I know this because that is how it's done."

"Son of a bitch," Shadow curses. "Nobody made *that* clear. I mean I feel attached to him but—"

"Cloud is an orphan," Tawny says. The old woman has a knack for interrupting and this time with the one thing bound to get Shadow's attention since she grew up as an orphan. "Fifteen years ago a badly injured gryphon arrived at the eyrie. Before he passed he told us a band of wild rogues, males who live in the human world, raided his eyrie. He'd been in the mountains and observed their entry. After a time the rogues began to cast gryphons from the high entrance, their wings bound behind them; the distance too short to become human and take wing again to escape their bonds, too far to survive the drop. He was spotted and dispatched his attacker barely making it here.

"Cloud was the only survivor, only a year old. We sent all we could spare and sent word to other eyries but we knew it was in vain. Talon was with the first wave sent south to assist. He's a great warrior and it's beyond me why no eyrie has chosen him to be a ranger; part of its royal guard.

"I don't know who found her among the dead but she was brought here and I took her in."

"Oh dear," Shadow whispers. How long had the child crawled among the dead gryphons? Her mother? Blood?

"We didn't think she'd make it. So young, losing her twin and everyone she knew. Her strong spirit has pulled her through but she's angry and distant, refusing closeness with anyone here. Perhaps she protects herself from further loss."

Tawny sighs as Shadow pulls her knees up as tight as she can. Her own pain is still far too close, binding her to the past in a pitiless wash of memories and grief. Fifteen years of it is unimaginable.

"I won't be around forever," the old gryphon says, looking all of her long years. She passes Shadow a towel. "There is nobody here who can get through to her but she seems to find you fascinating."

"How do you know?"

"I've never seen her shy with anyone, except you."

Talon falls into step behind Lev and the master of his guard. During his years as an aspiring ranger he'd suffered his share of broken bones at Soar's hands. In spite of Soar's larger size Talon hadn't spared any lessons about the dangers of underestimating a smaller opponent.

The smells of old sweat and leather lead him down a dark corridor and closer to the main entrance of the eyrie and a chamber generally used for guests to conduct private business. Lev's enormous crossed sabers reach past his waist and both bear the mark of Master Sky, the legendary blacksmith and warrior who trained Talon. It's enough to give him a need for challenge in spite of his dress; still barefoot and wearing nothing more than simple cotton trousers.

Talon still itches for a fight after finding Shadow in the black tunic and trousers of a prisoner. Her pleading hand shocked him into keeping his dignity and his wits about him. All he wants is to get back to her but here he is following her sire and his fiercest guard.

He'd once thought of his mate as no more than a common rogue and he swells up with pride, carrying his golden wings a little higher. Shadow is true royalty. Not that he'd doubted Swift and Feather that she was royal but that didn't equate to royalty. Hearing her sire, head of arguably the most feared and isolationist eyrie on the continent, claim her as his heir is enough to tip his world more than she already has.

Shadow was scared and overwhelmed and it's clear to Talon why she'd been such an enigma. Up until a few minutes earlier she thought she was human. If anyone can ease her past that way of thinking it's Tawny.

"Nice to see you again, Talon," the dark haired male at Lev's right wing drops back a couple of paces and holds out his right arm. Talon takes his elbow and grips it, squeezing as Soar's gloved hand holds his.

"Agreed, Soar," Talon replies, keeping a watchful eye on Lev. The Sire's head is turned slightly though his sharp hearing doesn't need help picking up their soft words. Evesdropping so openly is an obvious display of dominance.

"I hear you've adopted this eyrie as your home," Soar continues and as they ascend the tunnel narrows and the air cools. This conversation is something Lev wants; nothing else would cause Soar to speak out of turn.

"That is true," Talon hooks a thumb in his waistband. The last time he'd spoken with Soar, other than the minor face off in front of Shadow's apartment, they were both drunk at

Cooper's, the Calgary rogue bar. Unsure why they were fighting other than the usual male disagreement over who's tougher, their brawl had gone skyward and it had taken nearly a year for the large feather at the end of Talon's right wing to grow back.

Soar appeared to have repaired his missing tooth.

"I didn't know teeth grew back," Talon comments.

"Good dentist though it took some time to find it once I could see again," Soar points at Talon's right wing.

"Good dentist," Talon says lightly.

Soar grins, clearly enjoying the personal moment with Talon before he glances at Lev and sobers.

"It happens I was following Dame Shadow last summer. She was riding south and hadn't left her apartment for anything other than work in a week. I didn't recognize your truck at first. Not until you pulled into the gas station."

Ah shit, Talon. You were busted long before Lev showed up today. This isn't going to be pretty.

"I was about to intervene and run you off on behalf of her sire," Soar says, his back to Talon. "I would have only let you see me and you'd have come up with some excuse to leave her side to run off the competition. We'd have had a discussion and you would have walked away. Badass as you are my friend, word was you'd gotten soft, living the human life for a little too long."

The rumours had reached Talon's ears as well. Lev leads them into a chamber near the entrance where the gear of many more than two gryphons is stored neatly to the side. A real fire burns in one corner; the only light in the otherwise empty room. He's curious whether Lev's guard is roosting in the rocks outside or below taking the opportunity to meet the local females.

"Why didn't you?"

"The boat fell and before it finished landing on the ground you had her covered up as fast as ever. It was clear to me you're still very good. Maybe better. Much to my Sire's chagrin, I retreated and left you alone."

Lev stops and turns at the far side of the chamber, near the fire. Lit from below in the flickering light he looks like the devil himself; everything his reputation claims.

"Master Soar, see if our gracious friends can spare some of their purest moonwater. You know how much."

What kind of hellish punishment does Lev have planned if he needs the females' crazy magic moonwater? Nothing Talon has ever heard of but the gryphon is a recluse and stories about him help keep children from sneaking out alone; a terribly convoluted mixture of the rogue army attack on his eyrie, death, and the name Lev, one of the few survivors mean enough to live through it.

Soar nods gravely to the Sire and turns to Talon, leaning in more closely than either male is comfortable. Talon understands whatever he hears next is between him and his closest friend.

"You have taken on much more than you bargained for by claiming Dame Shadow but I imagine you've come to that conclusion already. Should I be punished for giving you an opportunity to impress her I will take more than feathers from you in reparation. Understood?"

"Understood, my friend," Talon's blood runs a little cooler as Soar turns and kneels to Lev before leaving them alone in the chamber.

"Talon, son of Stalker," Lev begins, his voice is friendly but the arms cross. "Approach."

With his wings held high because he's done nothing to be ashamed of Talon does and at the respectful distance of five feet drops to one knee, his relaxed hands resting on the other.

He knows what's coming. This is where Lev says exactly what he thinks of Talon. Everything he would never say in front of Shadow. Talon raises his chin, ready for praise or punishment.

Bring it on.

"Rise," Lev orders and Talon takes the opportunity to assess Shadow's sire. The gryphon is several inches taller and at least five hundred years old. Lev is old enough to shift completely; abandoning all hint of his human body. There is something of Shadow's chin in him, her long graceful neck and the set of her jaw. Her thick brown hair and petite body must have come from her dame.

Talon stares at the wall and waits, wings and tail perfectly still, as Lev takes a step closer. The unimpressed Sire looks Talon over as he moves around behind. Talon resists the urge to turn until Lev steps right up and grabs Talon by the base of his wings. With a growl, Talon's nails extend to claws and he shakes his shoulders, deciding which way has the least resistance so he can get around to defend himself.

"Easy," Lev whispers. Talon's movements cease but his nostrils flare and he turns his head, keeping an eye on the Sire. "She may have chosen you, rogue, but if I don't like you your next few centuries will be hell."

Talon's fingers flex, claws scratching at his palms, but Lev steps away before completing his circle. Lev's eyes move to Shadow's mark then he reaches. Fast and accurate, Talon's right comes up, grasping Lev by the wrist and holding it in place.

"I don't care if the Royal Council cleans your chamber pot, Sire," Talon hisses, well aware he's on the line if not leaning over it. "Nobody touches me there but Shadow."

"Hm," Lev snorts, stepping away and leaning casually on the wall behind him. "Let me guess; she's pretty, small and an easy mark for whichever rogue was lucky enough to stumble upon her."

Talon stiffens, waiting a chance to speak his peace.

"Then you let her get in trouble with a royal and ran back here to play ranger games with your friends. Abandoned her to Torrent who could have very well dispensed with his embarrassment by leaving her—"

"Abandoned!?"

Lev reddens at the outburst but Talon doesn't give a shit. The arrogant Sire thinks he's going to stand there smugly telling Talon off. Not bloody likely. He'll step in anything when it comes to Shadow.

"Let's talk about abandoned; she suffered every day for two and a half years without her brother. Not only did you leave them to the humans but when Condor died you let her fend for herself. The pain she carries is crushing and you did nothing!"

Keep your feet where they are, Talon, he says to himself. As he struggles to stay coherent, visions of Lev with a bloody nose make his knuckles itch. *If Lev is out of reach then you can't clock him.*

But the Sire takes a step forward forcing Talon to take a step back.

"What do you know of her pain? He was her brother but he was my son," Lev roars, static crackles between his feathers like he's readying to shift completely. Talon has pushed too far and if Lev draws full claws the shit will get very, very deep.

"I felt it even before I laid eyes on her, as fresh today as it was last summer," Talon keeps his voice down while his body language says someone will pay for Shadow's suffering.

Lev smirks. Thick feathers flow up the sides of his neck to mix with the hair at his temples. "So you went for her because she's weak and hurting too much to put up any sensible resistance."

"I chose her because this mountain could never hold back her strength," Talon takes another step away from Lev but the Sire takes two and they stand nose to nose, the peaks of their great wings pushing against each other. Lev's electric show has stopped and Talon prays it was just a display. He's not dressed for dealing with that kind of trouble. "I chose her because her bravery puts mine to shame. I chose her because her humility is as beautiful and innocent as a child and I love her before some half-assed excuse for a gryphon did her the disservice of taking her tears!

"When she heals and embraces her gryphon spirit she'll be a powerful reflection of her sire and dame and I'm proud she chose me to be at her side."

The soft scrape of an earthen bowl over rock is the only indication Talon is no longer alone with Lev. Soar has returned and put the moonwater near the fire. The gryphon wouldn't be master of Lev's guard if he couldn't be trusted and Talon knows whatever his friend overheard will never pass his lips. But the fire? It's not the pain of punishment which worries him; it's how he's going to explain it to Shadow without lying or telling the truth.

"It was her dame's dying wish they be hidden as humans," Lev whispers. Talon feels Lev's teeth against his throat and holds his chin high. "I did as I was told, flew south to a church and left them there. My only words were 'keep them together.' I let the world think their spirits flew free with their dame's. I silently cursed my dead mate for ten years, sure I'd done the wrong thing but her strangest desires were always proven out in the end. The band of warrior rogues returned and murdered several more of my gryphons including small children as we fled. The master of my guard was lost. His bravery spared the lives of many grieving survivors of the first attack and I'm certain Shadow would not have survived had I not given them up. They came for the females and the young, Talon."

"Sire," Talon says, inadequate and all he can think of.

"Do you truly feel her spirit in yours? Know her feelings as she does? Like I knew her dame?"

"Yes, Sire."

"And finally, is there any part of your rant you wish to retract before I finish our business here?"

Talon's eyes flicker open as he realizes the walls still echo with the word love.

"No, Sire."

"Master Soar," Lev says loudly and Soar kneels but is quickly pulled to his feet. Soar's look of surprise is priceless as Lev embraces him, nearly pulling him from the ground. "You have taken an excessive amount of shit over this, my friend. This is a good gryphon."

Talon looks away as Soar mumbles in acknowledgement.

"Leave us, Soar," and with a nod Talon is alone again with Lev. Beside the rough pottery bowl containing only a couple of cups of plain looking water is a leather pouch. Lev squats and unties the strips of leather holding it shut. Then he dumps a round wooden handle with a metal end and several chunks of raw iron into the water, carefully so he doesn't touch them.

"Sire," Talon starts. "I came here when Shadow took off because she didn't know she's royal. Her only hope was that I didn't miss her trial."

With a gesture to join him on the ground, Lev pushes his lips together before offering a smile. In the firelight his hair appears orange; his glistening eyes shamelessly reflect the flames.

"Sometimes we must abandon something precious for a time to protect it, yes?"

"Yeah," Talon sighs as he gets on his knees. As much as Lev's departure from Shadow's life initially disgusted him, it's his own abandonment which still has him angry. Talon had done the same thing when called for and can only guess it's earned him a small amount of the Sire's respect.

"On your hands, Talon, son of Stalker," and as Talon gets down, Lev swirls the bowl causing brief flashes of light. "I don't know what the females use this for but it makes an excellent cleaner, removing all traces of anyone who has ever touched the pieces."

It takes several minutes for the flashes to become fewer and farther between. Lev speaks again, this time in the old words like Talon's sire used to teach him the Earth's magic.

"My daughter has no guard, Talon, and a guard must first have a Master. This is not a task you can decline. Whether you accept or not is up to the Earth and she will test you now," Lev winks. "It won't take very long."

He places the bowl before Talon and sits back on his haunches.

"I was once the Master of my mate's guard, until I took my sire's place in the royal chamber. The same path is before you. Take the iron from the bowl and place it in the hottest part of the fire. It's nowhere near hot enough to melt it on its own but if you are truly free of doubt that you would put her life before yours the Earth will do the rest. She will shape

Shadow's mark that you will bear for the rest of your days. The mark you will give all whom the Earth chooses to serve with you in Shadow's honour.

"If you aren't the right gryphon for the job then the metal won't melt and you will not be Master of Dame Shadow's Royal Guard."

Without hesitation, Talon reaches into the water and pulls out the stones. They're surprisingly warm considering the icy chill of the moonwater and he singes his fingers placing them where the coals glow white. He's sure his hand trembles with excitement; from a prisoner on trial for his life to a chance to be a ranger and a master of the guard to boot.

Holy shit.

The change is nearly instant, first the pieces start to glow then they sink into the ashes, snaking several trails as the iron becomes fluid and creates its own mould.

"Ah," Lev exclaims as the concussion from a blinding flash of light knocks them both back several inches. "The handle."

Talon pulls it from the bowl and presses the metal end toward the iron. The redness fades and with a thunk the hot brand jumps, affixing itself to the handle.

"With its first heat, proudly claim your title, Master Talon."

Still on hands and knees, Talon presses the smoking brand so the three mingling horizontal lines of Shadow's mark sear his skin. The piece is long and he has to start at his bicep and slowly roll it over the curve of his arm. The smell of burning flesh wrinkles his nose and when the mark is done he can breathe again.

The Sire gathers up a handful of ash from the fire's edge and rubs it into the burn, cooling it and ensuring that when healed it will be clearly visible.

"Off your hands now," Lev holds the leather pouch open and Talon places the brand inside as he sits. "Nobody but its master may touch it. When you take my seat to serve Shadow's gryphons as Sire you will pass it on to the next Master of her

Guard. Should a gryphon not be meant for the commitment of service, the brand will stay cool no matter how hot the flame and the gryphon will not become a ranger. Clear?"

"Clear, Sire," Talon proudly replies.

"Fetch your armour and weapons, Master Talon," Lev stands, pausing to place his fingers under Talon's chin and draw it up in praise. "I assume you have several gryphons in mind who may be worthy of my daughter. There are several of her dame's guard who would be proud to be tested again.

"The attack on my eyrie wasn't random," Lev whispers. "There have been several others up and down the continent over the years including the home of that young catastrophe of Tawny's. I have suspicions but for now we have a risky trip ahead. Shadow's magic will protect the eyrie; bring back the light and the water, like her dame's did. Until we get her home she is in great danger, now that her existence is known.

"My hope is by tomorrow morning when we depart you've talked her into taking wing. She lost her child's roundness two years ago but I'm afraid like her dame her first shift will need some encouragement."

"Yes, Sire," Talon acknowledges as he dusts off old memories of his own sire giving him 'the talk.'

"Oh, and Talon?"

Lev pauses at the opening.

"Your female is unadorned. I trust you will take care of that tonight as well?"

After a minute Talon leaves the chamber taking a left to the entrance for a quick head clearing flight instead of right wherever Lev went, deeper into the bowels of the eyrie.

Jesus, did the Royal Sire just order me to screw his daughter?

Chapter Seventeen

Shadow shivers on a stone seat by the pool as Tawny puts a towel over her shoulders. Shadow was originally concerned for Tawny but her thoughts are now for Cloud; the orphaned teen all alone in this eyrie full of her kind. It looks like the girl does an admirable job of keeping everyone away by being more trouble than she thinks she's worth. Maybe simply remaining here reminds her of the roughest days following the loss of her family.

It isn't long before Cloud returns, a covered plate in one hand and Shadow's pack and some white garments bundled over her other arm. Tawny takes the clothes and helps Shadow dress before she's chilled. The clothes are pure white, or at least look white in the dim light; the shape their only similarity to the rough black set. The trousers have a gap in the back from which she presumes a tail would pass and both are light and soft and a little big, draping like Talon's shirt.

"Cloud," Tawny gestures at Shadow. With a roll of her eyes Cloud kneels and offers the plate.

"Thank you," Shadow says and as the girl stands Shadow tells her to stay put.

"Wow," she exclaims. There's a little dish of diced tomato and black olive tossed with cilantro, pepper and bits of lemon, a stack of steaming falafel, a large flour tortilla filled with coloured peppers and red onions and a heap of yogurty dip on the side. "You made all this?"

Cloud dips her chin.

"What's your name?"

"You've heard my name," Cloud whispers, triggering a growl from Tawny.

"But we haven't been introduced. I'm Shadow."

"Cloud," is the one word answer.

"It's pretty," Shadow says, thinking longingly of the outside. *How far did Torrent carry me? I could be above them.*

"It's stupid, boring and plain," Cloud's arms cross as Tawny's hairbrush flies through the air and nails the girl in the butt. "Oww!"

"Join me," Shadow tries, making room on her stone; partly to deflect Cloud's face to face attitude and partly to protect her from another hairbrush or anything else in Tawny's bath basket. "Now."

"Tawny…" Cloud whines, again acting like Shadow isn't there.

Tawny doesn't answer as she busies herself tidying. After a moment Cloud stands and takes a seat beside Shadow, fists shoved between her knees and careful not to touch her.

"After the meat I got for dinner I was scared there was nothing here I could eat," Shadow cuts one of the falafel in two before dipping one end in the yogurt and taking a bite. It's mouth watering hot and cold, spicy and tangy at the same time.

"We live in a mountain, child, not the desert," Tawny says. "A balanced meal is as important to a gryphon as to a human. Our caverns are very well stocked."

"Try it," Shadow whispers to Cloud.

"Tawny, she's sharing her food!"

Again Tawny doesn't answer so Shadow gives the girl a gentle elbow and she jumps.

"Did I do something wrong?"

"A gryphon never shares their food," Cloud whispers. "Only a dame will feed her young."

"A human will share something amazing with her

companion," Shadow feigns offense. "It would be considered rude of me not to offer and even ruder of you not to accept."

Cloud turns, making eye contact for the first time.

"I believe I am about as gryphon as you are human, Cloud, and you have to try this."

The girl's mouth opens part way as her eyes narrow but she's at a loss for words. She stares hard at Shadow, nostrils flaring just slightly and Shadow has to clear her throat. The itch from the previous time Cloud tried to persuade her returns. As Clouds inner indecision carries on, Shadow resists the urge to tell her never mind and finishes the piece of falafel. Then she moves on to a spoonful of tomato salad.

"Oh Jesus, that's good," she murmurs. Through the lemon there's the smoothness of olive oil and the sweetness of the tomato. Black olive and lemon is a combination she would have wrinkled her nose at before but the flavours co-operate completely.

Cloud reaches to take the remaining falafel piece and dips as she saw Shadow do. She sniffs it then takes a nibble before she reaches for the plate again.

"Once you pick it up you have to finish it," Shadow explains. "You touch it you take it is a human food rule as well."

Again Cloud appears puzzled but she finishes it.

"Try the tomatoes."

Shadow is ravenous and keeps going, barely noticing as Cloud samples everything. In the back of her mind though is the girl's comment about a mother and child sharing food. It's amusing to think but she wonders if Cloud feels the same closeness of the moment. Well, if not closeness then at least camaraderie.

"I'll take your things and find you a more suitable den," Tawny announces.

"Leave my pack, please," Shadow asks. Cloud's mouth is full and she stops chewing, concealing her hands under her thighs.

"As you wish."

Tawny gathers up Shadow's winter coat, boots, and the wet towels and makes her way from the chamber. Now that their only company is the moving water, it's definitely closeness Shadow feels with Cloud.

"They don't trust me," Cloud reaches with finger and thumb for the last olive.

"Why do you say that?"

"I know."

"Oh."

"I mean they always say the right things and I've never been without but I've heard them talk when they think I can't. Did Tawny tell you about me? Where I came from?"

"A little," Shadow allows. "It sounds a lot like my story. Lev put my brother and me with the humans to keep us—"

"They think I'm bad luck," Cloud interrupts, a trait Shadow is certain she picked up from Tawny to keep the conversation on target. Her target. "I know I scare them. They say the rogues will come for me again and when they do everyone here will die."

"Oh, Cloud, that's awful for them to think!"

"I can tell when I'm not trusted. I think it's my magic and I wish I didn't have it. They don't mean to mistrust, I mean they can't help it, it's instinct to trust or not to trust and I try and remember that but it still hurts.

"When I become an adult they can't keep me here and I'm going to make a human home where nobody knows me."

"Pass me my bag please," Shadow asks as she puts the empty plate at their feet. What she's thinking isn't much but it's all she can offer Cloud.

She knows you trust her. She wouldn't tell you that if she didn't.

"Where I come from there's a place my brother and I would go whenever we could. We'd rent a cabin… a den on the beach in a place called Tofino where the sky and the ocean could fight all day long even in the summer. My favourite time to go there was the winter and I would watch the clouds all day.

"You never know what a cloud is going to be: sometimes

protection from the sun, sometimes thunder, lightning, rain, the most powerful weather or maybe just passing by watching the stars with you and relaxing in the breeze. Some days if you're really lucky you can stand in the cloud it's so low and you just know that however it seems to be feeling the other side basks in sunshine shining brilliant white light all over. I saw it from an airplane a few times and there's always that beautiful part that will surprise you that you never really get to see but it's there. It's always there."

Shadow's hand finds the half box of chocolates in her bag but she doesn't pull it out just yet. Pressure on her shoulder brings a smile to her lips. It's Cloud, leaning closer, her wing around Shadow as her arm sneaks around her waist. She hopes not to spoil the moment and rests her cheek on the tangled red hair, remembering the coarse feel of Terry's dreadlocks.

"I think they're taking you home tomorrow, Shadow. I'm going to miss you."

A bit of food and a compliment brought out the warmth in Cloud's heart.

And your trust, Shadow.

"Can I give you something?"

"Yes."

Shadow gives Cloud the box of chocolates.

"They're half gone but I want you to have the ones that are left."

"What do they do?"

"They can make you feel better."

"They have magic?" Her eyes have gone wide.

"Not by themselves. Maybe it's the person who gave them to you or the people around you when you eat them. Sometimes I eat so many I'm sick to my stomach before I feel any better but maybe I'd feel worse without them.

"Maybe Tawny would let you use the internet to learn how to make them."

Cloud's vigorous nod is interrupted by Tawny's return.

"One day I will bring you some!" she exclaims as she gets to her feet.

"Cloud, child," Tawny orders. "Please find Talon and let him know Dame Shadow is waiting for him in the main chamber."

"Okay, Tawny," Cloud's attitude seems to have dissolved completely.

"Cloud?" Shadow calls to the girl's back. "Will you cook for me again?"

Talon has been dreading this for half a decade; speaking to Swift again. It's been that long since their messy ending. Except for a week ago at his Saskatoon house.

And the half dozen times she tried to kill him; obvious and incompetent as the attempts were she might have succeeded if Talon had never learned to fight and was maybe a third his size. It had been simple to disarm her and walk away.

"Talon," Swift's soft voice calls from behind the heavy curtain covering the opening to her den. The last time he'd been here she'd painted the walls white like inside a human house. Even the light of a single silver lantern hurt his eyes. "I'll behave. I promise."

She's dressed at least, standing at the far side of her chamber. Deep golden wings frame her excessively female body; their peaks high over her shoulders and a single large feather seems to caress the side of her calf. Swift looks ready to travel since the clothes she wears are human. Her sleeping mat is covered in the rough dark blankets typical of the eyrie, not the bright human fashions typical of Swift. Otherwise the room is empty with the exception of a single bag. Talon's muscles tighten with a flash of anger as he hopes his things are still in the smaller second chamber behind her.

"Relax," she gestures to the small opening. "I think it's time for me to move on from here. I was going to leave you the den but I don't suspect your royal mate will find it all that homey."

"No," he says, scratching at his thigh. This has to be brief or he's going to be rude to get it over with.

"I've acknowledged my poor behaviour at your home to your mate and I wish to acknowledge the same to you. I'm aware I disrespected you both and your home," she bows. It's the closest thing to an apology he'll ever accept and she knows it.

Swift gathers her bag up and steps over the mat, leaving dusty footprints. Then she glances at Shadow's bite on his shoulder and the ranger's mark on his other arm.

"We could have mated, Talon," she keeps her head down. "I believe there was love. But we never would have been a match. You're so insufferably *male* and gryphon and *ranger* there would have been too much conflict for us to ever really enjoy each other.

"Silence?" she shakes her head. "I appreciate you've stood and listened and I haven't humiliated myself by speaking to your receding back.

"I am pleased for you, Talon. A life of duty and pride is what you've always wanted. As much as I wanted you, I am proud to see you find her."

She moves quickly, startling him. Her words put him at ease and before he can defend himself her hand is on his throat.

Talon knows better. He remains still until her intentions are clear.

Slowly, oh so slowly, her hand releases then the tips of her fingers move to his chin and push it higher.

"Hold your head high, gryphon," she whispers. Her wings disappear through the door long before the curtain falls shut.

He does until the sound of her feet is long gone. In the small anti-chamber he finds what he came for. The familiar scents of his leather and oiled metal greet him. The bags themselves are canvas, stained and scuffed, and he loosens the ties holding them closed. Inside is his armour, so dark it's nearly black. Talon feels around the bag to verify it's all there. Satisfied, he unrolls the heavier bundle on the mat he and Swift once shared.

His rests his right hand on the hilt of his short sword as his left carefully moves along the heavy leather sheath then he draws the sharp blade. The raw ingredients were iron meteorite fragments from Ontario, similar to those used by Lev for his guard master's mark. Talon had sought them out in a remote area and lugged the chunks south to Sky's eyrie. Not only was the surly old woman one of the best rangers he'd ever met, she was also a master swordsmith.

During a ceremony attended only by Sky and Talon, she'd sliced his palm with it, spilling his blood on the virgin blade to make it lighter and stronger. The healed cut still tingles when he takes his skyblade up as if he and the steel are one. Anyone else would find the blade cumbersome, heavy and poorly balanced but to Talon it's an extension of himself.

Light footsteps betray another gryphon in the hallway and Talon freezes as he decides if the visitor will pass or intrude.

"Master Talon," a young female voice announces from outside the chamber. He recognizes the voice as Cloud, Tawny's troubled charge. He's certain taming Cloud is a fruitless effort but if anyone can keep the disobedient youngster in line it's Tawny, his favourite elder.

"Enter."

She does, kneeling to his left and keeping her head down. A gryphon shows pride by raising his chin. He also shows respect the same way by putting his life and his throat in the hands of authority. This little one shows neither. Rather than recognize her disrespect he chooses to ignore it. He's done enough of it himself over the years.

"Master Talon," she says quietly. "Dame Shadow waits for you in the main chamber."

"Acknowledged," he scans the remainder of his weapons. The crossbow needs to be loaded but everything else: boot and bracer daggers, telescopic baton and several other small blades designed to be concealed are all perfect. The leather harness for his short sword is still in good repair in spite of the years in Swift's closet.

"A skyblade?" Cloud gasps.

As much as he wants to growl at her for speaking out of turn he's proud as hell of it.

"Yes," he whispers as he repacks the weapon.

"A real one?" she pushes.

"Yes," he snaps, somewhat offended but her eyes are huge as they fly back and forth between the disappearing blade and his armour. Damn it. He'd been just as amazed by the first one he'd seen unsheathed and the ranger who owned it had been a hell of a lot more courteous. Cloud doubts her eyes, not his honesty.

"Yes," he tries again and holds the sheathed sword out to her.

Talon has to hold back a laugh when he realizes she's stopped breathing but can't when she barely keeps it from dropping to the floor.

He gives her a minute before he relieves her of it and rolls it up with his other weapons.

"Cloud, take these to the anti-room where Sire Lev and his guard are hosted."

The girl's mouth hangs open.

"Unless you can't manage the heavy bags."

Cloud scowls at the slight as Talon knew she would. There's only one way to get things done when it comes to gryphons. Their pride will never let them turn down anything as long as he presents it as hard and he's not disappointed. She holds her head so high she's nearly facing the stone ceiling.

"Very well," Talon touches her just under the chin.

Chapter Eighteen

Shadow waits in a corner of the main cavern with Lev and Soar when Talon steps from the tunnel. In spite of Lev's affection, her nervousness is easy to pick up. Talon's stomach doesn't lurch at their closeness now that he knows how they're related. His female's sire is part of the protective net he casts around her.

Shadow notices his approach and moves to join him, taking a few steps away from Soar in the process. Her unease ramps up until her focus is entirely on Talon. Something has gone on between her and the master of Lev's guard. Soar saw them together but Shadow doesn't know that. It's something else that puts the lead weight of grief in her heart.

"Talon," she smiles though she keeps her distance. Somebody's pure white garments hang from her and he's certain they're Tawny's. Even though she appears like a child in her dame's clothes the set of her shoulders says she's had it with surprises. Jesus, if he couldn't feel her inner turmoil he'd never know she'd been through hell today.

"Shadow," Talon replies with a bow of his head.

"I took off because it just got too weird," her brow wrinkles with worry as her mouth makes a little O. Then her arms stick out to tell him precisely what weird meant. "I mean I ran out. I spent the night at a hotel and when I went back to your place the next day you were gone—"

"Shadow, I—"

"Shut it, Talon," she snaps and he glances at Lev. Everyone in the chamber including the Sire can hear Talon being told off. Lev's firm nod tells Talon he's on Shadow's side. Each word Shadow speaks seems to lighten her mood ever so slightly so he'll let her unload on him here at least for a while.

"I bussed as far as Jasper and decided I couldn't face you in Parksville either then last night Torrent grabbed me out of my hotel room and I woke up in a hole in the fucking wall," she points twice in the air to emphasize her last two words. Yeah, she was held right where he thought but for her to wind up so close for days before she was brought in? Damn, if he'd just looked a little harder he could have eased her transition to gryphon life.

"Then all I had to eat was a plate of meat I could hardly see until I had to put on the itchy clothes—"

"I know, Shadow," Talon tries to hold her but she takes a step away, palms up stopping him like she did before.

"Tawny says I'm the leader of an eyrie. Lev is my father and I have a guard?" Her chin comes up like she's daring him to talk again and even though it sounds like a question he doesn't speak. "We're married or something? We bit each other and you touched my tears but I can't be mad at you for not telling that would go down since you wouldn't have suspected I thought I was human... still feel like a human."

Shadow grabs his branded arm in both hands then turns to glare at Lev.

"What did my father do to you?" she demands, lips red with anger and her scent clear through the fragrance from her bath.

"It's your mark, Shadow. I'm the master of your royal guard like Soar is master of your sire's," Talon drops to one knee, pulling his arm free and offering his hand in exchange. There's a little stress twitch under her eye and this is as far as he's going to let her go in public. Shadow seems to get it and as she looks around the crowded chamber she leans down to take his arm again.

"I know exactly what it means," she turns toward Soar and much to Talon's surprise Soar steps behind Lev. Damn, she's formidable but if she's going to have a blowout at anyone it will be him and not here.

"Where is your den?"

"Um," Shadow turns several times trying to get her bearings and points up. "Tawny says there's a tunnel up there with my things in it. There's a den all set up for me but I can't get up there or back down."

Talon stands and she lets him pick her up.

"I know the one, hold on."

As he spreads his wings the center of the room clears and after a few steps he kicks off from the ground. Shadow's shoulder gets up in his throat as she holds on for dear life. "I got you, tight turns."

And he means it. Talon has to circle as they climb high then they cross. His wings fold behind him as he lands a few feet inside the opening.

"Don't leave me up here, please?"

"Not unless you throw me out."

Instead of putting her down, Talon carries her through the long tunnel, not missing the irony that's it's more like taking a human bride over the threshold than anything else. Nothing would make him want their first encounter any different than it was but taking her on the wing has been a long time coming.

"We're in the den," Talon says and she unfolds, putting her feet on the ground. Although he can make things out it's pitch black to her. "Don't move."

But she doesn't listen and clings to his elbow as he goes to the dark light on the wall. Talon places his palms over what looks like a glass-smooth bulge and lets them part as he blows, a warm open mouthed sigh. Silver light floods the room and Talon has to adjust his eyes so he's not blinded.

"How did you do that?" she gasps.

He takes her hands and places them over the light then

pulls them apart.

"Blow, cold air, pucker your lips."

She does and the light goes out.

"Ha!" Such a small thing fills her with triumph. "How do I turn it back on?"

"Warm air; just exhale with your mouth open,"

In only a couple of seconds they stand in light and Shadow turns so quickly he has to check his balance before he falls on her.

"How long have you been able to read my mind?"

"I can't," Talon explains. "I have an idea what you're feeling but not what makes you feel it or what you're thinking."

"How long?"

Her stare makes his heart pound both because he's got her complete attention and because he dreads making her angry. He can't decide which is sexier.

"Before I saw you I felt this pain coming up behind me on the highway: failure, shame. When you stopped beside me I had to say something."

Shadow nods, her attention far away and Talon knows she's thinking about her brother.

"I'd quit drinking for a week," she whispers. "I was going where nobody knew me to buy vodka.

"Look, some things are really, really private. I don't want to know that you know if I'm upset."

"That's not all that's bothering you, is it?"

"No," she takes his arm and turns him so it's in the light. "Terry was all I loved for twenty-eight years and until I met you the booze was the only thing got me through. Not much of a future. No future at all really, without him."

"Condor," Talon tries. "He was Condor. I met him once ten years ago."

"Then you knew Condor better than I did. My brother was Terry. A big blonde adorable man with an alpha streak a mile wide. Nothing ever got him down. He'd stand up to anything like a giant fir in a west coast winter storm, arrogant as hell like a big fuck you to the world."

She pauses, her fingers tracing the air over one burned line after another, following their curves over his ash darkened skin like she's committing them to memory.

"When he died the world didn't feel right anymore. Something had shifted underneath me and it didn't start to feel stable again until the day we met."

"Shadow," Talon whispers, trying for a kiss but she doesn't look up from his arm. It's the closest thing to love she's admitted and he understands why she's so cautious to connect with anyone again; her brother gone in an instant, snatched from her arms.

"I thought I saw... now I'm sure I saw an angel come for him. We lived in six foster homes until we left the system. Some were more religious than others and we were expected to at least participate in the beliefs of our foster families. Lev says when we were six he introduced himself to Terry. It was then my brother lost interest in church but I didn't. I believed in angels and heaven, sometimes more than others and lying there on the road looking at my dead brother, when the angel came, I knew he was there to take him to heaven.

"Talon," Shadow's eyes are wet with the agony in her spirit. "The only thing that kept me from following him to the grave was that it was a sin and I'd never go to heaven to be with him. I believed Terry was an angel and one day we'd be together again.

"Then today, Lev walked in with the angel who knelt next to Terry's body."

"Soar."

"Yes, Soar," she sighs. "And I knew he wasn't an angel and Terry didn't go to heaven and everything I tried to imagine about him watching over me was a lie."

Shit, he can't even tell her it isn't a lie, because that would be one.

"Lev says the night he died they took his body from the basement of the hospital and the females blessed him then they put him back. I don't know what he meant. There was no service for him, nothing official anyway. His biker friends got drunk. When I could ride again I took his ashes to Tofino I stopped where the accident happened and fell apart for a while before I took him to the beach and left him there, in the waves and on the rocks.

"Even a little bit in the couch he loved. We used to rent a cabin there on weekends sometimes and hang out.

"Everything that's happened, it's all here," she holds her palm over the burn. Her heat makes it sting but Talon doesn't move. "On you."

"Shadow," Talon picks her up and she tucks her head in next to his chin and wraps her legs around his hips, arms tight around herself.

"I know," she answers before he can speak. "I'm stronger for it but right here, right now, I don't have to be."

"No, you don't," Talon kneels on their sleeping mat and waits for her to straighten up.

The thought of seeing her winged is entrancing, her tail moving, echoing the curve of her hips as it brushes against his. "Tomorrow we leave for your eyrie and I need you to do something for me before we go."

Yeah, she gets it.

Shadow nods, looking at the great spread of his wings. "How?"

Easier said than done. After some instructions about using her imagination and her body would do the rest and an hour of trying Shadow flops back on the mat in defeat. Talon's coaching would be helpful if she could clearly remember it happening to Swift but he won't turn human to show her. If his patience wasn't so completely unflappable they'd have bickered themselves into separate corners of the den.

"Nap," she announces around a yawn. It has to be nearly eleven and way past bedtime.

"Break," Talon points at the chamber pot and steps out into the tunnel.

"You didn't just read my mind did you?" she's so frustrated maybe a little argument would give her the emotional edge to pop out wings. Or take wing as Talon calls it but what she remembers of Swift in his kitchen was more like a room filling with angry feathers.

"Didn't have to, you were squirming."

Then she barely has her trousers back up before he snatches the pot away and disappears down the tunnel with it.

"There will be a clean one at the entrance in a little while," he announces as he kneels down behind her and grabs at the hem of her top. "Off."

"You want to—"

"No," he says as she lifts her arms letting him pull it up over her head. "If you haven't noticed, as good looking as I am I don't inspire any arousal in you at all and honestly you do nothing for me."

"Asshole," she mutters.

"Yeah, yeah," he tugs down her trousers. Shadow stands and lets him pull them off but he's right. She doesn't feel sexy at all nor does she want to. "Human females don't do a thing for Talon and gryphon males don't do a thing for Jenn. That's just the way it is."

"Whatever," Shadow crosses her arms under her breasts and tries to stare him down but he shrugs.

The dreams she used to have of him seem very gryphon now that she thinks about it. She'd just written the flying part off as a common theme of dreams. It was the rush of hunting him down that really got her going, almost as much as the fear of getting caught before they went at it.

I'll get you turned on, she decides. Nothing bothers her more than being told there's something she can't do. *I know exactly how hot you're gonna get. Then we'll see who wants to be human and go after Jenn.*

Talon sits back on his heels, mirroring her crossed arms and if Shadow can guess he's picked up on her resolve because his body language can only be described as defiant: shoulders back and wing's pushed higher to taunt her.

"I used to have this dream after we met, every two or three weeks," Shadow says, lowering her voice to sound as sexy as she can. "It always started I was really high up, looking at you a long way down, running through the sand, snow, whatever. I think you were scared of me and it made me angry that you'd be like that, fearful, afraid. A coward. But it wasn't enough. I wanted to feel your terror in my hands, in my mouth as I counted your breaths and your heart pounded like it was trying to break free of you and escape me."

Talon tries to remain emotionless but his fingers have taken hold of his cotton trousers and he won't look at her. Then a thick swallow. Sure, not turned on at all Mister Gryphon.

Shadow walks around behind him to give some realism to her dream, taking position where she would be.

"I drop down lower, flanking you nearly on the ground and I can smell you, hear your feet. Your steps are uneven as you keep trying to get away but I know it's pointless and so do you. Every time you look my way I'm a little closer," she takes a step nearer.

Talon pulls his wings in tighter. An itch runs down the center of her chest, past her navel creating a little heat between her legs. *Nothing to worry about*, she tells herself, *he'll be human soon, I'm anticipating him being human*. But his eyes move down her body like he's watching the itch move.

On her knees, she leans close to his throat.

"You don't see me coming," her fingers touch the feathers on his chest and damn if her mouth isn't watering. "Then I… I… "

She hears herself moan, surprisingly loud but it's all she can do. She's taken by surprise with the sensation overload in her back. It's not pain but pleasure as she releases something she's kept inside for far too long.

"Tal—"

But her lungs have emptied and she grabs at him as the light fades and a terrible weight threatens to pull her over. Their breathing echoes in her ears as everything goes numb.

Chapter Nineteen

Shadow is aware of growling and strong arms. She blinks in the blinding light and turns away as the movement makes her faint again.

"Talon?" her voice is loud in her ears. His growling stops then his frantic lips are on hers as he pulls her upright. Shadow's uncoordinated mouth can't keep up with the pace of his kiss so she gives up.

"Relax, *Arlette*, relax," he breathes. "You did it."

"Dizzy."

"I know."

His hand on the small of her back slides down and she takes in the odd feel of it running along her tail. Talon's thumb caresses little circles as it goes, feeling the bones through the covering of hair. "So long, oh wow."

Shadow watches him as her eyes focus.

"Your wings need blood," Talon explains. "Your first few shifts will be the roughest as your body gets better at storing the extra when it's not needed and making whatever it can't store."

Shadow moves as the tingling in her lips passes and he groans as she feels his erection underneath her. The heat she built up trying to make him change flashes brightly between them.

Without taking her eyes off Talon's, she gets her knees on the mat. The weight on her back is a surprise and her stomach tightens to hold her upright.

"Shadow, did Lev say anything about your dame?"

"Not really, why?"

"Because you're white. Pure white."

Talon helps her to her feet and she turns to look at her wings. Her tail wraps around her ankle and she shrieks, pulling her foot up and tipping over. Instinct moves her wings and she recovers her balance. When she looks down, her narrow white tail slowly uncurls then rests, reaching the ground before bending up with the bushy white tip six inches off the floor.

"A long tail is so fucking hot," Talon whispers as she notices his only goes halfway down his calves and is twice the thickness of hers. "I've never seen a more beautiful gryphon."

"I'm a gryphon," Shadow feels like she's seeing him for the first time. "And neither have I."

Damned if he doesn't blush. Shadow's tail swings between her legs and grabs his, coiling around several times like another way to hold hands only she feels far more connected.

"It feels like a fresh start."

"Then what do you want to do first, gryphon?"

"See in the dark," Shadow announces and Talon laughs, gesturing at the silver light on the wall. The sound is more a low sensuous growl than a human laugh. The knots it makes in her belly make it clear he wants it dark as much as she does.

She turns but Talon's firm hand on her elbow stops her in her tracks. Pulling doesn't help.

"Don't be prey," he reprimands. "Don't turn your back on me. Until you can fly and I know your limits don't risk it."

She tugs again and he lets go so she keeps turned to him as she approaches the light.

"I've been fighting and hunting for decades, Shadow," Talon explains but it's a little late. He doesn't have to be such a dickhead about it. "The last thing I want is to overestimate what you can do and hurt you. Symbolic surrender for now, nothing more."

Bullshit, it's because I'm a girl.

Shadow puts her hands on the light then blows, bathing them in darkness.

"Your eyes."

Talon's eyes are as black as in his kitchen. The outline of his wings is clear against the equally dark stone behind him.

"Yours are just the same."

But she's not really listening. Even the shapeless trousers do nothing to hide the muscle in his thighs. Talon's thick shoulders stand out in the silhouette of his wings and even in the dark there's no mistaking the outline of his cock against the heavy cotton.

Talon's tail twitches, disappearing behind his leg before returning to rest. Then again.

He's teasing me!

But her tail responds, ducking alluringly out of sight. As she watches Talon's eyes drop and he shifts his weight, absently adjusting himself. The feel of her long spine moving low against her butt is intriguing and as she reaches to feel it the diamond bracelet slides down her arm and brushes over his bite. Shadow's knees go weak as the cold gems vibrate over the raised tooth marks.

Talon's chuckle, too low for human hearing, is barely audible for her gryphon ears though she feels it in the air.

Jesus, touching it feels good and her hand creeps up. Tingles shoot everywhere through her body as she feels each and every bump; each mark seems to stimulate something different than the last. They harden as she goes becoming more and more sensitive. How can he not touch his all the time? But then he's a guy. He's used to knowing when it's inappropriate.

This time he laughs. She's overwhelmed by the foreign feel of stubborn pride and decides she's had it with the teasing, the symbolic surrender bullshit and making fun of her for touching herself.

Shadow picks up her heel and pivots on one toe, daring him to tell her what she can't do.

ELIZABETH MUNRO

"Don't..."

Don't what? Shadow doesn't remember, something about don't turn around. Unsure why she shouldn't and confronted with the big male she spins, knowing there's some kind of trouble coming. Talon's wings spread and his tail stiffens, vibrating like a cat about to pounce.

Shit, I'm in shit.

His growl is her queue to turn and run for her life.

Tucking her wings in she bolts faster than she ever thought possible. She's never tried to get away from anything but with her pounding heart egging her on she takes three glorious steps before she's hit from behind and pinned to the wall. Talon has her wrists together in one huge hand and her feet off the ground. His other hand pulls her head over his shoulder.

Talon's open mouth is on her throat.

The rumble in his chest goes right through her into the stone and after a moment a bead of his saliva or her sweat makes its way down to be caught between her skin and the rock. But as much as she's blind with terror everything below the waist is on fire and she squirms, desperate to find relief anywhere, even up against the wall.

"Don't turn your back, I said," Talon whispers and as he pulls his mouth away he swallows. She can smell everything going on with him even stronger than the smell of her own humbling defeat: dominance, arousal.

Victory.

"Don't tell me what I can't do," Shadow wrestles a hand free and gets a palm on the wall but his erection has captured her tail up against her thigh and as she continues to struggle he presses even harder.

"I'm going to put you down," so arrogant. Her blood boils with the need to put him in his place. "You're going to turn around and very carefully push my chin up and put your teeth on my throat."

Shadow slaps her palm on the wall and lowers her head feigning submission. No way in hell is he getting away with this.

"Okay," she gasps drawing in a few full breaths for strength.

As Talon steps away, Shadow jumps. She gets her shoulders on his chest and her feet on the wall and kicks for all she's worth. He goes over on the mat and as they go down she tumbles, wrapping her tail around his neck as many times as she can.

"Surrender," she orders.

"No."

He doesn't smell scared at all. The son of a bitch doesn't even get his hands up.

Shadow tightens her tail and gets on her elbows. Her wings are heavy but she can put up with it for a while. Right in front of her is his stomach so she opens wide and bites just below his navel.

"No," he says but when she gets a hand on his thigh his hands move. She knows exactly how to win.

Sliding her fingers up over his cock she finds the drawstring and opens it.

"No!"

"Yes."

Her hand goes in his trousers and he tries to pull away so she reaches past and scratches over the artery in his groin.

"We don't use teeth and claws there like this!"

But she doesn't stop. Expecting the loose sag of his balls she finds them tight to his body and runs her palm over before wrapping her hand around his thickness. Either excitement or fear kept him full and hard.

"Surrender."

"No."

"You want to."

"Yes," he bites out like simply saying the word bests him. Shadow pushes the waist of his pants down and draws her mouth near, tightening her tail oh so slightly. His salt meets her tongue as she explores his head with her lips opening just enough to pull it in.

Talon's high pitched 'please' causes her tail to release and she backs away proud of them both.

He sits, pulling her up and wraps his arms around her, stroking her tail with one hand. Then a kiss before his tongue works its way to her throat. Absolutely tender, Talon gets to his knees and lifts her up. After a moment he presses the tip of his shaft against her center, kissing her weak mouth as her weight sinks her down until she's filled with him.

Jesus, he's the most gentle and beautiful man Shadow's ever seen or felt. They've both dominated and submitted, true equals connected as one.

"I was so worried I'd overestimate you that I underestimated you, Shadow."

She works her tail between their legs and coils it around his to be close in every way she can.

"Read my mind, Talon. I can't explain what I'm feeling now," Shadows wings are lowered as are his. The time for dominance is over. "Tell me what it is."

"Trust." Talon's pure black eyes bore into hers. "Pure, absolute, trust."

The lazy smile on Shadow's lips says his beautiful white gryphon got as much from their foreplay as he did. Devious and adorable, the surprise of her attack nearly set him off in his pants. She could very well have shifted claws and fangs and done some serious damage but that wasn't her goal. Threat and imagination were what the lead up to coupling was all about.

Her mouth finds his; the heat between her legs mirrored in her tongue. Shadow uses her whole body on him, pushing away before he pulls her back down then her wings flare with his and like an awkward first kiss they bash together to find their perfect fit.

Talon gets his hands under her ass and lifts her as he thrusts up from below just as she nestles her wings around them both, under his. Mirroring her, he covers her completely like they're in a nest they made together of their own feathers.

"Talon," she whispers. There is no hint of the day's troubles or even the past few year's troubles in her, simply the balance of granting him a successful hunt and achieving that same victory herself. Both predator and prey.

As they move together Talon whispers in the old words; to her, to him and to the Earth. Part of him is back on hands and knees on the frozen riverbed repeating Stalker's words; first a promise for Shadow, that she'll learn the ways of the females' magic, how to respect the dead and prepare them for their return to the Earth and that she'll teach her daughters the same.

"Yes," she murmurs in his ear as if she agrees and she shouts, coming apart in his arms as she strokes him from inside tempting him to join but he only slows down, keeping her on the edge as he makes his own promise that their sons will learn the ways of honouring the Earth like he learned from his brave sire.

Only when she teases her bite on his shoulder with her tongue does he offer the final prayer. Talon takes the largest tooth mark on her hip between his thumb and finger rolls it between his fingertips. Shadow cries out a second time, throwing her head back. Her wings pull free and beat hard, nearly lifting her away. Friction sparks between their wings tinting hers in blue and his in black flashes of light. Talon's voice fades to a whisper and he holds her down, uttering the prayer he'll say every time they couple on the wing: fertility, conception and a healthy dame and offspring.

The cool metal of her new adornment presses on his chest as she clings, arms around his neck and wings high forcing their way above his. Then there's nothing but her soft laughter as her tail relaxes its powerful hold on his, tip twitching and softly striking his ass.

"Shadow, look," Talon says as they shudder together one final time and he lowers his eyes anxious to see her adornment. He expects the simple gold garment typical of a younger male such as himself and is as stunned by its composition as Shadow is by its very presence.

A deceivingly delicate sheet of silver-white platinum drapes over her breasts like satin. Talon follows the fine chains connecting the sides around under her wings and finds that rather than join like the others he's seen they twist together up along her spine before splitting to pass over her shoulders. There they widen, joining naturally with the front as part of the butter soft platinum weave.

Then there's the star field of tiny diamonds placed so perfectly he couldn't find them by touch alone.

"And it's only half as beautiful as she is," he catches himself speaking out loud.

"What is it?" she looks at him for only a second before holding her hands over it, running them down over her breasts.

"It's my adornment. It represents my hidden treasure, my hoard. It's modest and will grow as my hoard does."

Damn, it's hard to believe that's true but I said it so it must be.

"Adornment?" Shadow can't take her eyes off it. "Like Arden's?"

"Yes. When you're human it will be nothing more than a necklace. Look," he directs as he pulls it up. It appears to change shape enough he can expose her nipples. "It moves for me... feeding children."

"But..." she loses her voice and he's sick with her disappointment. True it's skimpy but he's proud of it. He's never heard of one that isn't gold or a white gryphon for that matter.

"It's not much..." he tries but her sadness only seems to deepen.

"Talon, it's amazing. It's I just met Echo and Mist and Tawny told me about being in season and I just hoped that maybe we could still," she lets out a big sigh and half a smile. "After last week I never thought I'd be unhappy about waiting for years maybe. What if we were human?"

Shadow seems to brighten at the idea of children and it

sucks to be the gryphon to shut it down.

"I wouldn't risk you like that," Talon lies on the mat and she curls up with him. Her tail wraps around, resting on his stomach and he fingers the tuft at the end. "A gryphon pregnancy lasts nearly two years and even though it's twins they're no bigger than human twins. A human pregnancy would last the same amount of time but would keep growing and growing, so big the dame doesn't usually survive."

"I see," the feelings he gets from her aren't any happier but he goes on since the rest is something the gryphon in her needs to know.

"That's not all. Human conceived children are completely human and are given up. I never want you to go through that."

"Given up?" Shadow pushes herself sitting and noisily figures out what to do with her wings. The noise is unnecessary; she's completely aggravated. "Like I was?"

"These days, yes."

"What do you mean these days?" Shadow pulls her tail away.

"A long time ago they were abandoned."

What he can see of the dark room dims with the fatigue that follows any Earth transformation, like manifesting her adornment. Shadow yawns, slumping to the stone wall. Taking wing requires protein especially until she becomes efficient with her blood supply and with the long flight to Vancouver Island she needs to recover as much as she can before they leave.

"I'm not going home again am I?" she takes his arm again studying the burn. "That's what this is, the three lines bound together: the past, the present and the future all together on you.

"Permanently.

"A week ago I thought I had to heal the past to even be in the present but now I know I'm already there. It's not so much my mark but a message only I could understand. Something I needed to hear."

As she pulls his arm close to kiss the burn he feels her

wings. The layer of white down beneath the fine feathers is so thick it's almost spongy. Her flight feathers are narrower than his but there are so many. And that tail. She uses it like a tool, longer and far more flexible than any he's seen, and she won't stop touching him with it. Even when she's still it explores, so insanely erotic his mind wanders as he imagines if she could coil it as tight as her fist.

"First we'll go to your eyrie," he reassures her. "Your gryphons haven't had heated water or light since your dame passed. It's not as cold as here, I'm told. Your magic will give them those things again and keep them safe like when you forbade Torrent from entering my house. The eyrie entrance is so low when the storms kick up the sea spray comes right in and it's coated white with salt."

"My?" she blurts out. "No warm water? But there are babies!"

"You're a good Dame," Talon gives her affection, stroking the back of her neck. "Sshhh, we leave first thing in the morning, Dame Shadow, and your gryphons will be proud to have you home.

"You don't have to give up your brother's apartment. If there are things you want to bring to the eyrie, we'll bring them. If you want to sell it, then sell. If you want to keep it just the way it is that's fine too, just keep in mind you'll outlive the building by centuries."

She nods against his shoulder as her tail comes up, caressing the edge of his ear.

"Did you really dream about me after we met?"

"I didn't know what they meant then. I understand them now."

"It'll be like that, when we get outside on our own, whenever you want."

"Yeah?"

"Fuck yeah," Talon promises around a huge yawn. "I gotta eat, coming?"

"No."

"Alright," he answers. Shadow returns his kiss then he

steps from the den and into the tunnel. It's clear she's not in touch with the physical change she's been through since she doesn't recognize her very gryphon need for food. "Get your trousers on. I'll bring you something."

Chapter Twenty

A shrill cry sounds from the end of the tunnel. Talon has the light on before it fades, adjusting his eyes to the brightness to give himself a moment of advantage before whoever it is reaches the den and has to do the same.

"Talon?" Shadow is on her feet as a loud 'ow' effectively covers up the purpose filled steps and feather sounds of several gryphons.

Then a chilling scream fills Shadow with the scent of dread and puts pure ice in his heart.

"Cloud," she bolts past as he grabs her and she nearly drags him to the tunnel.

"Dame Sha—"

Cloud's voice falls to a whimper as the four sets of feet turn to three. When Shadow raises her wings Talon uses their weight to keep her off balance and pull her away from the tunnel.

First through the opening is one of Sher's guard followed by Black-Eye and Cloud, suspended by her red hair from his big fists. The girl's hands scratch at his arm and he can only imagine how painful it is with the added weight of her wings. Cloud's trousers and tunic are smeared with blood as are her hands and Black-Eye's arm.

Last out is Soar before Talon loses sight of everyone.

Shadow's wings flare in fury and her throaty hiss sets his hair on edge. Talon's own dame once ran off a visiting rogue for picking up Feather's dinner instead of his own, so Talon lets Shadow go and drops to one knee to avoid riling her further. Soar has the sense to do the same and with his eyes on the ground is about as submissive as he could ever hope to get. Next to him is Black-Eye's kneeling accomplice. What the hell went on with Cloud to make Shadow react like this?

Talon prays he's doing a good job of keeping his threat down because he's the one who's going to have to stop her from leaving Black-Eye in pieces. The poor gryphon his dame went after fled the eyrie missing half an ear.

"Dame Shadow," Black-Eye announces.

Stupid fuck, she's past the point of listening. Stray sparks run down the long feathers at the tips of her wings and her sharp nails have thickened extending nearly an inch past her fingertips. She's too young to shift any more than this but it isn't enough to stop her from threatening him with all she has at her disposal.

As Talon fights the urge to stay out of the angry female's way, Shadow makes her move; one arm around Cloud to support the girl's weight and her other sinks long nails into Black-Eye's wrist.

"Release her," Shadow orders. A smart gryphon would but this one persists.

"Dame Shadow, this child has been accused of murder."

"Bullshit, fucknuts," she hisses and knees his groin hard enough to shift his armour and get his attention.

"I didn't," Cloud whines, able to speak now she's not dangling by her hair.

"Let her go."

"Do it," Talon says as he gets between his mate and Black-Eye. It's far from the riskiest thing he's ever done, getting in the way of an angry dame, but it's right up there. Shadow's maternal reaction to Cloud has turned the girl into something far more precious than Tawny's annoying brat. The danger to his mate's offspring has him ready to draw blood.

Then Black-Eye's arm retracts as Talon's wings take the place of Shadow's protective shield and create a wall marking both females as his. A glance over his shoulder shows Shadow backing away, Cloud nearly invisible in a cocoon of white feathers. Talon joins them at the far side of the chamber before dropping his wings. Cloud is so distraught Talon does the one thing reserved for a male's mate, female offspring or sibling.

He gives her affection, gently cradling the back of her slim neck in his hand and finding the pressure points that relax her. Loose red hair falls from Cloud's head in clumps as the standoff continues; the males at the tunnel haven't taken their eyes from the angry white gryphon and Shadow hasn't taken hers from Black-Eye.

"Dame Shadow," he tries again. "The child has been accused of murder."

"Don't speak to me again, fucknuts," Shadow hugs Cloud even tighter and with a nod of her head at Soar she points at the ground in front of Black-Eye.

"Dame Shad—"

"We have disturbed you, Dame Shadow," Soar interrupts with a carefully framed acknowledgment of their brutal intrusion. "A gryphon was murdered and Cloud was found with her hands on the victim's throat."

"I didn't," Cloud moans, desperately looking in Shadow's eyes.

"She has implicated another in the crime. Sire Lev suggests you may be sensitive to dishonesty as your dame was and Sire Sher and Dame Arden have agreed your validation of this child's story is sufficient to condemn or clear her."

Fucknuts is a far better name for the big gryphon than the one Talon can't remember. He stands until his cohort hits him in the back of his knee, buckling it and prompting him to get on the damn floor.

"Murder," Shadow whispers but the revelation that shocks Talon is the word dishonesty. Could it be her tears that made him truthful to her? But she nods at Soar like she knows exactly what he's talking about.

"Cloud? Are you hurt?"

Cloud pushes Talon's hand away and shakes her head, painfully holding her chin up.

"That's a lie, Cloud. You're hurt."

Cloud tries to drop her eyes but Shadow won't let her. She places her fingers under Cloud's chin and refuses to accept submission instead forcing the girl to remain proud. Shuffling at the other side of the room draws Clouds attention.

"It's just us," Shadow says. "Tell me what happened and pretend they aren't there."

"Yes, Dame Shadow," Cloud answers. The importance of her words isn't lost on her since the punishment for murder could be death. "I trust you will treat me fairly.

"I was turning in for the night and there were voices outside my den and she was scared and he was mad and she said she wasn't going away with him anymore because it meant Talon would be hurt and she wasn't going."

Shadow looks at Talon as she clamps down her worry then refocuses on Cloud.

"There was fighting and I looked out. She shrieked and all I saw was wings hiding them and blood running down her legs and then she fell to the ground and he stepped into the shadows.

"But it was too late I saw him and he ran at me. He said if I told I would be next."

Cloud shakes and Talon gets his hand ready to settle her down but she bravely pushes it away and gets herself under control.

"There were voices and he disappeared so I went to her. Shadow, she was always nice to me. She showed me human things and even helped me outside once to fly."

Oh no, Talon's stomach loosens. *Not her.*

He knows this story, might have even looked the other way so Cloud could have a taste of the sky. An unofficial right of passage; sneaking out. Punishable of course but gryphon children had been doing it for thousands of years.

"I put my hands on her throat and tried to keep her alive. I thought if I held on until Tawny got there she would be okay.

"I tried so hard to hold on to her, Shadow. I really tried."

It's the same thing Shadow said about her brother. One look at his mate tells him what he can already feel. Cloud's anguish hits too close to home. All he needs is the name and he's going after the killer himself.

"At first I thought it worked when the bleeding slowed but then I knew it didn't. Her heart stopped."

"Who?" Shadow whispers. Cloud's wings drop, displaying sadness and defeat.

"It was Torrent, Dame Shadow. Torrent killed Swift."

In seconds the room explodes in feathers.

Sher's bruised gryphon shouts at Shadow over the big wild cat fight between Talon and Soar. She can't make out his words over the high pitched growling and all she wants is a moment to deal with her own stirred up grief so she can comfort the scared teen she's started to love.

A gap between Soar's dark and Talon's golden brown wings gives Shadow a glimpse of Talon's fist striking his friend's already split lip then their wings slap stone beneath as the pair rolls across the den. Their fight is brought to an end by a stunning crash under the lone light. Soar has Talon from behind in a wrestling hold and after few tense seconds Talon's eyes droop and he goes limp.

"Dame Shadow?" The Black-Eye returns to his knee. "Is her story true?"

"It's true," she answers. *I thought I told you not to speak.* Sher's two guards retreat down the hall as Soar rolls Talon to his side. Both are bloodied, Soar's lip bleeds down his chin as his tongue explores the gash.

Her Talon has been with Swift. Not recently, but there's no way of knowing exactly how long ago. Had Shadow's encounter with Talon the previous summer been enough for Talon to break it off? And Swift said they'd been together a long time. Even if it ended a few years earlier Shadow can understand if he still feels responsible for her. She'd be disappointed in him if he hadn't.

Shadow shrugs it off and focuses on Cloud. For the girl to bear witness to a murder after surviving so much death already is far too much to ask of her fifteen years.

"Talon," Soar nudges him with his boot. "She's with the females now. Your place is with the living."

"Fuck."

"Yeah, buddy. Let's go for a walk."

Talon accepts Soar's extended hand and both flex their wings to straighten their ruffled feathers. There's a bruise on his jaw and several scratches on his chest since he's not wearing leather like Soar.

"Shadow," he gives her the smallest nod as he speaks to the floor. "My reaction was inappropriate."

"Talon," she calls and he straightens with a loud sigh.

What can she say that's not going to sound like an apology? I sorta liked your ex-girlfriend? Or go with something formal and call him gryphon? The seconds drag on as Shadow finds two words that work.

"Thank you."

Thank you for taking care of Cloud, for being honourable and caring about Swift even when you knew there was nothing left to do. Thank you for giving me a chance to let Cloud speak and thank you for the past, present and the future. Shadow hasn't yet thanked him for any of the complicated pieces he's fit into her life. She's not sure which one he understands but the tightening around his lips acknowledges her gratitude.

Soar takes his elbow.

"Dame Shadow, we'll be stationed at the tunnel entrance until we're certain Torrent is in custody or is no longer in the eyrie."

But she looks away, her focus already on Cloud. Still unable to speak to Soar, she's not disappointed to hear their steps recede into the dark tunnel.

"She was the only one who ever came close to trusting me," Cloud shivers. "Until you came and showed me what it's like to be trusted she was the only one who ever did.

"Sometimes I would go to her den when I couldn't sleep and we'd talk. She knew I don't think of this eyrie as home and promised she would help me find a good place. Maybe a human home or another eyrie. She was sad since Talon stopped coming here and when she started spending more time with Torrent it made her happier."

As much as Shadow wants to be reassured about Talon and Swift it's his story to tell. It would be terrible to use the traumatized teen for gossip. As Cloud finishes speaking she trembles and falls asleep, breathing deeply in Shadow's arms. It feels like four in the morning although it can't be much past one.

Swift was more than another gryphon in the eyrie. She'd been one of Cloud's few friends.

Shadow smoothes worry from Cloud's forehead with her fingers, kissing the last of it away before pulling the rough blanket up.

The scent of blood from Talon and Soar is quickly overwhelmed by Swift's in rough red patches on Cloud's knees and hands. Shadow tucks the blanket tightly under Cloud and disappears down the hall, hands outstretched until she's certain her eyes can handle the blackness.

The two gryphons are perched at the tunnel opening like pigeons on a telephone line though they would probably find the analogy offensive. They kneel with their wings neatly folded at their sides, tapering tips pointing at her as she nears.

"Can you leave us alone, please?"

"No, Dame Shadow," Soar answers. "Sire Lev is safe with the remainder of his guard. I have been ordered not to leave your den until we are certain there is no more danger to you."

"I see you've left it already," is her tight reply.

"Go, Soar," Talon mutters and Soar reluctantly makes his way up the tunnel. He doesn't go all the way to the den and judging by his grumbling isn't happy she's held him to the letter of his orders and not their spirit.

Shadow is wary of the ledge and Talon's words about being prey so she kneels beside him as close to the drop off as she dares. Even though she's built for flight, going over the edge is still something she never wants to do.

"I saw her the night before last," Shadow needs to talk about Swift. "We had dinner in Jasper and she said I needed to talk to you. She reached you in Parksville and said you'd come for me the next day but Torrent got to me first."

"What? I've been here nearly a week."

"She said—"

"Nearly a week. You didn't know you're a royal gryphon and he would have had you punished if I wasn't here to explain for you."

"Oh God, it makes sense."

Swift called Torrent, not Talon and for some reason regretted whatever put her in league with him. Talon had been on trial too and Swift wanted out rather than see him hurt. Shadow's tail coils around his and he pushes his closer, accepting the gesture. She leans forward enough to make out the hurried movements of a few gryphons in the silver lights.

"Before Terry died I was dating someone," she says. There's nothing she'd dare say suggesting she understands since her loss is so different but maybe she can draw him out. The only reward for keeping it in is pain. "He was really nice, caring. He would tell me all the amazing things he'd do for me. I'd struck out a few times and he seemed different. As kind as he was on the inside I thought he was as tough as Terry on the outside.

"Then there was a day I got home alone. He was meeting me there but two other guys got there first," Talon turns as she continues and she can't help but feel ashamed. "My apartment was trashed and as they ran out I challenged them. I felt so brave thinking he was there beside me and I took a swing at one like Terry taught me, tagged him and broke my hand but he hit me and as I went down I saw my knight disappear down the hall like a solid coward."

"You've gotta be kidding me," Talon hisses.

"I woke up in Terry's arms; ambulance, police. Terry went through my things and gave them a list of what they took. I didn't have a lot of jewelry but it was all gone. Most turned up in pawn shops over the next few days and Terry bought everything he could find rather than wait for the police. There was a ring he gave me I never got back which was sad because it was the only piece that meant a thing."

Shadow's fingers feel the weight of Talon's bracelet and he notices, turning enough to take her hand and kiss it.

"This is as special to me as the ring was. Losing it was terrible."

She gives him a moment in the hopes he'll reciprocate with something of his own but other than giving her wrist a gentle squeeze he goes back to brooding.

"About a year ago the bank sent me to Toronto for some office culture thing: airfare, hotels, teambuilding stuff. Some of the girls and I went out for dinner and a couple of drinks. The drinking was bad then so I made some excuse for not going to the hotel with them and had a few more.

"I don't know if it was the gin or what but before I knew it there was this guy at my table buying. When we left we got about a block away and a couple of guys jumped out of an alley. One had a knife and the other wanted my purse.

"I was starting to think I attracted crooks and took a step away. I'd learned my lesson about fighting and one was armed but the guy exploded. In a second the knife hit the ground. One was on his ass and the other was limping away in tears.

"Thought I found my hero and we went to my hotel room but he was gone before he even got his belt done up. Left me feeling really, really empty. I mean, was it asking too much of men to have a real hero who treasures my heart as much as his own?"

Talon's head moves and she realizes his attention is on the chamber below as he tracks every moving thing he sees. Uncertain when her attempt to open him up turned into a confession, she finds a way to refocus on him.

"Last summer I hoped I found it in a man. Today I'm certain I found it in a gryphon."

"See to the child," he answers as he leans forward, hands on the cusp of the drop off.

Chapter Twenty-One

"Ready?"

"What if I put my wings away and you carry me down?"

Do I have to say it? Talon watches her toes curl around the ledge. Her heart beats so hard he could hear it with human ears.

"Everyone down there sees the white gryphon," Talon figures he has to point it out. "I will if you insist but you'll look bad."

"No pressure," Shadow mumbles. The vicious Dame he saw in the den is embarrassingly timid.

"None," he kisses at the side of her neck. Talon still feels the buzz of hunting the night before and had woken her for more to make up for the cold shoulder that followed. Cloud slipped out shortly after they received word that Torrent abandoned the eyrie, taking Feather and several others with him. His sister was either involved with Torrent or thought the price of defying him was too high given what happened to Swift. Both reasons put knots in his gut. She should be in the upper reaches of the eyrie with the females.

And with Swift.

"Cloud went to prepare your breakfast," he nudges.

Shadow offered no explanation for her attachment to the girl other than her actions proving it's maternal and Talon responded without thinking, openly crossing the line from guard to sire when he doesn't even like Cloud. He never understood what Swift saw in her: rude, disrespectful and awkward to be around.

There are rules for children. For any other gryphon behaviour like hers is earned. Even then her mouth would get her in more trouble for her years than most gryphons start in a lifetime. It's a bad mix of Tawny's privilege of age and the uneasy aura of death he'd first sensed in her home eyrie.

He touches Shadow's waist above her bite and steps behind her.

"Take a step, Shadow. Glide, bank, keep your eyes off the lights so you can see. Push me away when you want to fly on your own."

Then she falls forward, arms outstretched while her wings remain at her sides.

"Shit."

Talon jumps, digs his fingers into her hips and takes their weight on his wings. Only a second later Shadow gets her wings out, looking more like a startled infant than a creature taking flight. With his wings held forward to avoid turbulence from hers, he guides them to the right, avoiding the wall ahead so they cross the main chamber.

She's steady, crossing the room and pulls his hands from her before sticking her arms out again with her fingers splayed.

Left, left, left! Talon wills her to turn but she doesn't. Shadow's wings are bone straight, too tense even for gliding and judging by the tilt of her head she's looking down, unaware how close she is to taking a header into the stone.

With a burst of speed Talon renews his grip and takes her left into the second half of their figure-eight to the ground.

"What?" she demands, squirming in his arms as her right wing brushes the stone wall. "Oh."

"Yeah."

They descend, dropping through the turn and as they make their last pass across the room she pushes him away to land on her own. Talon angles his wings to brake and takes his weight on his bent knees but she's going a little too fast and is top heavy with the unaccustomed weight of her wings. As she cart-wheels her arms, she runs to catch up with her upper half and comes to a staggering stop.

She turns, searching wildly then shows a flash of white teeth as she spots him.

In spite of the nearly botched landing she's aware of her audience and with a graceful nod pretends her landing was as smooth as his. In the white light her adornment is spectacular, nearly as bright as her wings and she gets on her toes as he approaches.

"Breakfast?"

Talon is too stunned by her lack of flying instincts to comment so he offers her an elbow and leads her into one of the tunnels.

The dining chamber is much less crowded than usual given the absence of females and Talon leaves Shadow where he can see her while he goes to the kitchens. The dining chamber is a cave like the main chamber only much smaller; one tunnel leads to the big main chamber and the other to the eyrie entrance. Its lower ceiling makes it feel brighter.

Cloud is long gone but the girl left Shadow a couple of grilled cheese sandwiches and some fruit which Talon collects along with a bowl of venison, hard multigrain bread and apple pieces for himself.

Shadow found them a pair of cushions and she looks eagerly past him for Cloud, he supposes.

"She will be with the females," Talon kneels.

"Doing what?"

"Preparing Swift," his voice fails and he glances around hoping nobody heard. The only gryphon who appears to notice is Shadow and he pays too much attention to his food in order to avoid her questioning stare. He knows exactly what she was trying to do the night before with the story of her ex-lovers and as much as he didn't want to hear it he was glad he didn't have to talk. Talon is prepared for her questions today.

"Oh."

She's momentarily distracted by her appetite, starting with a grape then eating half a sandwich in two bites. "Where?"

"Above."

Shadow looks up, fingers feeling for a strawberry. Talon decides that the mix of strawberry and venison is one of the more unappetizing combinations he's encountered.

"The females will prepare her for the afterlife. No male will see her again."

She frowns, little lines forming between her brows.

"I was hoping to see Cloud before we leave."

"We're not leaving," he chews another piece of nearly raw venison.

"But—"

"Nobody may leave the eyrie until Swift departs."

It's getting easier for him to say her name but not by much.

"Torrent did."

"That was disrespectful," he grinds out.

His sister should have known better. His sister should be here caring for her best friend.

"I should be there," Shadow exclaims. The accompanying flare of her wings gets attention from several males who are busy with the youngsters. "Tawny said I'm not an adult until I go and you can't and I want to be there."

"No, you're not an adult," Talon sighs.

"And I should be when I meet, um, my gryphons."

"Yes, you should," he's relieved she's eager to attend. "This isn't your eyrie so you aren't required. You are however, welcome."

Shadow's participation will go a long way to tightening the bond between her eyrie and Arden's. After the misunderstanding with Torrent and the murder, the Jasper eyrie is vulnerable and will need friends as it recovers.

"You're a good Dame, Shadow," he tells her as his venison covered fingers tip her chin up. She smiles proudly then her nostrils flare taking in the smell of meat.

"Oh," she breathes.

Talon pulls his hand away but she follows and leans over his dish. She's too close and he warns her with a growl. Shadow's sharp grunt shuts him up though she's still very unwelcome so near his meal.

But it isn't the venison she wants. As she gets nearer she sniffs, tongue in the corner of her mouth so he responds expecting a poorly timed kiss.

Instead she gives him the cheek and touches her lips to the corner of his mouth.

"I've been craving something since last night," she trails off as her tongue comes out and gingerly traces down his jaw. "Wow, wasn't sure what it was until now."

She sits, licking her lips and as Talon wipes his mouth he realizes he's let blood run freely down his chin in his effort to keep his mouth too busy to talk.

"Can I get you some?"

"I'll try a piece of yours."

"No," it comes out a little harshly.

Jesus, Shadow. I'm not your dame.

"I get it," she sighs, a little offended. "Cloud said only a dame shares her food with her child then I made her try what she made me for dinner."

"Oh, damn," Talon curses. So that's what happened. "I'll get you some."

Talon takes his bowl and stomps to the kitchen. Feeding the orphan? That can't be good. And Cloud accepting is definitely not good. It explains why the two are close since his mate is trying to adopt a stray. The only one who may not realize it is Shadow.

Talon fingers a necklace in his pocket and can't help but wonder if Swift would be alive if he'd given her what she really wanted, a mated bond. Would he have been any happier? Or would he have abandoned a relationship with her anyway, seeing her only when her season drove them both past hate and straight into the hunt? He'd made the necklace for Swift with the magic of the Earth; no stipulations, neither one having to commit to anything for her to accept it but changed his mind. It would have been lost in the dozens she wore already as nothing more than a human trinket.

"Will you do something for me?"

Shadow tries not to be obvious about licking her fingers and nods, satisfied by the meat in a way she never imagined. As she devoured piece after piece Talon talked about her gryphon body's needs and blood but the talk of blood just made her mouth water more. Even though they bathed and changed after breakfast her sensitive tongue finds hints.

"Wait," Talon says.

She feels his hand in hers and stops even though she's charged with enough energy to sprint all the way to the top of the mountain. She fidgets, rolling from heels to toes until Talon gets his hands on her shoulders.

"Anything," Shadow says. They're only a few minutes up a long tunnel leading from the chamber where the trial had been held. Today it's empty and even in the weak light she could make out the clean spot her body made on the floor.

He holds a gold chain. Even though it lacks the sparkle of the silver lights, it's as intricately woven as a satin ribbon and not really a chain at all. And judging by the way his fingers curl he's hesitant to part with it.

"I left her five years ago," Talon's hand closes and the necklace disappears in his pocket. "We'd been together nearly two decades; not a long time for gryphons. She wanted to bond with me, made it clear from the start and I wanted to be needed. After years learning to be a ranger with Soar he was recruited by your sire and I'd been passed over one too many times.

"I can't believe I'm telling anyone this," he looks away and allows Shadow to get close, her head tucked under his chin; near yet giving him privacy.

"She wanted to do it right, she said, bonding when she was

in season. I'd gone to give her this as a promise next time we would but we fought. She wanted to move to an eyrie in the city. There are some led by a human style democracy and they are close to being recognized in the grand council.

"It pissed me off. Unimaginable. If you asked her we were headed in two different directions; she to commitment and me to disappointment but she was too willing to shed what it meant to be a gryphon and I preferred the old rhetoric and the past. She wanted something I didn't have the courage to give. She was right. I was selfish accepting her attention, settling for being wanted for what she saw in me and not for what I valued in myself. Then I was cruel when I punished myself and walked out. I told her good luck and never gave it to her.

"Until I lost her I didn't know how close I'd come to having the life she wanted. I loved her, Shadow, and leaving broke my heart as much as hers."

"Do you regret taking me?" Shadow asks, scared Swift's death has given him second thoughts.

"Oh God, no," Talon grabs her head in his hands and fisting his fingers through her hair, he brushes her lips with his. "Don't ever worry about that. She was right. I got involved with her for the wrong reasons and staying with her was driving me straight to disappointment."

"This," his lips seal over hers. The taste of venison joins his male scent and she pulls both in through her partly open mouth. She growls as she's overcome by the unbelievably primal scent. "Is what I wanted for so long."

As they resume their walk up the steepening tunnel, Shadow's tail wraps loosely around his. It seems to have a mind of its own, or at least be more in touch with her feelings than she is. Unless she consciously wills it to keep still it wanders all over him. The climb goes on for another ten minutes before she pauses, reaching out with her hearing. Echoes of something female come but no matter how hard she tries the sounds are unclear.

"There is a barrier and I can't go any further," Talon says as he squeezes her hand. "I can never know what you learn today just like you can never know where my hoard is."

"Okay."

"Here," Talon holds the necklace out and Shadow takes it, cradling the long heavy ribbon in her palm. "It's my hope she can wear it because I treated her like our decades never happened and I hurt her. I was a shit and too big a shit to admit it. If she can't wear it, leave it behind and let me believe she took it with her.

"A few minutes ahead you'll find a narrow gap in the side of the tunnel, follow it. I'll be in the main chamber below when you return."

"Talon," she calls. He's quick and has nearly disappeared around a bend in the tunnel. Hurrying to catch up she has to call him again before he stops. Shadow holds her hands at her chest, fingertips together like she's made a delicate box, then opens her palms offering the invisible contents.

"Talon, this is my heart," her lips press together as he glances at the imaginary treasure. "It's been damaged and broken. It's known unbelievable loneliness, emptiness. It's fallen for yours, Talon, son of Stalker."

He laughs, just a soft purr of air from his nose as he presses it to her palms and kisses.

"Has its owner fallen for me too?"

"Undeniably, Talon," Shadow whispers. "I've fallen in love with you."

"*Arlette*," he answers, crushing her in his arms and forcing her hands and her heart back into her own chest. "I love you."

Chapter Twenty-Two

Shadow climbs for another ten minutes before finding the side passage. She doubles back down the steep, slippery path to where Talon's scent is strong before she finds the jagged hole in the wall.

The passage isn't as tight a fit as it looks and most of the way two winged gryphons could walk abreast over the floor that's been worn smooth by countless female feet. The weight of the necklace is heavy on her heart. If she's too late to put it on Swift then she'll have to bear her failure all on her own. Talon has done his best to resolve the mess he left behind and the rest is up to her.

The clear sounds of laughter reach her interspersed with conversation and outbursts of tears; sounds typical of a wake. The air cools significantly as the soft glow of real flames outlines the end of the tunnel and carries with it the scent of wood smoke. Shadow adjusts her eyes and steps into a small room. Nearly thirty women fill it and even in the close quarters they are clearly grouped in twos and threes. A single fire in the corner provides light and their shadows dance, infinitely tall, following their voices into the limitless space above.

"Shadow?" Dame Arden asks and Shadow bows. Arden's son and only heir is gone and accused of murder and she can't help but think it's due entirely to the trouble she started at

Talon's Saskatoon home. "Welcome."

"Thank you, Dame Arden," Shadow bows again. The women around her appear strange and she realizes they aren't winged. Many gawk at her white feathers. "I came to… um. I mean the Vancouver Island Eyrie wants to…"

"I want to honour Swift, Dame Arden," she tries. Screw protocol; she doesn't know it anyway. "As a gryphon and a friend in whatever way I can serve."

"A kind sentiment," Tawny speaks up. Behind her Shadow sees Cloud: alone, overwhelmed and lost. "Here we are simply sisters, none of this Dame business, eh?"

"My sisters," Arden announces. "Swift's spirit will be blessed with three wishes."

"Thank you, Shadow," comes from a couple of them and another pair embrace, overcome by the news.

"Cloud," Tawny says. "Please fetch Shadow a tunic."

"I met your dame many years ago," Tawny says as she leads Shadow to the fire. Near it is a large bowl full of very clear water. At the bottom is a ring of bright stones which appear to be huge gems. "She was fourth in line for her dame's seat and just an infant. She was absolutely tiny and it was rumoured she took after her dame's dame, a white winged gryphon who claimed to be the daughter of the first royal. Though in truth the family feared your dame was sickly. She was deeply loved and they treasured each day they had with her. She flourished however, eventually claiming the heart of Sire Lev."

"Oh?" Shadow answers but Tawny doesn't say any more. Cloud approaches and kneels near the bowl with Shadow.

"First your wings, child," Tawny instructs. "This is a place for emotion and sharing, not stuffy gryphon pride. Our sister Swift, her sprit is with us to celebrate. We honour her as Earth dwellers since that is where her body returns."

"How?"

"Like when you took wing," Cloud whispers. "And they won't call us 'child' anymore after this."

Shadow concentrates and within seconds the lightness of

her back becomes pounding in her head. Clutching her temples, she squeezes her ribs in place with her elbows and for several agonizing heartbeats the pain batters her insides. As her inner pressure subsides, she shivers as the room becomes uncomfortably chilled.

"Over it goes," Tawny declares and stuffs the tunic over Shadow's head.

"I have this," Shadow says. With one hand she pulls out Talon's necklace while feeling her adornment with the other. It's long and as Talon said, nothing more than a plain necklace of the same white platinum.

"Talon?" Tawny holds her hand over Swift's necklace.

"He said he would like her to wear it but he doesn't know if it's allowed."

"Of course it's allowed, child," Arden says. "Put it in the bowl. I'm pleased he chose to acknowledge her. The rejection her sprit carries is the largest stain we have to heal."

Shadow drops it in the water and is startled by the brilliant flash accompanying the searing sound it makes breaking the surface.

"He's been holding on to it for quite some time for it to be that dirty," Arden comments. "The males ask us for moonwater from time to time although I can't imagine they grasp its significance. It purifies without causing damage. It will amplify magic, for instance if Tawny heals a gryphon while her hands are wet with it she can do more than without."

"And I will in a moment!" the old gryphon announces from the other side of the room.

"Roll up your sleeves," Arden instructs. "And wash your hands until the water is quiet."

Blue light still snaps around the chain as Shadow does what she's told. The moonwater is cold and goose-bumps spring from her skin and rasp against her sleeves. When the flashing stops she takes the chain and waits, careful not to touch anything for if she gets dirty she'll likely need another electric cleaning.

"Come, Shadow," Cloud takes her elbow and helps her up.

As the women part, Shadow can see Swift on a narrow waist high altar. Her body is covered in a simple drape and the warm fire light can't hide the unnatural whiteness of her skin or the rows of neat stitches closing the devastating wound to her throat. The pounds of gold once around her neck are gone. Four claw marks are visible on one side and as Shadow gets closer the fifth from Torrent's thumb comes into view. She can only imagine Cloud's terror witnessing the attack.

"Put it on her," Tawny says softly. "Her spirt is with us and will bond with anyone who shares a trauma she cannot take to the afterlife. The gryphon blessed with the connection will seek others in the room and through conversation or even simple contact we help heal Swift's spirit."

"That's beautiful," Shadow says, deeply touched by the intimacy of the ceremony. She closes the clasp under Swift's neck and turns the chain until it's behind her out of sight. Only then does she smooth it out, drawing the long loop down and flattening it between her breasts.

"Ah," Arden sighs as Cloud takes Shadow's hand. "The room feels lighter already."

"Now, trousers down," Tawny announces. Cloud laughs at the look on Shadow's face as the cold air hits her bare thighs and bottom. Then Shadow yelps as Tawny's wet hands grab her scarred leg. "Hold still."

"Um," Shadow breathes as Tawny moves her hands again and again.

"You should have been brought to me immediately when this happened," Tawny mutters. "Or I to you. Barbaric. When the human doctors remove the metal come see me and I will repair the holes. You should have no more trouble."

Tawny stands. Beads of sweat stand out on her wrinkled forehead.

"Thank you."

"There is food; eat, talk. There is peace in the room and it shouldn't be long until Swift leaves us."

Shadow helps herself to a couple of the hard crackers Talon had with his breakfast and Cloud joins her, crouching in a niche along the wall by Swift's feet. Shadow's desire for meat disappeared with her wings.

"Thank you for breakfast."

Cloud grins around a mouthful of red meat and sighs. Her eyes sag from lack of sleep.

"Swift was upset I saw her die," Cloud admits. "She loved her time with the children and the young and it bothered her to see one of us so frightened.

"I told her how brave she was. How proud I am. Even though she had a terrible disadvantage in the narrow tunnel she fought with all her heart.

"One of the dames here broke her ankle in front of her daughter a few years ago and carried a terrible guilt ever since. It upset her child so much. Swift felt the same way as the dame, I think, about being killed in front of me so they made a connection.

"The dame came to comfort me and we talked a long time until we felt better. Swift was able to see how I healed and Tawny says that made her spirit lighter."

The groups of women have broken up and they approach Swift alone for the most part. They hold her hand and talk to her. One laughs, telling a one-sided version of an event in their childhood. Shadow's thoughts go to Talon and images of him with the loud blonde. Then she's overwhelmed by feelings of futility and a vision of Terry dead on the road. Swift's frustration she could never really connect with Talon stirs Shadow's complete hopelessness. She's aware of the parallel between the pain and emptiness when Terry died and when Talon left Swift only Swift faced the real future of seeing Talon over and over to renew her loss.

"Excuse me," Shadow kisses Cloud on the head and stands without pain for the first time since the accident. As she approaches Swift's body her breath hitches then eases.

"Hey," she takes Swift's hand. "Maybe you know me better than you think if I have the privilege of standing here now. I'm proud to count you as someone he cared for. He loved you and I think he did the only fair thing he could."

Something male touches Shadow and she whirls but nobody behind's her and no male is in the chamber.

"You have a visitor, Shadow," Tawny approaches. "Don't question."

Shadow closes her eyes and rests her lips on Swift's cheek. The closeness brings her a vision of the accident she'd never seen. The bare arms on leather tasseled grips can only be Terry's; everything in black and white, gray and gray.

I never thought of his last moments, Shadow realizes. *Not how they were for him. He knew from the moment the truck appeared I'd be alone.*

Her knees buckle as the impact knocks the wind from her lungs and her head turns sharply to the left. She's blind to the room as Swift's fingers tighten their hold. The present has her clinging to a dead woman and not broken over the roof of a truck. Shadow sees a blur of sky and paint then nothing but her body broken on the ground as Terry's vision tunnels to blackness. He knew she survived. He knew everything she went through since and he's proud.

"Terry?"

But he's gone.

"Many of us are blessed like this," Tawny says. Swift's fingers have relaxed and Shadow should be alarmed by the whole thing but she isn't. "They travel a long way to connect with the living through a spirit still bound to its body. We are of the sky and the Earth and when we pass our halves are returned."

"She held my hand."

"Yes, she is ready now. When your turn comes you will make a wish for her, something your magic can grant."

Shadow looks away as the drape is removed, leaving Swift's tall white body naked and exposed. The women rush to wet their hands and place them on Swift.

"Hurry," Tawny breathes. Shadow follows her to the bowl then places her wet palms on Swift's left shoulder. "The cloth was soaked in moonwater to keep her spirit from leaving too early, stained with wounds from her life. Now our hands keep it down until the blessing is over."

Tawny is at Swift's other shoulder and Arden cradles her head in her elbows, her hands between Tawny's and Shadow's. Cloud is somewhere by Swift's feet and the women jostle for positions that allow them all to touch her. Some manage both hands but most have to turn sideways just to lay a single hand on her.

"Hear our wish sister!" Arden shouts, bringing silence to the room. "My sister, leave us without fear. Be brave. Your spirit is strong and beautiful."

"Hear our wish, hear our wish," the women chant. As the room warms, Shadow has to press on Swift to keep her hands down. "Hear our wish, hear our wish."

With each twitch of Swift's body she becomes markedly warmer, the chill of death evaporates with every word of the women. Swift's body is shaken by deep shudder that vibrates up through Shadow's sweaty palms.

"Hear our wish sister!" Tawny interrupts and again the room falls silent, even Swift's weak shaking stills. "My sister, leave us healed. Be loved. Your spirit is whole and beautiful."

Swift answers with a jolt as her body gets hot and those who can lean forward to hold her down.

"Hear our wish, hear our wish," the chanting continues as the struggle to hold Swift escalates. Sweaty arms rub together and beads run inside Shadow's tunic, soaking the waistband of her trousers. The difference in temperature between Shadow's front and back is like opening an oven. A hand slips from Swift's trembling body and Shadow knows it's her turn.

"Hear our wish sister!" she yells over the mayhem. "My sister, leave us protected. Be safe. Your spirit is treasured and beautiful."

"Hear our wish, hear our wish," they chant, voices breaking. Shadow tears so heavily even the blistering inferno before her isn't enough to dry them. Arden's shoulder shakes with effort as much as her own and Swift's necklace slides out of place. A look around shows every face wet with tears.

"Fly!" Arden bellows and together they wipe their hands

over their cheeks, soaking them in tears then shoving them under Swift. She's weightless and with only their fingertips they raise her high above their heads. Swift's head falls and her back arches as she draws a final breath.

Swift's piercing screech echoes up through the infinite height of the room. As her lungs empty they scramble to hold on with their tired slippery arms as Swift's body gets heavier and heavier.

"Fly Swift!" Cloud yells and others whisper good-bye. Shadow sees the youngster through the forest of limbs, an adult now, her eyes wide with joy.

"Fly, my sister," Shadow whispers.

They hold Swift until the echo of her cry fades completely then lower her to the altar and cover her up. Some linger, others dip scraps of cloth in the moonwater to wipe their hands and cheeks clean before tossing them in the fire.

Several women tend to Swift, wrapping her in soft linen and stitching tight seams to hold her.

"We may depart," Tawny says and Shadow looks longingly up into the blackness above.

"Someone did this for my brother, didn't they?"

"Yes," she answers. "His spirit flew free."

Chapter Twenty-Three

"Do you all have, um, treasure?" Shadow whispers at Talon's side. She picks at her food like she doesn't understand how much demand the next day's travel will put on her.

"Only males," he pushes her plate a little closer but she ignores it. She emerged from the tunnel with Cloud. An adult now. A gryphon. Both are for that matter. The strength he previously felt masked by pain is clear in her like it's been brought up from the bottom of a swimming pool. It's balanced with her grief, which while still present, is integrated and under control.

Finally she picks up some lightly cooked meat and sniffs it.

"Do you buy things like my brother did?"

"Your brother's sports memorabilia was a hobby. A gryphon's hoard is gathered on the wing. Precious stones, metals: all hidden in secret."

She nods like she understands but then asks the same question as her hand absently strokes her adornment.

"So you don't buy things at a jewelry store?"

"No."

"But this—"

"Our bond gave your adornment its form. There's nothing like it in my hoard. Dragons acquire finished pieces through trade or conquest. A gryphon's hoard is scavenged from the

Earth."

"There's really dragons?" Shadow sits up straighter to get her feet underneath her butt.

"Not supposed to talk about dragons," Talon mutters and she snaps her mouth shut. At least she's stopped talking about his hoard.

Let her wonder if dragons are real or not, he shrugs. Gryphons aren't supposed to tell stories.

"You need to eat, *Arlette*," he says around a mouthful of very rare venison. "I can, of course carry you but I'm sure you would rather fly to your eyrie yourself."

Shadow snorts, indignant at the slight snub. In spite of spending thirty years as a human she's still a gryphon and any challenge to her pride pisses her off.

Good.

They eat silently until a pair of small children shrieks. Mist and Echo's dame has returned along with a few other female stragglers. She looks as the others did: tired and content. It's infectious and the mood in the chamber levels out a little further. Shadow watches the children and gives him a smile he can't read.

"Seconds?" he offers.

"No thanks," Shadow answers so he takes her bowl back to the kitchen with his.

Lev and Soar find her before Talon so he slows as Shadow stands, using her left leg like it was never hurt. Tawny he suspects.

Talon greets Soar with a clasp of elbows. Soar gives him a nod and runs his tongue over the cut on his lip. It's not as spectacular as other injuries they've exchanged so it doesn't warrant comment. Talon's intent hadn't been to harm Soar anyway. A good gryphon will always stop a friend from getting out of hand.

"Hello, gryphon," Lev says to Shadow. "You are the very image of your dame."

"Really?"

"Our friends are honoured you chose to join them today. I

missed you this morning." Shadow searches his face for something intangible. From what Talon remembers of Condor, other than years there isn't much to differentiate sire and son. "There were arrangements to be made for our return so I was by the entrance where my satellite phone works. Additional gryphons will join us by morning.

"Master Talon?"

"Sire?" Talon accepts Lev's invitation and kneels before joining Shadow, surrounding her with one giant wing as her tail coils around his. Then his hand finds her stomach, low over her womb like the day they met. It's not Lev he feels possessive around; it's Soar even though Soar's service to Lev precludes anything other than professionalism. The rules are different however between males. Soar is big and dangerous and if the looks of the unmated females around the room are any indication he's very desirable mating material.

"There are several gryphons arriving with whom you will meet."

Talon nods. They must be the remnants of Dame Treasure's guard.

"I wish to share something with you, Shadow," Lev pulls a small pouch from his pocket. "Don't open it quite yet. I want you to understand what it is and what it has been through to find its way to you."

Shadow holds it in her palm, not even probing the deerskin with her thumb to find out what the object is. Her curiosity fills Talon and he's tempted to do it himself.

"First, a small history of our eyrie. My sister was meant to take our dame's seat however she was impatient and mated to another royal. When Master Sky, our greatest warrior and Dame to his eyrie removed herself to teach combat full-time my sister took over. Soar is her son, your cousin if there were a gryphon word for such a relationship."

Talon interrupts with a loud laugh. Grandson of Master Sky he knew but his own kin as well? Soar's grin says he's as amused by the idea as Talon. Lev however looks like he isn't. Neither is Shadow, whose pointy elbow makes a brief visit to

Talon's bare ribs.

"So I came to be heir," Lev continues. "And in need of a mate to fill my dame's seat. I'd learned of an eyrie in northern Europe blessed with four pairs of royal offspring and hoped one might find me interesting. I made the journey alone, on the wing as is tradition, and when I arrived the eldest was spoken for, already Dame of the eyrie, and next two were gone.

"I was three hundred years old and they told me the remaining female was young and small and in spite of the best care had failed to grow or take wing. I'd come a long way and wished to meet her anyway.

"As I waited for her to be brought to the royal chamber the Dame explained about her dame's dame who legend said, was a small white winged gryphon who made outlandish claims regarding her parentage to excuse the fact she hadn't taken wing until she was nearly forty. The Dame dismissed the tale as nonsense but there was nothing I wasn't willing to take on including teaching a small gryphon to fly.

"She stopped my heart, Shadow, when I saw her," Lev strokes Shadow's chin and she tenderly returns the gesture. "Treasure was no bigger than you. From that very moment I could read her feelings, she was very scared, lonely. Even surrounded by gryphons who loved her she knew she was out of place but she was brave nonetheless.

"I swore I would do whatever it took to make her mine, to put happiness in her pale brown eyes and joy in her spirit every day.

Talon pulls Shadow closer, knowing just how Lev felt.

"Her Dame insisted Treasure offer me the hospitality of the eyrie so she led me down to the baths. I'd been on the wing for what felt like weeks and couldn't have been any dirtier. Treasure told me no gryphon had come to meet her and as I realized we were headed to the warm baths she could comfortably share she stopped and held her hands up.

"A flash of heat seared us then she took my hand and told me no gryphon would enter the baths until we left."

Lev pulls open the ties on the pouch.

"Wearing nothing but this, a gift from her brother, she took wing for the first time at my side and I proudly became her mate."

"Oh," Shadow whispers as a ring containing a single large sapphire and two diamonds falls into her palm. "My ring?"

She weakens in Talon's arms as Lev moves in to help hold her up.

"It was stolen."

"Yes," Lev admits. "But not by the men who broke in to your apartment. It was Dame Treasure's and it was her wish you have it. Condor gave it to you and took advantage of the robbery to take it back. He wanted to add the diamonds, one for each of you, and return it."

Ah ha, Talon realizes. Like Feather's ruby, given then stolen to be charged with the magic of the Earth and grant Shadow the strength to really fly.

"He passed before he could do it so I completed the work for him and have held it close until today when it is returned to your hand."

But she's frozen, seeing nothing but Lev then her head tilts to the ring.

"I hope I made it as beautiful as he planned, Shadow," Lev prompts. "Put it on."

Shadow chews her lip. Then with a teary smile she places her other hand over top. For a moment Lev's brow wrinkles with the worry Talon shares that she might put it back in the bag. Talon can only guess the magical stipulation for real flight has something to do with her brother but precisely what, he'll never know.

"Terry," she points a thumb over her shoulder. "First day with the new wings, eh. What do you think? Am I doing okay?"

Then the damn breaks and she fights to keep her lips still as she breathes hard through her nose. She blinks up at the chamber far above and smiles as her waves of grief calm.

"It was good to…" she trails of. "It's been a really good

day, Terry."

Shadow slips the ring over the big finger of her right hand and dives for Lev. Talon moves to stop her before she can paste magic tears all over his chest.

"It's okay, Talon," Sire Lev says as he holds his daughter. "You and I are the only gryphons immune. They can't change us any more than they have already."

Shit, is that really why I can't lie to her? All that pain for the truth I'd tell her anyway? At least he doesn't have to worry about touching her tears again. If Lev isn't concerned about the breaking bones thing Talon won't be either.

"I will leave you to your rest, Shadow," Lev says softly as she releases him. "We have a long day tomorrow. Master Talon, I will send for you when the others arrive."

"Sire," Talon replies.

For Shadow, the flight to the west coast would be insufferably long without the magic from the ring. No amount of food would get her in the air for more than a couple of hours at a time and after only eight or ten she'd need another big meal and a full night sleep.

"First day with the new wings?" he asks and she laughs.

"I was, um, heavier when Terry was alive and a little clumsy. He used to ask me that about my feet, hands, mouth, whatever I couldn't seem to use properly."

"You seem different, Shadow," Talon says, so proud of her. She's taken to being a gryphon very well considering the culture shock.

"I grew up today, Talon," she says, fingers in his chest feathers. He used to cringe from public displays of affection but he wants everyone to know she belongs to him. He's graced with a glimpse of her dazzling smile and she wraps a hand behind his head, pulling him down for a kiss.

"Dame Shadow!"

Shadow sways with the little voice and they look down to see Mist. Shadow's big white feathers are in the child's death grip as she balances to get down on one knee.

"Hello, Mist," Shadow exclaims. "How are you?"

"I am beautiful," the child announces as she wobbles, trying to see if her other knee is any more reliable.

"You are, child," she runs her sapphire covered fingers through Mist's curls.

"My dame needs you."

"I'll catch up with Lev for a few minutes," Talon says as Mist leads his mate away.

"Tell me about dragons, Mist."

"We don't talk about dragons," she says patiently, hopping twice on each foot.

Talon laughs. Dragons are one of many things children are taught to be imaginary and therefore not worth discussing. If Shadow ever gets to meet one she'll be in for a shock.

Chapter Twenty-Four

"*Arlette*," Talon calls, lightly shaking her elbow.

Shadow sits with a start, feeling around for Mist. Her dame was one of six gryphons honoured with bearing Swift from the eyrie and Mist refused to wait with anyone but Shadow. Talon took their evening companion with good cheer though he excused himself to see Lev when Cloud arrived with hot chocolate and cookies. The last thing Shadow remembers is Mist's soft snore and her chubby hand clutching a glass angel; a gift from Swift.

"We're in the den. You slept through the flight up."

"Okay," Shadow swallows. It feels like there's sleep in her eyes and mouth.

"Breakfast, chamber pot," Talon orders as he strides from the den.

Shadow smells old leather soaked in a heavy layer of what can only be described as Talon. He wears dark clothes like Lev and Soar and his steps don't sound like bare feet. They sound more like boots. Armour? It makes sense but if they're just flying somewhere why does he need armour?

Breakfast is simple: meat, raw fruit and what Shadow has come to think of as gryphon crackers. Nothing with Cloud's touch at all. The den is already empty of Shadow's belongings so she follows Talon down the tunnel.

ELIZABETH MUNRO

"I couldn't let you sleep any longer and expected you to get ready a little faster."

"You didn't say anything about hurrying, Talon. Have you always been hot and cold?"

He makes some sort of ambivalent grunt.

Well, you are today, Shadow thinks, irritated and still half asleep. *Or just cold, maybe even icy.*

"You woke up full of ranger," Shadow accuses.

Talon puckers his lips and lets them open with a pop before picking Shadow up so they're at eye level.

"We have a long trip," he admits as she runs her fingers over his tied back hair. Is this who he is when she's work? The relaxed man she knew as Mark is buried deep. His armour is thick, almost to the point of being hard and matted sheepskin sticks out around the shoulders of his leather vest either for insulation or to protect his skin from the sharp hems.

Then Talon turns and without another word jumps from the tunnel. Squeezing her eyes shut to ease the lurch in her stomach, she pulls her wings in. Dropping instead of circling like the previous day Talon's wings flare at the last possible second, catching them as they hit the stone floor running.

"This way."

They hurry up a tunnel Shadow doesn't remember using though the increasing cold of fresh air tells her she has. Torrent would have brought her through this passage while she was still unconscious from whatever he did to her neck.

"Here, Master Talon," Lev calls from the far end of a smoky room. In addition to a fire in one corner several white wall lights reveal more than a dozen armoured gryphons, their dark pungent smells mix with the welcome scent of winter. They are only hushed for a moment as they kneel to Shadow and return to their preparations. The sight of her white wings doesn't get the attention she'd come to expect from the Jasper gryphons.

"What's going on?" Shadow asks as Lev's expected greeting, caressing her neck, erases the worry that made her ask the question in the first place. Her sire carries the big crossed

200

swords she saw two days earlier and as she grabs for Talon's hand she grips the solid wooden stock of a crossbow strapped to his thigh. Why didn't she notice before? There's a sword on Talon's back, a dagger bound to his upper arm. His leather chest piece has several handles protruding from it.

"We'll make some room," Lev gestures and the males step away like they know better than to stand between their Sire and his daughter. "Get her ready."

By the time Shadow notices their presence, three large women bearing the same winding burnt lines as Talon kneel and the oldest, in the front, adds a bow.

"Dame Shadow," Talon introduces. "This is Firn, Rapid and Dove."

The latter two bow as their names are spoken. It's impossible to tell what colour their hair is under their old-style leather football helmets. Firn stands out; what remain of her right cheek was never stitched up before it healed. Firn and Dove wear old dark armour like Talon's. Rapid's is new and soft as suede.

"Hello, rangers," Shadow tries, hoping to sound official but her eyes keep dropping to the weapons. The knuckles of Firn's fingerless gloves bear cat-like metal claws and the surrounding leather is stained darker than the rest. Jesus, nothing says expecting trouble like big armoured bodyguards.

"Dame Shadow," Firn says. "Master Talon has welcomed us into your service."

"Thank you, Firn. Please stand." Shadow would hate to run into Firn and her friends in a dark alley. On their feet the three are at least six three plus the lift on their heavy boots pushes them even higher. It's a hell of a lot of firepower.

"Rapid," Firn points to a heavy leather bag as Talon steps behind her and spreads his wings like a curtain to hide the four women in a corner. They quickly get to work, pulling out armour as new as Rapid's: a fresh sheepskin for underneath, vest, trousers and soft treadless boots that are more like thick insulated slippers. Shadow looks at Rapid then to her own gear.

"Any gryphon aware of your unique colour is still in the

eyrie," Rapid explains. She has a soft lisp and though her face is unmarked, most of her front teeth are missing. "This new armour should be sufficient for me to act as your decoy, Dame Shadow."

"Decoy?" she echoes. "No decoy."

"Master Talon?" Rapid calls.

"Decoy," Talon insists and Shadow narrows her eyes at him, not in defiance but with concern for Rapid.

"If I could serve you any more I would not hesitate, Dame Shadow," Rapid says. "Your love and concern for me is accepted with gratitude and very much like Dame Treasure's."

The gryphons surround Shadow and with well practiced hands they pull the sheepskin over her head. A narrow strip passes down the center of her back where it's laced up to the sides beneath her wings.

"We served in your dame's guard," Firn speaks as they work, going through the same process with the sleeveless chest piece.

"Her guard master passed defending her as we stole her away but not before a terrible, terrible fight," Firn points at her cheek. "Dove is my child. We delivered you and gave Dame Treasure blessing as Sire Lev took you and Condor away.

"The survivors…" she trails off. "There were many black days."

Shadow puts a hand on Firn's shoulder partly for balance as the thick leather trousers are pulled over her cloth ones and partly to squeeze in thanks. The trousers are similar except they lace up above her tail instead of having a simple hole for it to pass through and a drawstring front.

"I am royal by blood and defied my eyrie mating to Sire Lev's guard master. He passed two decades ago defending us from the *animals* when they came a second time."

"Oh, no," Shadow gasps, horrified at the loss this family has suffered at the hands of the rogue army. As horrible as her own.

"Nothing for it now, Dame Shadow," Firn replies as the last boot is pulled on. "The armour was Dame Treasure's.

When Sire Lev located you we were ordered to bring it right away."

"Who is protecting the eyrie?" Shadow asks.

"Those who remain," is Firn's cryptic answer. A wide leather collar like Talon's is laced up behind Shadow's neck as Dove braids her hair.

Shadow frowns. The Vancouver Island gryphons have been through enough. How few are looking after them in their cold, dark cave while the biggest ones are crammed into a hole in a Jasper mountain?

"Wait—"

"Hold still," Firn orders. Shadow hadn't noticed the long slender pockets on the sides of her boots until the ranger started jamming knives in them. "Or I'm certain Master Talon will make you."

Sure enough, Talon's arms cross and even with his back to her she's sure his look says to keep out of the ranger business.

"I use my only good knife on tomatoes," Shadow protests only loud enough for her new guard to hear. The rattle of Talon's wings says don't push it so she shuts up but only because she can't think of anything else to say.

"I can assure you these knives are better," Firn insists as another is strapped on using a heavy belt around her waist and thigh. Then one up her pant leg into a cleverly concealed pocket. "If you don't know how to use them leave them be. I promised Master Talon you wouldn't take a finger off on your first day with the new gear."

Shadow laughs, remembering sharing the first day thing with Talon and he gives her a wink. His smile dries up just above his lips and her unsettled feeling returns. Talon notices she's dressed and gives her a nod before approaching Lev and Soar. The three get their heads closer than their wings and size should allow and try as she might Shadow can't make out any more than the occasional click of their tongues.

The last thing they put on her is a vest like all the others wear in addition to their dark chest pieces. Not heavy leather, its function appears to be more like a pack or purse.

"See," Firn explains as she pulls out a flask. "The ones around back aren't for drinking. Moonwater, just in case. Get it?"

She does. Just in case there's a dead gryphon.

"We tend to use more than necessary when we have the luxury of being in the eyrie. Each flask is enough and we each carry several. Between the four of us there is one for each gryphon on the trip. Otherwise there's drinking water and jerky in the front pockets. We cached more food and water on the way here so your vest carries enough to hold you over if the weather grounds us."

"You're set," Firn announces as Dove rechecks all the buckles and ties.

Shadow's guard steps back to huddle with Talon for a moment before he excuses himself, leaving them with Lev and Soar. Nobody has lied to her but the mood has darkened. She feels like she's wearing a corset and ski boots since the footwear is stiffer than it looks. The bare arms are cause for concern since it's winter in the Rockies.

"You're bothered," Talon says as he looks her over. He only brushes the ties with his fingers and doesn't adjust any of them. Shadow feels like he sees her as nothing more than a collection of knots.

"I told you not to read my mind."

"And I told you I can't help it."

Shadow acquiesces. Of course he's worried about her. She's worried about them all.

"Lev and his guard will fly above us, you and me in the middle of the lower wing below. There are four food caches between here and the Island otherwise we travel straight through and should arrive before dawn. If you need sleep, I'll carry you."

"I'm sure I'll be fine," she says. God, he looks tired and she doesn't want to be any more of a burden than necessary.

"This is what I do, Shadow," he says. "I'm a lot of things. This is one of them."

Warrior gryphon. Judging by the age and wear of his

armour he's been one longer than her thirty years can appreciate. Shadow takes his chin and forces him to make eye contact until she's satisfied there's still something she knows under the surface.

"What bothers you?" Talon asks.

Shadow forces a smile. Other than the huge guard and the first step from the eyrie...

"Nothing."

"Trust me?" Talon asks. Then he's soft again like some switch has been thrown; kissing her, fingers in her hair before he straightens up at Lev's approach.

"What the hell is she doing here?" Shadow's sire demands.

Shadow looks past Talon toward the door. Cloud scans the room and smiles when she sees Shadow. She's dressed in mismatched armour and wrings her hands. Her long red hair has been hacked short, blunt chunks three or four inches long stick out everywhere since she still suffers from the tangles.

"Sire's pinfeathers," Talon mutters barely audible over the talk and shuffling in the room. "Get her out of here, Dame Shadow."

With protective hiss for Cloud, Shadow shoves him with her chest.

"If I want her to come, she comes," she insists, angering Lev and Talon. Shadow tunes out their shared growl as she turns, determined she won't be pushed into leaving without Cloud.

As she makes her way across the room however, Shadow nods to gryphon after gryphon. More than one bears terrible healed wounds like Firn; gashes line up with gouges in their armour. How many of them lost their own 'Treasure' the day she was born or later when the rogue army returned? How many are here ready to do it again or have loved ones back on the Island who are sick with worry?

The Dame in Shadow turns to Lev and Talon, giving them a brief bow acknowledging what she was about to do. Bringing Cloud would mean two inexperienced gryphons to protect and Shadow's word would make them fight as hard for the teen as for her. They would be spread too thin and had already made their plans based on defending only Shadow. They may even be spread too thin already.

"Hey, look at you," Shadow exclaims to Cloud. Her hobbled together armour is a child's reflection of what every other gryphon in the room wears and its sad lack of protection cements Shadow's heartbreaking decision to leave her behind. "Let me see."

Chin high, Cloud turns. Her tail sways as she holds her wings up with happy pride.

"I found pieces the rangers cast away," Cloud explains as she completes her turn. "I've been working on it for a while and stayed up late finishing it for the day I would finally fly from this place. To your eyrie. With you."

Oh, damn. Shadow is torn between joy Cloud wants to join her on Vancouver Island and guilt for turning her away.

"Today's the day?"

"Yes, Dame Shadow," her eagerness is wonderful.

"Let's step out," she takes Cloud's elbow and they move into the tunnel. The air is so much fresher than the hot noisy chamber full of fighters and their sweat. Shadow and Cloud don't belong there.

"Cloud," Shadow whispers.

"Please," Cloud drops to one knee and holds up her palm while pulling out a small dagger with her other hand. A tuft of her red hair is caught around the handle. "I will kneel at the entrance to your eyrie and open my hand to promise my blood to your eyrie, my spirit to its gryphons and my love to its Dame. With all my heart, Shadow, I will follow you anywhere."

Shadow gets down on the floor and takes Cloud's hand, running her thumbs over the smooth young skin.

"I'm so glad you want to come and you are welcome to join me."

"Thank you," she sighs as she puts the knife away.

"But they're keeping things from me, Cloud," Shadow hopes it comes out in a way that makes her want to stay behind. "Look how many there are. They're expecting trouble."

"You need me then," Cloud closes her eyes and Shadow feels the scratching in her throat like in the bath when Cloud tried her persuasion. All it takes is a swallow and a deep breath to recover her voice.

"They will have two of us to protect if you come because I'll insist you're as precious as I am. Even then you would only have half the guard which may not be enough.

"Cloud, I would never forgive myself if anything happened to you. We grew up together yesterday, true sisters. We've both known loss and loneliness and what it's like to be surrounded by people who don't understand us."

"But not this trip," Cloud sits back on her heels in submission. She knows there is no getting around the big but.

"Not this trip. You will come, but not with us."

"I understand, Dame Shadow," she pulls Shadow up as she stands and accepts a hug.

"You will come, but not with us."

Cloud stiffens in her arms like she's hurt but then she smiles and kisses both of Shadow's cheeks. Maybe she's just never been hugged.

"I love you, Shadow," Cloud whispers and dashes away into the darkness as a flash of orange dawn light sets the tunnel behind Shadow on fire.

"It's time," Talon says softly. "You did the right thing."

"I thought we would say thank you to Sher and Arden before we leave. This eyrie has been through so much because of me."

"They have withdrawn to their chambers until Torrent returns. He is their only heir and the gryphons here must heal from his act if he's ever going to serve them as Sire. Lev has given our formal thanks to them already."

"But you'd still like to see Torrent punished," Shadow says. Talon's eyes flash and he pushes her against the wall, his hands against the stone at her shoulders. It's a quick, rough and desperate act to avoid her question. It's also sexy as hell. After two days touching his bare skin and patches of golden brown feathers the Talon scent overload from his armour mixed with the sharp smell of steel bound to his back works like a charm. Shadow abandons whatever it was she'd asked about.

Then on an unspoken queue the room behind him empties. The orange light flashes and moves around the tunnel as the rangers step around the corner to be swallowed by the waiting sun.

Shadow's stomach knots. This isn't going to be a leap of faith in Talon's arms like the day before.

She's about to be reborn.

"Hold still," Talon says as he pulls her helmet on. It's as snug as the rest of the pieces and he laces it up tightly under her chin. The soft inside is lined with sheepskin.

The last gryphons to jostle past are Shadow's guard and as quickly as the tunnel was jammed with activity it's only Talon, Shadow and Lev.

"Dame Shadow," the corners of Talon's lips tease as she takes his offered elbow in one hand and grabs Lev's with the other. Only twenty feet further they turn left and she squints at the blinding dawn light.

"Holy shit," Shadow breathes. She knew she was in the Rockies but the peak they face is at eye level so they must be a hell of a long way up. "What if I forget and put my wings in and fall?"

"I will of course catch you," Talon is impatient as Lev drops behind them. "But I can't believe you'd do something so embarrassing."

The sky opens brilliant gold before them as the stone gap nears and Talon has to pull her within a step of it. Snow and rock fall away vertically below and as her pupils narrow to pinpricks vertigo tricks her into thinking she's falling out already.

"Like yesterday—"

"Enough, Talon," Lev hisses. "This is my job."

And with a solid boot to her ass he launches her from the opening.

Chapter Twenty-Five

Shadow doesn't seem to weigh anything in Talon's arms. It isn't as easy to keep their speed up at night without daytime thermals. Her heart beats a little harder so he knows she's awake but she stays relaxed and doesn't try to move. The night is clear and the moon nearly full so they have a decent view of everything but not nearly as far as they'd like. Although there isn't much to see other than ice and rock, the view is still magical even when the ice is the colour of the moon and the rock is plain black.

Shadow endlessly questioned the whistles and chirps of the guard right up until the first food cache, demanding Talon translate. It was mostly orders from Soar, the Master aloft, assigning areas to scan and sending the occasional gryphon even higher for a better view.

After eating, Shadow speculated about other things Talon could do with his lips until he was so completely distracted he missed his turn to go up and earned a shout from Lev. But shit, even bound up in leather she teased him with the sway of her long tail until he'd charged at her to make her stop. Shadow dropped behind, he figured to sulk, and when she didn't return to her position after a few minutes he wasn't alarmed. It wouldn't take her long to figure out this wasn't the place for foreplay.

Then she crashed into him from above, head first and grabbing his ankles. He was flipped on his back and into a tumbling dive so quickly by the time he was in position again she was in hers like nothing had happened. At least after that she'd kept quiet, paying attention to his instructions.

Then bless her, she made it until midnight.

When she wandered into him for the third time Talon got no complaint as he folded her up in his arms and she quickly fell asleep. Even with the magic granted by the sapphire ring she doesn't have the stamina of a ranger who would race another across the country for fun. Now the eastern sky is a shade less dark than the west so dawn is coming and daylight will offer them a little more safety.

"Talon, where do we come from? Don't start with when a daddy gryphon and a mommy gryphon love each other very much. I've heard that part."

Talon laughs and so do Firn and Rapid on either side as Soar orders them higher. Talon's come to appreciate his guard; Firn in particular. She isn't shy about her love for Lev and his eyrie and Talon suspects the two have found companionship with each other since losing their beloved mates. Rapid is rebellious and pushy and Dove is trimmed from her dame's gentle feathers. Gentle only when she feels like it however; more than once Firn broke ranks to answer a challenge from one of Lev's guard, usually proving herself to be the better ranger. Typical pass the time stuff.

"Should I put you in school with the children once we get to the eyrie?" Talon answers.

"Not if you tell me."

"Even if I tell you," he insists but she's pleased with the idea. They settle into their new elevation far above the cloud lined valleys they passed over all night, each deeper and thicker than the next.

A low whistle from above gets Talon's attention and he pulls Shadow in tighter. Two short chirps from Soar tell him there's trouble behind; the long pause between the sounds is an indication of distance. On the bare edge of the horizon, low enough to have remained hidden without their change in altitude.

The group picks up the pace in response. As far away as the following gryphons are it's still too close.

"Our legends say we were once the pets of the gods, Greek, Norse, whatever," Talon starts. "It's so long ago we don't really know. The story is one of us bravely defended her master. The cleverness of her actions led him to believe she could be sentient which is saying a lot because the gods found none other than themselves to be sentient. He whispered to her in the old words and she became partly human, retaining her wings and her tail and he fell in love with her because she was more beautiful than any goddess he had ever seen.

"She seduced him and as he slept she went to her sisters and brothers, changing them as she'd been changed. When she returned he tried to make her a gryphon again but she remained part human. Because she was pregnant kept her new form. Mist could tell you this, you know."

"Mist wouldn't say seduced," Shadow retorts.

"She will when she's older," Talon answers as Soar chirps again; more gryphons, far but flanking their right and keeping their distance. They turn left and Talon shifts his eyes as black as they will go, scanning the horizon ahead. They can't be more than thirty minutes from the final food cache. If it's anything like the last one, a small tunnel, he can focus on defense while Shadow is safe in the rear. Soar will have to decide if they confront them there or if they push on to the eyrie.

"But she'd fallen in love with him and together they gathered the gryphons she'd changed and hid on Earth.

"By the time her children were born, a son and a daughter, she had been found out and the remaining gryphons were cast to Earth with her. As punishment, the selfish god who made her part human was stripped of his godhood and together they ruled the first eyrie. It's said all royal females are descended from her and blessed with the magic of the gods inherited from their sire.

"We've been bound between the Earth and the sky ever since."

"But not everyone believes this," she counters.

"Stretch your wings," Talon says and lets her go. Shadow has to be ready to fly on her own if he's the last thing between her and a challenger. Within seconds she glides to his left and takes her place between him and Firn. The pace they keep is punishing for her and after a moment of lagging behind she loosens up and is able to hold position at his left wing.

A final signal from Soar says he can't keep their problem from Shadow any longer. A third group appears over the high ridge ahead.

"Here Shadow, now," he barks, instantly regretting his tone but on some level she's relieved like she's glad the waiting is over. As Talon lifts his left wing and pulls her in she rolls, hooking her right leg around his waist. Without taking her eyes from his she holds on silent and ready for his instruction.

Talon snaps the crossbow from his thigh and pushes it into Shadow's hands.

"We're surrounded, *Arlette*," he whispers.

Take the group to the left, Soar whistles and like two large birds they make a graceful turn.

Talon knows what's coming; they'll take on the group back to the left. It's not the one to which they were being herded. The ridge under the third group could be hiding anything. So could the thick valley cloud below for that matter and with the rising sun lighting the surface it will be much harder to detect danger hidden below. If they're quick enough about eliminating the first group then they'll still have a lead on the other two. If they try to get between two groups they'd just wind up caught by both with the third coming in fast from behind.

"Fasten the thong around your wrist so you don't drop it —"

"It slides," she notices the figure eight of leather that slides along the loop already around her wrist. "Got it."

"If they get too close we'll run for it, the guard will get in the way and we make for the eyrie like our tails are on fire."

"Okay," she breathes but a little sob slips out as her thighs dig in.

"You have five shots, a last resort while we run. If I have to fight I'll drop you and fight and you keep going. I'll catch up."

"How do I reload it?" her voice shakes.

"You don't," Talon's hand finds the back of her neck as he whispers, soothing her. "It's just like a gun, looks like a crossbow."

It's true that's all it is. The bolts it fires are a combination of bullet and arrow, about six inches long and launched by an explosion of black powder. No need to reload, just a bitch to replace if he loses it.

"What about my father?"

"Right now he's just another ranger and a damn good one," Talon looks ahead at their targets. They look big like he has double vision and he blinks to clear it. He makes out eight coming in fast as they drive to shorten the gap. Then fifteen or sixteen. Shit, each had a passenger like he does and now it's too late to change course.

Climb, Soar whistles. The tactic is sound. Climb then dive at the last minute, crossing under their opponents and forcing them to turn and follow while Soar drives them on ahead.

In theory.

"Talon—"

"The eyrie will survive without him, not without you."

"Talon—"

"We're going to do everything we can to make sure it doesn't come to that, okay?"

Ahead of them, the approaching gryphons climb at the same rate, silhouetted by the lightening eastern sky. Their opponents want to time their dive to collide with the Vancouver Island gryphons and engage them in close. If they wait too long or go too soon then they're playing catch-up while Soar drives them on.

Soar's goal is to dive first, cutting under the rogues'

descent path as well as if they waited too long.

"We're going to dive, keep your wings in as tight as you can. If we drop too slowly we're in trouble."

"Okay, I'm ready."

"That's my girl, *Arlette*," he encourages as he silently ticks off the same seconds Soar counts. The pressure in his lungs from their upward sprint burns as he drives still higher, guiding the lower wing in behind the upper.

"Brave, brave, *Arlette*."

Soar's click is so faint the oncoming gryphons could never hear and Talon's response is automatic. They drop like a silent torpedo; heads down. Shadow releases the hold her legs have on him and tucks her pointed toes in between his shins, removing even more drag. Coupled with the bit of draft from the upper wing just in front the fall is dizzying.

For a split second they're tugged backwards as the attacking gryphons pass inches from Talon's feet then there's the deafening clap of wings catching air. They take off before they fully arrest their fall to convert some of their downward momentum into a burst of speed.

Once they're back in formation, Soar drops down to the lower wing and Dove moves aside to make room at Talon's left.

"Screw the last cache, my friend. We make for the eyrie."

"Agreed, Soar. Even if we have to go the long way."

For a moment there's only the quiet swish of wings in the frozen air as they push, growing their lead by a small amount. Then Soar laughs. The long way means around the Earth. Right now they're headed east and turning around will only invite one of the following groups to join in. With all the gryphons on their tail the coming fight looks worse and worse.

"No," Soar announces. "The guard will turn and deal with this bunch."

"Master Soar?" Shadow calls.

Talon feels her fear. The adrenaline echo through his veins must be nothing compared to what's rampaging through hers. He swears silently for letting himself be worked up by her and decides the first chance he gets he'll make Shadow something to give him the ability to tune her out. That is if he ever has the heart to leave her long enough to do it.

"Dame Shadow," Soar nods, the closest thing to a bow a gryphon can manage on the wing.

"When we get there tell me about Condor."

"Of course," he bows again. "Three minutes, my friend."

Shadow doesn't feel much better and neither does Talon but he understands why she did it. She promises they'll meet up safely at the eyrie. Even scared shitless she's trying to lead with confidence however she can.

Talon gives her neck affection as Soar returns to his station. It seems to help but Talon grinds his teeth as he realizes that he's squeezing too hard. She's become limp in his arms and he backs off before he makes her too weak to fly.

"Kiss me," Shadow says as she tries to hide a shudder. At first Talon thinks it's due to fear but when their lips meet they're cold.

"Eat something," he orders. He's seen it before; stress in a younger gryphon depleting their reserves. It has to be twenty or thirty below freezing which isn't helping. And he feels her worry as a knot in his belly that won't go away. "Relax, *Arlette*. Think about when we get to the eyrie. Condor and Soar were good friends and he can tell you a lot about the gryphon Terry was."

"Okay," she whispers as her teeth chatter. There's nothing but jerky in her pockets and she gets a piece out.

Fuck, it's started.

The sounds of battle reach him through the frozen thin air and fighting gryphons tumble away in two's and three's. A single gryphon falls, wings limp, rolling as he or she picks up speed toward the mountainside below but Talon can't spare a longer look. Two have broken away from the main fight, one on the tail of the other, and he can't tell if they're both taking chase or if one is trying to stop the other.

"Eat," he orders again, digging a chunk of jerky from his own pocket for her.

"Yeah," she chews, working the frozen jerky between her teeth. "What about you?"

"I'm a long way from needing it, Shadow. I can fly all the way to the eyrie if I have to."

Through the sound of his own wings Talon hears the two gryphons behind him. A final glance tells him it's three. Shadow see's them and after a moment frozen in his arms she digs her thighs into his hips and steadies the crossbow on his shoulder.

"Eat," he tries again. In minutes he'll order her to run for it and she'll need every bit of energy she can get.

"No, glide," she shouts.

Talon knows why. She wants a steady platform to be sure of her aim and she's right. He can keep two busy, one between him and the other, but a third will always find a way to flank him. As much as he hates to let them any closer it's the only play that makes sense.

"Let them get closer," he insists to make the rounds count but the idea scares her and he's starting to think of plain old fleeing. Not a ranger-like tactic at all but if Shadow can keep her head in the face of such fear he'll have to as well.

"Okay," her arm relaxes and she eats another piece of meat. Shadow's shivering has stopped but she doesn't feel any warmer. Her next piece comes from his pockets and she eats it as she takes the rest. "Where are we?"

"Between Lytton and Hope," Talon answers. "When I let you go you're going to fly to the sun. It'll help hide you and I'll know where to look."

The smell of jerky makes his stomach rumble. Talon is a lot closer to needing it than he let on but he can at least hunt the first animal he sees. Shadow can barely land.

"Ready?"

She hitches her thighs up around his hips and lines up for her shot.

"Glide," she whispers and in the second his wings are still she startles at the sharp report of the crossbow.

"Shit," she whispers. "Again."

A few more beats of his wings to speed up and Talon coasts for another second.

One fewer sets of wings pursues and the disorganized flutter of a dead or badly injured gryphon disappears below.

"Oh, God," Talon can feel her stomach heave and his first thought is anger she'd waste her precious protein throwing up. "I killed her, Talon! Oh, no!"

She slaps the base of his wings, banging the dangling crossbow against his back.

"Spitting fire," she gasps. "I didn't..."

"You did or she would have," he growls. "Keep the crossbow."

"Okay," and for a split second their eyes lock as she holds his cheeks in her hands.

"I love you, Shadow," he promises. "I'll see you in the sun."

"Fight your ass off, Talon," she says as she gets her feet on his hips. "You have my heart."

Then she's gone and Talon turns, shifting his hands to claws since he prefers weapons he can't drop as his first line of attack. He's confused they don't both rush around him for Shadow. They do as Talon does, making a tight circle to stay in place.

Talon doesn't waste any more time figuring them out and bursts into a full-blown charge at the bigger gryphon on the right. They've spaced themselves too far apart and Talon has no trouble taking him on before the other can join in. His body position and failure to meet Talon by charging him head on stink of inexperience and invite a hard landing below. As his opponent continues to coast closer, Talon beats higher so gravity can assist in knocking him from the sky.

Talon's roar drives out the last of his humanity as he bears down on the young gryphon. Everything slows as the cold blooded hunter inside takes over, focused on nothing more than the pulse in his victim's throat.

His name is gone. His senses are aware of the smaller, more experienced attacker coming toward him but he'll be too late to stop Talon from claiming his first prize.

It's over quickly.

Talon knocks his opponent's knife free with a blow from his bracer and wraps his legs around the male's thighs. His right fist drives the gryphon's chin up out of the way and as they roll Talon's weight pushes him over backward. Both are covered in a red curtain of blood as Talon's clawed left crushes his opponent's windpipe up against the inside of his protective collar.

There's no cry of pain or yell of defiance.

Talon is already positioning himself for his next kill as he drops the dying gryphon.

This one is experienced. Older and weather worn, he draws his lips back exposing a single thick sharp front tooth-plate but it will take more than that to make Talon back off. The black-eyed animal in Talon locks his stare with the shifted black eyes of his opponent for only a moment. Instead of wasting his time trying to figure out where the enemy's featureless eyes are looking, Talon concentrates on his hands. They're held a little too far back for a frontal assault and he gives away what he plans to do with his bare feet. They're covered in golden hair and lengthened like a lion's paws with razor sharp claws spread ready to lay him open.

That's bad news. The oncoming warrior only needs to hold Talon still to get his feet up and tear him to shreds.

Talon rolls at the last second, turning sideways. His butt hits his attacker just above the knees, a move as effective in the air as on the ground. Even more so. The gryphon's lower body swings from the impact and his hands are too far back to do any real damage. As Talon passes beneath the slashing claws his dagger bites deep into the exposed calf of one leg and cuts open the other.

With his feet up and head down, the wounded gryphon has no choice but to dive to get enough speed to turn and re-engage. It's a move Talon hoped to force.

Talon dives faster and they collide again as he wraps his legs around a wing and a thigh. As his pinned opponent screeches in pained frustration, Talon gets both hands at the base of his free wing and with a vicious jerk pushes it up, tearing muscles and tendons and dislocating the big bone.

As his second kill drops to be finished by the Earth, Talon turns toward the main fight. A few shuddering breaths allow him to reclaim some of himself and he shakes his head to knock loose the hunter inside.

He quickly sizes up the situation. Dove and Firn are easy to make out. Their fighting styles are nearly identical and he'd seen enough of Firn on the trip to have a good sense of her. Rapid's lighter armour is nowhere to be seen and she could simply be below, tangled with another gryphon. A burning above Talon's knee turns out to be a small dagger driven through the armour on the side of his leg. Cursing, Talon pulls it free. The wound only weeps through the leather and will need attention eventually but not now. Not while he still has a job to do.

There are a couple of Lev's guard missing as well as many of their opponents. Soar's out of place laugh reaches Talon as two gryphons position themselves behind an occupied Lev.

Talon swears under his breath. He's certain no gryphons have passed him so he yells for Lev's attention and jumps in to the fray.

Chapter Twenty-Six

Shadow kicks off to carry as much of Talon's momentum as she can. The image of her lucky shot buried between the female's collar and chest piece won't go away. The gryphon's gloved hands immediately dug the little missile free but blood cascaded down both elbows as she did, emptying her body of life as she cast the crossbow bolt aside. Shadow covers her mouth to keep her food down even though it keeps the tumbling dying gryphon in her as well.

She's too scared to do any more than fly so all she remembers is the sun. The last of the heat she carried from Talon fades and she fumbles, dropping several pieces of jerky as the dangling crossbow makes her arm swing of its own accord. Behind her Talon sounds confident and she hesitates, circling once in the hope he's coming but he isn't. He grapples with one of his attackers before dropping him and going for the second.

She doesn't look back again.

The sounds of battle fade as she loses the fight with her stomach. A single heave purges Shadow's meal and she doubles up, compromising the lift of her wings as they involuntarily join her in a head down ball. The icy peak in her path barely hides the sun; both large in the thin air. Its warmth is nothing but cold light and Shadow understands why Talon was so insistent she eat her reserves and gave his up.

Shadow shudders, bitten to the bone by the wind and pulls another piece of jerky from her pocket, losing a second in the process. Maybe the female she shot will be okay, Shadow hopes.

She can't be okay, her inner voice chastises. *If she is then she's after Talon.*

Talon roars only once as the grunts and cries disappear completely. The pure animal sound is chilling. She's terrified by the monster inside him and drives forward, losing altitude in her panic to get away. Shadow spits her half frozen beef morsel in her hand and drops further as she vomits again. The sun bounces from the snow and cloud filled valley below and she keeps her head up to protect her eyes from the glare. It seems to help with the nausea so she sucks on the meat, carefully scraping the thawing surface and forcing the bits down.

Talon should have said they were between lost and hopeless, not Lytton and Hope. A quick inventory says she has only a few pieces of meat left, not enough to get her anywhere significant now the cold has set in. Shadow jams her freezing fingers up under her chest piece and pulls the local geography from a memory. Years before Terry had doubled her around the interior of British Columbia for a cheap vacation between university graduation and her new job in Parksville.

East of between Lytton and Hope is the Coquihalla Highway. Shadow recalls it as the orange hi-lighted line on a map as Terry marked out day three in a new colour. The tang of the ink is nearly real as is the snap of its cap as his hands popped it back in place. To clear her vision, Shadow rubs her eyes on her shoulder but the soothing friction only adds to her mental numbness. The orange of the sun turns grey as weakness reaches her wings.

If Talon hasn't caught up by the time she gets to the busy highway she's sure he won't be coming. And she sure doesn't have the stamina to wait. Her food won't last but at least she can flag down a ride.

"Talon," she pulls out another piece of beef. "Damn you

hurry up!"

But her cold lips aren't enough to keep the morsel in her mouth and as her teeth rattle it falls, slapping against the crossbow when she tries to grab it.

Then another drop in altitude. Shadow's legs kick as her body tries in vain to make its own heat.

Shit.

With Lev safe, Talon decides he's spent enough time protecting his mate's sire. Only one of the two following groups of rogues joined in, hitting them from the north-west. If Talon flew east he would have led them straight to Shadow so he stuck with the guard, eliminating as many of their attackers as he could. The last group is nowhere to be seen but Talon can't stick around any longer.

"Later," he shouts at Soar as he reaches around to stabilize the sheath for his short sword and slides the blade home.

"Get out of here," is Soar's reply. "And I want to see tails or they don't count."

"Same to you," Talon hollers and with all the speed he can muster he turns toward the sun.

The tingle of his connection to his skyblade fades, uncovering a mild itch around his wrist. It's nothing like he felt from Shadow back in the eyrie but it's worrisome. The itch could be from the cold or fear; threat she perceives or fatigue. She was in rough shape when he'd sent her ahead but away from the fighting and with sufficient food she could have kept going for a couple of hours, long past the fifteen or twenty minutes he'd been tied up.

But damn it, staring into the sun hurts like a bitch.

To rest his eyes, he watches the cloud below. The sun has cleared the peak ahead and much of the valley radiates hostile yellow-white light. The spot temporarily burned into his retinas floats on its own, faster and faster as he involuntarily follows with his gaze. He scans every direction for motion with his peripheral vision but there's nothing; no movement at all.

As he picks up speed, the crack of his crossbow reaches him followed by a weaker echo off the rock around. Talon's eyes turn to the direction from which it came but the sun smear hides everything except a couple of dark smudges.

A flash of light makes its way through his blind spot and he surges forward to greet the sound of another crossbow shot. Four winged shapes, dark enough to be seen through the last of the sun's afterglow, fly clear of the clouds and surround his white winged gryphon.

"Shadow," he calls and one of her stalkers turns but she doesn't and judging by her uneven flight she's not listening. In fact she's barely flying as she rolls to her side with both hands on the crossbow. The two gryphons to her right move and she tracks one to the side. A flash from the crossbow's last round is followed by one of her attackers grabbing at his leg.

That's my girl, he silently encourages as he begins his descent. Pinning one in the leg isn't enough and he can't do any more than swoop down and grab her but Soar is only ten minutes behind. He can sprint that far at least.

Then there are more shapes in the cloud directly below Talon and he's sure where the last group of rogues has gone.

The crossbow is spent and the four gryphons with Shadow close in. Talon pushes even harder, focused only on the feel of Shadow in his arms. Letting her fear swallow him up might not be smart but it could give him the edge they need as he runs for her life.

A fifth gryphon appears below Shadow and has to coast so he doesn't overfly her stuttering progress. His armour is like hers, light brown and new, untested by blood, sweat and battle. In contrast to his light armour, the male's long black hair appears as dark as his brown and gold wings.

Torrent.

When Shadow tries to glide she doesn't even have the strength to hold her wings steady against the air. One folds painfully and she cries out as she rolls over to try again.

"Fly!" Talon yells and Torrent looks but carries on unhurried above her.

Then the weight of a big male surprises Talon from below and he rolls clear letting himself drop, picking up speed and distance. He doesn't know the male but his dagger is wet with fresh blood. The stitch in Talon's side tells him whose blood it is. With his attention on Shadow, he hadn't noticed the six on his tail. Each beat of his wings brings a fresh burst of warmth to the inside of his chest piece.

Talon drops to gain more speed. Now that he's injured he'll be lucky to recover from the dive to catch her but there's no choice at all.

Shadow's wings give out and as she falls from the sky Talon is sickened by the loose unconscious sag of her head. The air fights her descent giving her wings an unnatural bend. Torrent looks back and with a wave he dives for Shadow, catching her in his arms.

"*Torrent*," Talon yells.

Torrent responds by repositioning Shadow's body. His hand takes the back of her head and with a rough pull to expose her throat Torrent wraps it in his teeth.

"She's not yours," Talon growls but he's struck from above before he can see if Torrent's gesture means dominance or death.

Stars fill Talon's vision as he tumbles. His helmet is barely enough protection and without it he's sure his skull would be fractured. But that's only the start of his problems. As Talon faces his attackers his exposed legs are bound by a pair of heavy steel balls connected by a thick leather cord. They whistle through the air as they circle and one stings as it crashes into his shin. Another blow that should have broken a bone but other than pain it feels quite solid.

He can't hold an opponent or fight one off without his legs.

The six gryphons don't waste any time. At least three of them don't. The other three disappear after Shadow. Talon draws his skyblade, certain this is the biggest fight of his life.

Three to kill then west after his mate.

But it's not to be. A second pair of balls binds his left arm to his wing and all he can do is coast. Hating himself for ever letting Shadow from his sight Talon starts a slow turn but one of the three gets him from behind. The muscle rupturing dislocation of his right wing is followed by a blow that should rip his neck from his head. Then Talon falls, nearly blinded by rushing wind and incalculable shame.

Some master of the guard you turned out to be, you pathetic ass.
Don't I know it.

Talon tumbles into the clouds. From beneath their surface he can see the sky through every speeding second it takes to reach the ground. Landing on the rocks hurts less than he expected. From two hundred feet up? Three? Initially surprised to be alive, Talon wishes simply to be dead.

When he lands a second time he knows he bounced then he slides head first down a gravel patch, roaring with pain as he's battered by every bump. He comes to a rest between two trees, hitting one hard enough to knock loose hundreds of pounds of snow and add indignity to his useless body.

Talon only has a few minutes to size up his situation. His satellite phone is on his left and his bound arm can't reach it. He can't shift to human to free himself of the leather around his arm and wing until the dislocation is set. The right can't reach the phone or to free his left.

Truly screwed, he's intensely aware of his heart's struggle. Its uneven rhythm and the weakening flow of blood from his side say he's done. There's a small patch of blue above between the trees and Talon hopes its enough for a searcher to find his body so his spirit can be freed and his sire can live out his days without shame.

The only sign of life is a bird above. Talon's failing strength grants him enough energy to alter his eyes and as the flier comes into focus he recognizes the young red haired gryphon struggling bravely overhead.

"Cloud," he hisses, a mist of blood accompanies his broken voice. "You stupid little gryphon."

Everything turns gray as Talon tries to sit.

"Tawny's gonna…" he heaves. His body numbs until he's nothing more than fading eyes and thought.

Tawny's gonna kill you for running off!

And with a final desperate squeeze, Talon's heart surrenders.

Chapter Twenty-Seven

"You need to eat," Feather says.

Shadow leans against the stone wall in exhaustion. It's nearly impossible to hold the spoon with her frost bitten hands when they're bound in moonwater soaked cloth. Then she has to negotiate around the bandage over her nose.

"It hurts," she says. Her fingers won't work without pain and Feather won't feed her. "And I'm so sleepy."

Yawning pulls at her damaged nose.

"Eat, Shadow," Feather insists. "Or by the time you heal on your own the frostbite will claim your fingers and the tip of your nose. If you eat you'll heal before the damage is done. It isn't too late."

"What?" Shadow's brain is still stupid and frozen. She's finally warming up after what could be hours by the fire in the stone room. At least on the outside.

"Eat."

"Okay."

Shadow leans toward her bowl and rattles the chain connecting her steel collar to the wall. Her fingers can bend at least as she aims another mouthful of beef broth past her lips. She remembers something about running away with Talon; finally going home like he promised but it all went wrong and she got cold. "Where am I again?"

"You were flying," is Feather's patient answer. "We found

you in the cold and brought you here but you still froze your fingers and your nose."

"Feather?" How did Talon's sister get here? And why is she lying?

"Yes," the brunette smiles. She wears nothing but trousers and gold and Shadow focuses on her bowl rather than Talon's sister's breasts. Shadow wears the same, trousers and her adornment, so she is only slightly more covered. "Another spoonful. If your stomach stays good we'll get some solids in you."

She looks so much like her brother: the deep brown of their eyes and serious shape of their brows that all but disappears when they smile. Her wings are the colour of a golden eagle just like Talon's.

"Where's Talon?"

"I don't know," Feather says but the pain on her face is clear. Another lie covers up something very bad.

Shadow winces as the spoon gets under her nose. The soup is plain, nothing more than unseasoned broth but with her appetite returning her mouth waters with impatience for more.

"Hungry."

"Good," Feather says. "Finish the last of it while I check your hand. The moonwater isn't doing the healing, you are, but it's effective in controlling your pain."

The combination of heat from the fire and dry air stings Shadow's skin as the damp cloth is pulled back and she hisses, stomping one foot on the ground. All the nerves in her fingers are alight and she closes her eyes, hoping each shaky breath is one closer to relief. The sound of her bandage being wrung out is the only sound as she breathes through the pain.

"See?" Feather squeezes Shadow's wrist to get her attention. "There's a lot more pink. You're doing a good job."

"I'll take your word for it," she sighs as the cool cloth is replaced and Feather torments her other hand.

Sent on ahead? An image of Talon dropping a blood covered gryphon as he turns on another then wild heart stopping fear as she tried to fly into the sun. There's nothing like pain to bring clarity, such as it is.

"I didn't see him again," Shadow says as her eyes water. Feather removes the dressing around the tip of her nose then carefully dries her tears with spare pieces of cloth before tossing them in the fire. "Where's Talon?"

"I don't know," Feather says again and pushes a plate of meat chunks toward Shadow. Again the lie. Does Feather know that she can tell? Did Torrent take her from the eyrie before anyone knew? She can only hope.

"I was cold," Shadow says between pieces. "Why the chain?"

"Not up to me, Shadow," Feather pulls up a corner of her sleeping mat to reveal the dagger Firn had tucked up her pant leg. When she's sure Shadow has seen it she puts the mat back down.

What the hell?

"But now isn't the time," she mouths and Shadow nods.

"The prisoner is recovering?"

Feather's eyes fall to the hidden dagger before she scrambles around and kneels to Torrent. The gryphon framed in the doorway throws his shoulders wide and rattles his wings. His tied back hair makes it easy for the firelight to bring out the yellowing bruises from his impacts with the shield around Talon's house.

"Son of a bitch," Shadow hisses and rests a hand over the dagger. To her the gryphon is no longer royal by any stretch of the imagination. Killer? Liar? Maybe. But royalty? No way.

"My love," Feather bows. "She is healing."

Damn, Shadow curses. *Now things are complicated.*

Torrent crosses his arms and sizes up the two females. Shadow gets a hand on Feather to pull her away if the big male comes for them. Did he see the dagger? She doesn't know what to do with one and hopes her hands aren't too messed to use it. Terry only taught her to disable and run and in spite of the fact she's no longer afraid of Torrent her only option is the same as in her hotel room, wait for an opportunity.

"Feather," Torrent offers his hand and pushes his wings forward to invite her in. She responds, hurrying into his arms to accept his embrace.

"Sshhh," he croons as his fingers get around behind her neck and she relaxes though she chokes on a sob. Torrent's eyes don't move from Shadow, his stare so lacking in emotion it chills her. "I'm proud of you, Feather."

Feather nods as her arms reach up around Torrent's shoulders.

"What's going on?" Shadow asks, having lost interest in satisfying her hunger. She had been so immersed in the experiences of her new life that she hadn't considered Feather might have a place in Jasper. On her knees, Shadow waits for an answer. It doesn't matter what they say, she'll see the truth in their lies.

Feather turns. Her eyes glisten but her cheeks are dry. Torrent wraps an arm around Feather's waist, the other loosely takes her throat.

"Where is your brother, Feather?" Shadow whispers. Her hands cover her stomach as if to hold its heaviness in before it can topple her.

"My brother," Feather's trembling lips press together.

"I know how he cared for Swift. I went to the chamber in the top of the mountain. You must have known her well if they were together so long. Maybe she was a friend?"

"The best," Feather whispers, her voice constricted and Shadow doesn't need magic to know it's the heart-felt truth. Torrent stretches his fingers and they work their way into the gold around her neck.

"Murdered," Shadow says.

Feather's eyes flash.

"Disloyalty," Feather says but she doesn't believe it.

"Where's Talon?" Shadow tries again.

This time Feather doesn't answer. Torrent tightens his hold; fingernails thicken and stretch into inch long claws held just over her windpipe.

Right-handed attack, Shadow's mind forces her to shut up as she pictures Swift's terrible wounds. She has to stop pushing Feather about Talon because it only increases Torrent's threat. Something has changed between Feather and the big male she calls 'Love.' Now Shadow understands why she left with Torrent. Either the price for disloyalty was too high or she felt she could still do some good at his side. But good for who?

Feather's wings flare and she erupts with a vicious hiss.

"My dead brother was a fool!" she yells. "Too much like our old fashioned sire."

It's the worst possible news Shadow could receive. Dead. Feather says he's dead. It's Terry all over and Shadow slumps into the wall.

"There's no game, we can't even hunt to feed ourselves," she carries on. "Our males work in human businesses so we can shop in their grocery stores. Commons eat out of fucking cans! There's no pride left. Where are the herds? The clean air? It's Sires like yours who hold us in the past and shame us every day we have to serve humans."

"No," Shadow whispers, still reeling from the word 'was.' Feather believes every word she says. She's as sincere about the lives of common gryphons as she is about her brother.

"He didn't survive. You'd have been better off—"

"Feather," Torrent's hand on the back of her neck silences her. As his fingers work her voice fails and she licks her lips, eyes roll lazily with a feeling Shadow knows all to well. "Fetch her more meat, beautiful gryphon."

"Yeth," Feather slurs, unaware of the saliva collecting in the corner of her mouth.

Just because she believes Talon is dead doesn't make it the truth.

Until Shadow sees his body she's not going to believe. Torrent steps aside, guiding Feather to the opening before she can wander into the wall. She's barely on her feet.

"Prisoner," Torrent says as Feather shuffles down the corridor. "Talon was defeated and fell hundreds of feet to his death. He won't be coming for you."

"Liar," Shadow hisses, certain Torrent, like Feather, only believes what he was told.

"But someone else is," he condescends. "It seems Cloud followed you from the eyrie and we will see she finds her way here."

"No!"

Shadow jumps to her feet to shut Torrent up but the chain is too short for her to stand and she's brutally jerked to the floor. A hard landing on her elbow jars her shoulder and she cries out for Cloud and for Talon and everything Torrent has done to them.

"I'd thought her incapable of attachment to anyone but her long flight proves a deep connection with you."

"You cheap piece of shit," Shadow sobs, mindful of her tears. "You lying cheap shit."

As she pushes herself sitting and tests her arm the back of Torrent's hand knocks her down again. His boot on her braid holds her and he grinds his toe into the stone floor, pulling her hair and rocking her head side to side.

"Do you know what this place is, prisoner?"

"You pinfeathered—"

Shadow is cutoff by a fist to the stomach that leaves her frantically scratching at the steel collar as her flattened lungs spasm.

"Fifteen years ago I led a raid on this eyrie," he gloats. "Much to my surprise there was one survivor. The gryphon who let her live said she told him 'no' and he walked away. Well, he did from her but not from me."

Head shaking in disgust Shadow finally draws air. She knows why. Cloud's persuasive magic worked even then.

"Quite by chance I spotted you twenty years ago when we went after your eyrie again. Just a child but I was quite certain I would make you my Dame when you were older. There was no guessing who your sire was since your twin looked just like him. Then I found you with Talon," Torrent rolls his eyes. "Bonding with you so you would rule Jasper at my side would finish the job my friends started thirty years ago: destroying Lev's eyrie. Without an heir, it will eventually die.

"Though my friends and I have dissimilar goals, in the

short term erasing the steadfast traditional eyries serves us both. It expands my territory and reduces the number of eyries which object to the inclusion of democratic colonies in the grand council. They give me rangers and in return they will have the support of the Jasper Eyrie."

Torrent's thumb strokes the stinging red spot on Shadow's cheek.

"But Talon had already claimed you and well, we all wound up in Jasper. He would be executed for treason and my dame would put you in my care with the noble goal of taming you. Then Sire Lev to the rescue but its all worked out.

"Talon is dead and you are here. You will never offer your blood at the entrance to Lev's eyrie. It will remain dead."

Shadow keeps her mouth shut and straightens the bandage on her nose as a kick cramps her thigh.

"The rest of your life is mine, little gryphon, and this is how it will be. You will keep Cloud in line or she dies. You will not upset Feather again. She's not all there since losing her brother and if you hurt my consort, Cloud dies."

Nod.

"You will be very, very good or I'll teach Cloud how I like to hunt."

"Son of a bitch, Torrent."

Shadow closes her eyes as Torrent spreads his wings in threat. Whatever it takes, he'll never get Cloud.

"Feather? Thank you."

"You're welcome," interrupts Feather's humming and Shadow suspects Torrent gave her neck another dose of sedation before she returned with more meat. Feather is satisfied that Shadow's split lip is clean and removes the dressing on her nose. Stupid thing to try for the last word with Torrent. Her eye feels as fat as her lip.

Feather had returned glassy-eyed and mysteriously happy.

She's pleased how well Shadow has healed even though the fresh pink skin is overly sensitive to every flicker of the fire.

Shadow's nose burns inside with each breath and when it makes her sneeze she's convinced her ribs are only bruised and not broken. When Terry broke his he followed each sneeze with harsh language and a shot of rye. She's definitely not in that sort of shape. Not over her physical condition at least.

Jenn would have been a wreck after a beating like that. She was badly shaken by the break-in and being battered would have shattered the ancient teacup of self esteem she bore saucer and all. Royal Dame Shadow on the other hand is surprisingly stoic about it. Or as much as can be expected: chained, frostbitten and knocked around, her concerns aren't for herself. Until there's real proof she's lost Talon she'll be ashamed to cave-in when there are two to serve and not to mention an eyrie waiting for her to return it to life. But without Talon and her own heir, its life will only be as long as hers.

Healing her bruises and looking after Cloud and Feather are no more than things to do to get the hell out of here. She's not sure if finding Talon alive is on the list because that includes the possibility he isn't. The small taste of love and family she crammed in to a few days is worth fighting for.

"Feather—"

"You don't believe he's gone," she says.

"No," Shadow puts a hand on her adornment. "Tawny's mate passed and hers is gone."

"True," Feather says as she tosses Shadow's used bandages into the fire. "But it doesn't mean anything. A human found his hoard before he passed and her adornment disappeared."

Shadow gives a slow nod.

"Come here," Shadow shapes her wings like she's seen the males do and Feather initially backs away, confused by the gesture. "Please?"

Then Feather accepts, resting her head on Shadow's shoulder. She's stiff in Shadow's arms but only at first then she lets Shadow stroke her forehead as the fire burns down.

"You said you went to the upper chamber," Feather

whispers.

"Yes."

"Will you bless me Shadow, when I pass?"

Get me a gun, Nuke. They won't let me die.

It's the plea of defeat from a woman who's lost everything. Although Feather looks calm on the outside, inside she's torn with grief. And Shadow isn't going to run from the need of a friend. If Torrent is right about Talon they'll need each other.

"I'd be proud, Feather," is Shadow's choked answer. "But I will serve you for many years first."

"Serve?" Feather laughs. "We serve. You rule."

"If being a Dame was about rule and orders I'd shout until I get out of here. I serve, Feather. Nothing more. Nothing less."

Chapter Twenty-Eight

I should be dead.

Talon stares up at the night sky. He hurts. His neck, head and shin ache and the big joint where his right wing connects is twice the size it should be. Other than the cold, he feels reasonably intact. Maybe the tumble down the hill fixed the dislocation but that was hours ago. The white stars above aren't dulled by city lights.

"Stupid little gryphon," he mutters, remembering Cloud's passage through the morning sky above. "Where were you going?"

Due south? Talon lies in the Talon-shaped snow as he pictures her fly past. South-west.

"Good girl, Cloud," he amends, warmed by a measure of affection.

Gryphon, she's a gryphon now.

"Lead the way."

Upright, he frees his left arm from his wing then his legs. Although there is still pain in his right side the movement doesn't cause any more bleeding.

"Hot damn, Shadow," there's nothing more than a lump at the base of his skull where it should be shattered. "The truth was from your tears. And the pain that day? What did you do to my bones? You made this battered ranger unbreakable, didn't you?"

Her magic is truth and protection and she gave him both. The burning in his wrist tells him Shadow is alive — in danger — but very much alive. If Torrent only wanted to dispose of her he would have already done it.

Bring her home, Talon, he inhales and though her scent is gone, he turns south-west where his heart aches less.

But first he needs reinforcements and dials Lev on the satellite phone. A quick, clean extraction of Shadow and possibly Cloud isn't a one gryphon job.

The Sire is as backwards about the state of the human world as traditional gryphons can be; he's never even taken a human name but the gryph loves his gadgets.

"Lev," is the one word greeting as Talon works his wings, beating them gently at first then stirring up a cloud of ice and snow as he tests the stiffness of his mysteriously relocated joint.

"Sire Lev, this is Talon," he kneels in snow and gravel, partly from habit and partly in recognition of his botched escort job.

"You're not at the eyrie."

"No, Sire."

More than twelve hours have passed since the battle; more than enough time for Lev to reach the eyrie on the west side of Vancouver Island and notice that Talon and Shadow aren't there.

"Location?"

Talon mutters to himself as he remembers how the GPS in the device works and relays the coordinates.

"Where is my daughter?"

"Torrent took her, Sire."

The string of ancient curses on the other end of the phone is impressive.

"Thoughts?" Lev asks when he's finished.

"I was three hundred feet up when they dropped me, Sire," Talon says. "I should be dead."

"You have her tears to thank, ranger. Don't let it make you

237

reckless."

"Yes, Sire. They went south-west," Talon says. Cloud's decimated eyrie is south-west of where he stands; south of Hope. Gryphons are superstitious creatures and would have stayed away. It's the perfect hiding place for Torrent and the rogues who accompanied him. "She's alive, Sire. I'll know when I'm close."

"You're certain?"

"Certain, Sire," Talon insists. The wind changes, giving him a hint of something he's lost. "My guard?"

"We lost three, including Rapid, Master Talon. The females are in the mountains, presumably near you. I'll bring those who remain to intercept your path and order the females to join when they are able. Keep me apprised of your progress."

"Acknowledged," he answers as Lev disconnects.

Shadow is smart and much tougher than her size suggests and Talon is certain she plans on staying alive. He doesn't have to walk far to find a clearing sufficient for take off and after a small, stiff legged run he's airborne. The scent of his lost skyblade guides him deeper into the valley.

Feather excused herself to get more food and water for Shadow then again to empty the chamber pot. She was despondent and weary since her induced good mood faded and Shadow tried to be as small a burden as possible. A stitch developed under her sore ribs so she did her best to find a comfortable position until Torrent took Feather away.

But sleep is hard to come by. She's unaware how much time has passed since she was separated from Talon. Without Feather to comfort, the minutes fill with worry instead of rest.

The unattended fire burns down until the distant sound of raised voices makes its way to her small den. One voice is female and the male voice is even louder. The female falls silent but not before Shadow is certain the female is Cloud.

Cloud is unceremoniously dropped at the opening then screeches at the two males before crawling on all fours into Shadow's arms. She's ice cold; her mismatched armour frozen stiff over her body.

When Shadow can finally get a good look at Cloud, she's alarmed by her condition. One ear is entirely frozen grayish white, the other only around the edges. Frostbite has also marked Cloud's nose and hands.

"Gryphons?" Shadow asks the males. She'd prefer to stand but if humble kneeling gets Cloud help she'll do it as long as needed. "Please bring moonwater, bandages, clothes and food."

One of them snorts indifferently and the other strides into the room swinging a heavy chain. He grabs Cloud by the elbow and pulls her a few feet away before chaining her to the wall. Cloud's knees knock and she falls into Shadow's arms.

"Please," Shadow tries again, placing a hand on the jailer's arm.

The big gryphon's eyes drop to her touch; to the pink skin of her hand and he offers a curt nod before barging out and leaving his companion at the door.

"I d… d…" Cloud stutters, shaking uncontrollably.

"Didn't come with me," Shadow finishes and Cloud nods though it's hard to tell if she has any control over the movement. "I don't know what I looked like when I got here but your ears look bad."

The tip of Cloud's nose is white but her fingers seem flexible in spite of their deep redness. The ties on her armour are too frozen to untie so Shadow makes sure the guard is turned away. She slips the knife from under the mat and cuts all the ties she can before concealing it.

By the time Shadow has undressed her, the male has returned; his arms full of the items she'd requested. She shields Cloud from his eyes with her wings as he puts them nearby.

"What's your name, gryphon?"

"Tundra," he says then hesitates, unsure if he should leave.

"My name is Shadow. This is Cloud. Thank you, Tundra."

Tundra tilts his head to the den opening as if to say he'll be outside if they need anything. He takes station in the tunnel.

Cloud's arms are a mottled dark pink in contrast to the bare whiteness of the skin her armour covered and Shadow dresses her before duplicating the makeshift dressings Feather used.

"Shadow—"

"I didn't notice if you had a helmet or not," Shadow interrupts her with a spoonful of broth. There's no argument from Cloud about being fed. Shadow's long tail comes around and holds Cloud's shorter brown one, easing the twitching the cold brought on.

"I had one," Cloud says. "But..."

"Yes?"

Cloud gags and keeps the broth down before she continues.

"I saw the fighting in the sky and stayed low and went around after you and Master Talon," she lowers her eyes. "I saw Talon chasing after you and six of them attacked him. They dislocated his wing and he fell a long way.

"Something caught my eye as I flew after you and when I doubled back it was him."

"Cloud..." Shadow whispers as she goes numb. Cloud stills Shadow's shaking hands with her own bandaged ones as broth drips everywhere.

"He passed, Shadow."

Shadow hears sobbing and reaches for some cloth for Cloud's eyes before she realizes it's her own crying. Cloud's wet bandages touch Shadow's bruises as the bond between the two grows. Dame and daughter: alone and together.

"I poured moonwater over him to protect his spirit. Then I tied my helmet to the top of the tree above as a marker and came here."

They stare at each other until Shadow's tears dry. As honest as Cloud is, she still hopes it isn't true.

"I know why they're keeping us here, Cloud," she mouths.

Shadow and Cloud are survivors of two eyries Torrent and his friends tried to destroy so the terms Torrent gave for their lives don't make much sense. If he really wanted Shadow's eyrie dead why keep her alive at all? Or is there far more going on than he said. He only told her enough to make sure she'd comply. Not that she has much choice when chained to the wall. That he cares for Feather is the only thing Shadow understands.

"We're bait to bring the rest of the guard."

Cloud swallows and glances at the hidden dagger. "It's all we've got."

Maybe not, Shadow thinks. Call it denial or whatever. Talon is alive he has to know it's a trap. He'll be led to the cave just as Cloud was. Shadow sets off her built-in silent alarm, concentrating on Talon and the only thing she can.

Danger.

Chapter Twenty-Nine

The Welch Peak Eyrie east of Chilliwack should be
deserted. Talon's hidden perch is crowded with gryphons
watching the guards in the eyrie entrance. He's still full from a
much needed meal of black-tail deer so he ignores the rangers
behind him. Lev and the others quietly fight over two deer they
killed as they caught up. If the females were with them the
males would have some manners but a group comprised
exclusively of males has a feeding hierarchy not necessarily
related to rank or status. If Talon was hungry he'd wait. Being
a guard master means nothing and as the newcomer he'd have
to fight if he wanted to eat first.

Talon tunes them out so he can focus on Shadow. Her
mood is confusing and faint and he's certain distance disguises
what should be obvious to him. She's anxious but not afraid.
He rubs his bracer wrapped wrist on a sharp stone and releases
a low growl as he tries to welcome her anxiety. It's illusive and
never feels the same way for more than a few minutes.

"Master Talon," Lev's voice is barely audible.

"What?" Talon snaps.

The Sire knees him roughly in the thigh as he settles on
the ground beside him. Soar prefers to encourage Talon's
impatience by granting him a friendly elbow to the head as he
gets down on the other side.

"She's there," Talon tries in a more professional tone though he wishes they'd shut up.

"You're the only gryphon here who's been inside," Lev says. It isn't a statement. It's an order for intelligence. With two hours until dawn and the females in the guard expected soon there's a little time to plan.

"At the first fork in the tunnel, the right branch leads up to the great chamber—"

"And the left down to the guest dens," Soar interrupts with an annoying statement on common eyrie layout. Lev remains thoughtful, his black eyes focused on the eyrie entrance. At his age his eyesight is ten times better than Talon's; the best it will ever be before the years begin to take it away.

"Yes," Talon agrees. "There's a set of larger family dens below the great chamber, down the tunnel to the right once you get in there. Those dens are at the same level as the visitors, only a few feet of stone separate them; they alternate in the stone, side-by-side but separate. The cooking chamber is attached to the main one. Left tunnel is to the baths. Center tunnel goes up and splits again, unmated females to the left and the royal chambers to the right."

Talon shudders. He searched the females' chambers for survivors and found nothing but silent, bloody death. It's sickening to think his Shadow is captive in such a cursed place.

"The royal chambers consist of guard dens to the left and right of a long tunnel, at the end are several connected dens, a private bath and another tunnel to the upper chamber."

"Unusual," Lev comments. "No audience chamber?"

Jasper and Welch Peak holds the only royal dens Talon has ever entered. The lack of an audience chamber doesn't strike him as odd.

"Perhaps one of the guard dens," Talon sighs. "Maybe I thought they were all guard dens because of all the dead guard."

"No," Lev shrugs. "It's logical given what you described. I suspect Shadow is in those upper chambers. They are designed to be the most defensible."

"Perhaps, but she's below either in the guest dens or the family dens. I can't tell which. It's a maze down there."

Enough stupid questions.

"Curious," Lev mutters. "And her mood?"

"Indecipherable." Talon grinds his bracer on the rock again. The itch isn't getting worse but it's wearing him down. "She's anxious… angry but she's holding strong."

Talon shifts uncomfortably on the stone shelf as he realizes she's aroused.

"She's thinking about me," he says. "Shit."

"Yeah," Lev says.

"A warning," it's Soar.

"She's not where we expect," Lev says. "And she wants you to be worried. They want us to go to the upper chambers."

"Mm, that's where their fighters will be."

"And no trouble getting here," Soar says.

"I suspected this would be the place," Talon admits. "Cloud flew over me after I hit the mountain. I figured she was following Shadow."

"Clever gryphon," Lev whispers. His voice softens, belying his image of Cloud changing as Talon's has. If she's in there then the young gryphon is the only one who stayed on Shadow's tail.

More of the guard settles close to the ledge as the last few get a turn with the carcasses. Deer blood soaks their rock. The males' scents begin to merge as one, urging cohesiveness of the group. Two gryphons who had been circling above the entrance dive and enter and two more take their place watching the skies above.

"The guard in the entry has been watching us," Lev says and Talon is more than impressed with the Sire's vision. "But they do nothing. They could be aware our forces are incomplete."

"It's a trap alright, Sire," Soar mutters. "That they wait tells me their forces are weak and they rely on surprise and close quarters."

Then two more gryphons fly out, circling hundreds of feet from the entrance before going higher to join the two already aloft.

"A surprise they'll get. S… Something's wrong," Talon blurts out, startling Soar. In a second he's on his knees ready to leap from the ledge. Shadow's mood has abruptly changed to terror and alarm and Talon lashes out at Lev as the bigger gryphon pins him to the ground.

"Speak," Lev orders.

"We can't wait," Talon grunts, ignoring Lev as he tries to roll and get away. He can almost hear her scream, the picture of a dark haired gryphon fighting for her life triggers the hunter in him. Talon fights harder against the weight of both Lev and Soar. "Terrible…"

"We go now, Master Soar."

"Take the four aloft," Soar strategizes as Talon savagely kicks. The rest of Lev's guard crowds around. "Then inside we split up. I'll lead four down into the visitor dens. You and Talon take the rest through to the main chamber to the family dens. Talon knows the way and he goes with you. Your team splits; Talon down to the dens and you defend from their warriors in the royal dens. When we're done below we'll deal with any who follow you.

"Talon, if you figure out where she is we go straight for her."

Talon nearly tosses Lev and Soar off. The thought of Shadow's small dagger covered in blood won't go away. His mouth waters anticipating revenge as the dozen rangers take to the sky.

"It's pretty," Shadow whispers.

The pain is gone from Cloud's healthy pink hands and shining on the middle finger of her right is a ring she didn't have back at Jasper. Three emeralds look black in the firelight.

Her left ear is a worry. The right is whole and pink as is the center of the left but the outside edge only turned a darker grey as the rest of her frostbite healed. Since she's still unable to lie down, Shadow's thigh serves as a pillow for sleepy Cloud.

Tundra's big wings block the fire's heat as he adds more wood and stirs up the flames.

"Sire Sher found me as I was leaving," Cloud says. Shadow absently works her fingers through some of Cloud's smaller tangles. "For a second I thought I was in trouble but he only wanted to talk.

"He said he and Arden and Tawny were proud of my strength and that I survived without my eyrie. Sire Sher didn't expect me to stay when I became an adult and promised I will always be welcome in Jasper. Then he asked why I chose to follow you."

"What did you tell him?" Shadow asks although she feels the answer in their spirits. She smooths Cloud's hair as she concentrates on worry for Talon and love for her young gryphon.

"I told him I love you, Dame Shadow. That you love me and I think Talon does too. I thanked him for giving me a place and a chance. He gave me the ring and said he was proud of me again and when I put it on it made him happy."

"I'm proud of you too," Shadow adds as she lifts Cloud's chin.

Cloud saddens as she thinks about what to say next.

"I remember this place."

"Yes," Shadow softly agrees. "This was your home before you went to Jasper."

"No, not just this place. I remember this den; the tunnel down here. I think the rock remembers because it still smells of my dame."

"Oh, Cloud…"

"It's okay, Shadow. With you here with me, it's okay."

Cloud's bravery is admirable but maybe it's not bravery at all. Perhaps it's enough that she can feel close to the dame she barely remembers. Shadow closes her eyes and thinks of the families she met in Jasper and imagines Cloud and her rambunctious twin testing their patient dame every chance they got.

"I wonder sometimes about my sire," Cloud muses. "Was he away? Does he know I—"

"Gryphons," Feather speaks from the hall. Shadow hadn't been listening for her stealthy steps. "Torrent wants you to join the patrol above the mountain. I'll keep an eye on them until your replacements arrive."

"Feather—"

"What are they going to do?" Feather's light laugh is convincing. "They are chained and weak. Get up there now."

As the two disappear up the tunnel Feather rushes to Shadow's side. Key in hand, Feather reaches for Cloud's collar.

"Feather," Torrent says from the doorway. It's a warning and Cloud shoves herself under Shadow's wing. She trembles even though it's been several hours since her body warmed.

Shadow's eyes make contact with Feather's and in that moment she sees herself two and a half years earlier. The life is gone from her spirit. Shadow shakes her head, uncertain if Feather's final act is suicide or an attempt to make amends for helping Torrent.

"After what happened to Swift I thought I could protect my brother and you by coming here. I knew Torrent wanted you and it didn't matter before we met and you mated with my brother. But now he wants you dead. I thought if I kept Torrent close I could keep him from hurting you," Feather says. "Maybe I still can."

She puts the key on the mat where Torrent can't see then grabs the dagger from beside Cloud and stands, turning to face the gryphon she once loved.

"Feather," Shadow tries as she palms the key. "Put the knife down."

"No," Feather answers, taking two steps to the side out of reach. Torrent hasn't moved. Torrent watches her, momentarily saddened before his emotions lock up. "The devil I know."

"Feather," she tries again. "I know you believe Talon is dead and you're not thinking straight. I still hope, Feather. You're not alone. Please put the knife down. Please? Everyone understands."

"It's too late." Feather holds the knife up level with the ground. "Disloyalty. The knife has been drawn."

"It's too late," Cloud echoes and while Torrent's attention is on Feather, Shadow opens the lock around Cloud's neck. If they're going to die today it won't be chained to the wall like animals.

Torrent charges as Shadow puts the key to her own lock. Feather moves with impressive speed and as she turns she viciously swings the knife into Torrent's path. But he expects her attack and brings his armoured leg up, aiming to kick her head. Feather gets an arm up to block and there's a crack as his boot connects. She sags but stays on her feet, her broken arm at her side as Shadow's shaking hands get the key in her own collar. With a shout, Cloud pulls her over and they roll clear while Torrent spins to a stop where they had been on the mat.

The key flies over Cloud, striking the wall behind the fire with a metallic clink then landing in the burning wood and embers. They tumble out of reach and Shadow cries out as her bruised ribs take Cloud's weight and her chain pulls taught.

"Feather!" Cloud yells as Torrent begins to circle.

Shadow nearly sits on Cloud to keep her against the stone wall. The teen's warning growl gives her chills and there's no mistaking Cloud's desire to get involved. In spite of being unarmed Cloud tries to get away. She may have been as close to Feather as she was to Swift.

Torrent doesn't waste any time moving in on Feather. She keeps her knife up, fingers loose on the handle as they face each other for what could be the final time.

"Your brother would have done well in my guard, Feather," Torrent whispers. "I didn't ask much of you and Swift; simply get him on board. Instead she fell in love with him while you did nothing more than wring your hands with ethics."

The corners of Feather's mouth drop with heavy sadness as she brings her knife hand up to wipe away a rivulet of blood from her temple. She doesn't say another word as she drops into a crouch. Even though she's half naked against Torrent's armour, she seems only intent on provoking him into finishing her off. Shadow sees no other reason for Feather's actions.

Torrent doesn't draw his daggers as he comes closer. She holding her ground against his first step, then backs away toward the fire as the distance between them shrinks. Torrent's wings, high with dominance, are a fearsome contrast to Feather's; lowered with what can only be shame. Cloud growls again, pushing past Shadow but moves no further. She doesn't resist when Shadow takes her arm, holding the teen on the floor.

Shadow raises her hands to Torrent like she remembers from her dream.

"You won't touch her," she proclaims but there is no heat and Torrent laughs.

"This isn't your home, female. You have no magic here."

Feather releases a screech and dives at Torrent, making brief contact with the knife as he dodges and doing no more damage than a scratch to his arm.

Feather's former lover doesn't play with her any longer. As she gets into position for another attack he is already behind her. With his arms over her wings, he pins one down over her broken arm as the other grabs her wrist to take control of the knife.

Torrent picks Feather up off the ground and turns, giving Shadow and Cloud a good view. Then he brings the knife down and slides his hand over hers, taking complete control of the blade. Instead of driving it into her throat he holds her still as if granting a reprieve. A section of his hair falls forward and for a moment it's the only moving thing in the room. Second thoughts? Shadow can only hope but the set of his jaw says this is a display of power and control.

Nothing more.

Cloud screams and with alarming strength pushes Shadow

away. Shadow is in no shape to hold the bigger female down though she grabs at her heels as they slip from her fingers.

"No," Shadow yells. She tries to flare her wings in warning but one hits the chain as her voice fails.

The knife descends but only a small amount as Torrent shifts his weight to his rear foot. His boot comes up at Cloud and she catches it on the hip as she grabs his arm and sinks her teeth in. Feather tries to get loose but Torrent has her broken wrist and she drops to her knees. The weight of Feather's body against Torrent's relatively weak thumb pulls her right arm free and she uses it to hang on Torrent's left. The knife pops up and before Torrent can make his muscles stop pulling he drives a deep cut along his cheek.

Torrent drops the bloody knife and knees Cloud in the stomach, knocking her stumbling across the room. Shadow pulls her chain tight to get between Cloud and her attacker though she can't get close enough. Not nearly.

Feather refuses to let go of Torrent, holding on as he picks her up and throws her through the air. The only sound is the devastating crunch of breaking bones as Torrent slams her into the wall. Feather's spine and head land squarely on the uneven stone and she drops, still and lifeless to the ground.

Cloud moans; her body stiff. She gets to her feet and looks at Feather. One wing is beneath Feather's broken body; the other is raised, extended toward the center of the room and partially covering her head.

"Next," Torrent hisses as he kicks Shadow's bloody knife to Cloud.

"No," Shadow tries.

Cloud picks up the knife and in spite of her obvious pain she advances.

"Cloud, please?" Shadow begs but there is nothing she can do.

Chapter Thirty

The Sire's guard swarmed the four gryphons patrolling above the Welch Peak Eyrie and took out two as the fourth turned on one of his own. Lev gave the big gryphon he called Tundra a wave. As Tundra disappeared into the dark they turned their attention to the mountain below.

Then Talon led the charge to the eyrie. Not because it was his job but because he was helpless to do anything other than snuff out the cause of Shadow's distress.

Once inside, they found one guard in the entry.

Talon silently brought them directly to the great chamber since he was certain Shadow was in the family dens. To their surprise the chamber contained what looked like the bulk of Torrent's forces and confronted with the wild cries of Lev's guard, many took advantage of the great space to make an unsuccessful run for the entrance.

"Feather!"

A female's cry reaches Talon from deep within the family dens. It's impossible to tell whose voice has called his sister through the echoes and twist and turns of the stone tunnel ahead.

Talon doesn't bother fighting the rogues in the chamber. He's fueled by the scream and blinded by Shadow's terrified desperation as he disappears alone down the tunnel in pursuit

ELIZABETH MUNRO

of the fading echoes.

Only half way down a pair of armed gryphons blocks his path and Talon wakes the vicious hunter inside, draws his skyblade and picks up speed. They crouch, human-made weapons drawn, and the hunter snorts at their overconfidence. Talon's diving roll aims to hit the ground two feet behind him. He carries enough speed to impact just below their bent knees. One falls forward into a well coordinated landing. The other drops awkwardly to the side, his right leg severed just above the ankle.

While the wounded gryphon is still figuring out why he can't stand up straight, Talon bounces to his feet as quickly as the gryphon he knocked over. His raised skyblade draws attention up and away from his left hand which has shifted to full claws; a first for him, driven by his urgent rage. He barely has time to notice his unusually boney fingers' skin toughened and yellowed and ending in sharp black claws.

Blue light from Talon's wings shines on his sword as he dodges a dagger, grabbing his opponent's hand as it pass just under his throat. He crushes the other's fingers against the handle, twisting as he feeds the skyblade under the doomed rogue's ribs and stopping only when the bloody tip appears up out of his shoulder.

Talon releases the skyblade only long enough to use his opponent's dagger to eviscerate the other, who out of sheer ignorance of his injury still stands.

Another female's cry stings his ears. The hunter doesn't understand the human words but he knows his mate's voice and her urgency. With a boot on his first kill Talon uses both hands to draw his skyblade free and without a backward glance at the two nearly dead gryphons behind him he bounds further down the tunnel.

The only light in the dead eyrie tunnel comes from the sparks of threat on his wings. At the end of the featureless descent the tunnel levels and straightens and half way down firelight shines from a den to the right.

Another gryphon blocks his path. She's fully furred and

feathered, the slight roundness of her breast and absence of male genitalia confirm the adversary is female but that doesn't make her any less dangerous. Talon knows from experience that so completely shifted she retains little of her human self and even if she's poorly trained she could be as deadly as Talon on a good day. She's alone, seated peacefully in the center of the tunnel, and Talon assesses his options.

Although this opponent wears no armour her natural weapons are sharp and capable of granting a devastating death. Her raven black talons and wings contrast with her warm golden hindquarters.

Even seated she makes an intimidating silhouette against the orange glow behind her and Talon is certainly impressed. His instincts tell him he'd be better off taking a pass on this one. But age doesn't always imply experience and his terrified mate on the other side doesn't make a graceful retreat an option. In spite of her outward look of confidence something tells Talon this isn't what it seems.

A full shift is a waste in such tight quarters and is far better suited to aerial combat. The hind legs are awkward when upright and unless she can get Talon in an embrace on the ground they're utterly useless. It can only be a display to discourage an attacker but he has to be sure.

As the black gryphon's golden tufted tail curls around her black talons the shrieks further down the tunnel mask the struggle of combat and Talon moves closer. He feels the pressure to act and knows he's running out of time. The scuffle ends in the echo of snapping bone the black gryphon's tail slaps the stone in a nervous twitch.

It's game on.

Talon breaks into a run. The gryphon before him rises; her wings wide with threat. She prepares by drawing her claws but sitting has cost her a precious advantage. He leaps, gathering as much air beneath his partially extended wings as he can. It's a move she can't counter in time though she bends her knees to jump in the air to meet him.

She's too late.

Talon's boots hit her square in the chest, giving him some distance from her ebony claws as his skyblade comes down into her left shoulder. She sinks her other claw into his thigh, the nails only making it a half inch through his armour as her left arm and wing are nearly cleaved from her shoulder. They roll to a stop. The fight hasn't left her in spite of the fact she's nearly in two pieces. A slash of her claw rips Talon's protective collar from his neck as he scrambles for a dagger and pulls her on top of him.

His gamble that she's too close to death to support her own weight and get at him with her hind legs pays off but not completely. Two claws tear at his thigh and open the knife wound from the day before.

The skyblade is too long to use this close so Talon uses her weight to drive his dagger deep into her chest.

He shoves the dead gryphon aside and runs for Shadow's den.

Talon stops in the entrance to the fire lit room. As the hunter rages inside for vengeance, Talon struggles to retain control. His white winged mate yells a familiar name; maybe his, maybe that of his *child* dangling helplessly in Torrent's grip. One hand is buried past the second knuckle of his yellow clawed talons into her side and the other holds the back of her head. Throat exposed, Cloud's eyes blink before she offers him a weak smile of recognition. Shadow's bloody dagger is on the floor beneath her. The third female carries the scent of his sibling and though she's crumpled against the wall, the weak beat of her thready heart says she isn't gone yet. And then there's what Torrent did to Swift.

The fucker is going to die.

Torrent growls as his fused upper and lower tooth plates move toward Cloud's throat then he too shows pleasure at Talon's arrival. With a smirk which would set Talon off all by itself Torrent laughs, mocking the hunter with nonsense syllables. Talon is impatient to leave the arrogant gryphon with several gaping bloody holes and ignores what can only be jabs about his sister, common parents and his size and strides into the room like Death rides on his shoulder.

This is your end, Talon hisses in the old words.

Torrent only registers surprise for a moment then opens his jaw wide, making the joint crack as he tosses Cloud at Shadow.

The honourable Talon wouldn't kill an eyrie by destroying its only heir, Torrent gloats.

But the hunter doesn't see the logic. The only honour here is avenging the damage Torrent has done to the females in Talon's life. Talon drops his weapons so he can squeeze Torrent's spirit from his body with his bare hands and starts with a blow that should shatter his skull. Torrent dodges and Talon narrowly misses shattering his hand on the rock behind.

Talon's wings tighten around his body to let momentum hurry him around and his left elbow catches Torrent on the chin. Although it isn't as hard a hit as his first attempt, he feels Torrent's flesh rupture under his elbow. As they face off again Torrent is already making his move by knocking Talon's guarding left clear with his right bracer. He follows up with a navel to throat slash of his claws. Talon is caught on the chin but Torrent has both arms raised, leaving himself vulnerable.

A single step closer is enough for Talon to take control. He starts with a fist to Torrent's stomach and when Torrent drops his hands for protection Talon is ready. Talon catches both wrists and holds the claws at bay while bringing a knee into Torrent's side and with a satisfying snap a rib breaks beneath the heavy armour.

"Talon!" a male behind him yells, not in alarm but instead attempting dominance.

Fuck you, the hunter thinks and pulling Torrent's arms up and apart he swings another right. Then a couple more as Torrent staggers and Talon goes for his throat.

Cease! A new voice declares. *You will not harm him further.*

The hunter knows he must listen to his Sire but all he can do is watch as Talon rains blow after vengeful blow upon the battered and bloody gryphon before him.

"Talon," Shadow whispers. She doesn't understand the words Lev speaks but he clearly wants Talon to back off. His fists pummel Torrent, many blows unanswered. It can't have gone on as long as it seems. As much as Torrent deserves it, destroying Jasper by killing its only heir is as atrocious as his own acts against Shadow and Cloud's eyries.

Shadow checks the wad of leftover cloth on Cloud's side but it isn't enough. Blood oozes out from underneath and the teen's hand comes up, cradling Shadow's cheek.

"Sshhh," Cloud comforts. She's pale and Shadow pulls her closer desperate to keep life inside her.

When Shadow looks up it's just in time to see Lev and Soar cross the room as one. Talon's enraged cries are cut off as he's tackled, leaving Torrent to crumple to the floor.

Lev sits on Talon's chest as he continues speaking words Shadow doesn't understand. At first he mutters with quiet urgency then louder as Talon fails to calm. Talon roars in defiance until Lev's hand comes down, slapping Talon's cheek and knocking his head to the side.

"Enough, Master Talon," he declares.

Talon gasps for air as his struggles still. His black eyes return to normal and he looks at Lev like he's only just noticed him in the room.

"Sire," Talon mumbles and turns to Shadow. "I'm…"

"Talon," Shadow says for him. "You're Talon."

Whoever the monster was who strode in after Torrent is gone.

Lev stands, staying between Talon and Torrent. Soar offers a hand and pulls Talon to his feet. He sways for a moment before coming to Shadow. Talon's eyes flash to Feather and Cloud as his face falls. Looking at them is too much to bear so he focuses on Shadow. She won't let his courage leave now that he's made it to her side.

"I was too late," he whispers and Shadow reaches for him,

pushing his chin up in praise before he falls to her shoulder.

"She didn't believe you were dead," Cloud coughs and Talon rests a hand on her head.

The den opening fills with gryphons, Firn and Dove in front followed by two of Lev's guard.

"Sire," Firn says. "I thought I told you to save some for —"

But she stops as they spot Cloud and Feather.

"Get this disgrace from my sight," Lev orders with a click of disgust. Soar steps aside as the two rangers haul Torrent from the room. "When he can fly, toss him from the eyrie."

Firn and Dove cross paths to get to Cloud and Feather. In unison they pull flasks from the rear pouches of their vests. Dove wets her hands and places one on Feather's head and the other between her shoulder blades. She's as still as her dame is pushy.

Firn shoves Talon aside and rests her hands on Cloud's stomach.

"What is your name, gryphon?"

"Cloud," she says. Her voice is barely above a whisper.

"You will do as I say, Cloud," Firn instructs. As her hands move she glances at Shadow and Talon.

"Can you help her?" Shadow asks.

"Quite," Firn answers as she wets her hands in moonwater. "Keep still, Cloud. Stay awake."

Cloud nods bravely and moans as Firn grabs the gaping wound in her side.

"She followed me," Shadow cries on Talon. "When Torrent defeated Feather, Cloud stood to defend me."

"Ah," Firn breathes. Sweat drips from her brow and steam rises from her hands. "More water."

Shadow's hands shake as she pours a slow trickle over Firn's; once on the wound then on her belly. Talon adds his hand to steady the flow. Only a few feet away Dove still hasn't moved. She sighs and shifts her weight.

"Cloud," Firn says. "Do you wish to be a ranger? A member of Shadow's guard?"

"Yes," she wheezes.

"In that case you must obey the guard's master. In a moment Master Talon will order you to draw your wings in. Do it then and not a moment sooner," she turns to Shadow and continues. "Her blood loss is great. Once I have stopped the flow and she shifts, the extra blood volume from her wings should keep her alive but she needs more care than I can grant.

"Human doctor, do you understand?"

"Yes," Talon whispers.

The seconds tick far too slowly and for too long until Firn nods.

"Cloud," Talon says. Shadow jumps at the force and authority of his voice. "Draw your wings in."

Barely conscious, Cloud grinds her teeth but nothing happens.

"Cloud, now," he orders more loudly and her eyes open. The longest of her flight feathers fade as she grimaces then the next and when the long bones begin to disappear a slight pink returns to her gray cheeks.

"Hurry," Firn sits on her heels. "Human doctor, Talon."

Talon gets Cloud in his arms as gently as he can and Shadow scrambles to help him wrap her in the sleeping mat for the cold trip.

"Where's the key?" Talon asks and Shadow points at the fire. Soar kicks at the embers looking for the small piece of steel.

"Master Talon," Dove interrupts. "Her back is broken and her skull is fractured. She can't be moved."

"No," he whispers and holds Cloud tighter.

"We have dead here, Master Talon," Lev says and Shadow understands. She won't be going with Cloud to the hospital.

"I will do all I can for her, Talon," Dove says. She still hasn't moved and Firn pours moonwater over her daughter's hands. "If it comes that there is no hope, I swear she will not suffer."

Talon nods and Shadow watches, heartbroken for him, as a single tear makes its way down his cheek.

"Talon," Shadow wipes it away before anyone else sees. "I love you, Talon. Cloud is ours now. Get her help. Your place is with the living.

"Mine is with the dead."

Chapter Thirty-One

Cloud sleeps in the small second bedroom of their rented Tofino beach cabin. Surrounded by magazines, clothing stolen from Shadow, Talon and even Lev, Terry's resurrected iPad and a number of bits and pieces scavenged from the rock strewn stormy shore, not much is visible other than her short, spiky pink hair. Talon explained that although her nesting is extremely delayed, something expected of a child who hasn't yet taken wing, it's completely normal and a good sign she finally feels at home.

Shadow was reluctant to make the last leg of the journey to her new eyrie until Cloud was well enough to fly so Lev gave the order to evacuate the eyrie and Tofino is enjoying an unusual tourist boom. The motels are full of gryphons and the local Co-op is experiencing meat shortages.

Cloud's new look is complements of a local hairdresser; she was left alone while Shadow went down the street to buy them tea and something sweet for desert. When she returned the woman had cleaned up Cloud's self inflicted hack job and was soaking her hair in dye.

"Tony is bummed."

"He's what?" Talon asks, arms around Shadow as they watch her.

"Bummed."

"The owner's kid?"

"Yeah, they're the same age."

Tony's parents own the cabins occupied by Shadow, Lev and females with children. Accommodations on either side are taken up by the guard and any others.

Shadow studies the wear on Talon's face. Very human stress and trauma plague him and he takes wing daily to seek refuge in his strong gryphon spirit. Only today he admitted to suffering nightmares of running through endless tunnels, unable to find his broken sister, adopted daughter and chained mate.

"He says it's not fair his hippie parents saddled him with Tony when city folks like us got the really cool names."

Talon laughs but underlying the sound is a protective growl.

"Cloud says she'll break his fingers if he tries to touch anything she covers with clothes."

"That's my girl."

"I think he's just happy to have another kid his own age around since he's gotta work here after school while we've rented all their rooms," Shadow says, thinking of Cloud's week of firsts: first car ride in Talon's rig, first haircut, first bra, first kiss. News of the first kiss had been girl talk and something Shadow found amusing though nothing Talon's fledgling paternal instincts were ready for, not by a long shot.

Talon was winged and invisible when he helped Cloud stagger into the Chilliwack emergency. She refused to speak to anyone in the hospital and the night before she was to be discharged into the care of social services she'd taken wing with Shadow in her room. They'd walked out the front door to Talon and his waiting truck.

"She's so strong, Talon. With all she's been through… every challenge makes her stronger."

"Sounds like something I told you the day we met." Talon pulls her chin high and gives her a soft kiss along the curve of her jaw.

"Hey Talon, I see you got the new *Seventeen*," Lev calls.

He's around the corner in the small living room. Shadow has to wonder if it's just his strange sense of humor or if he's completely out of touch with the way humans do things.

"That's Cloud's," Shadow answers. "We got you a copy of *Six Hundred and Seventeen.*"

"Arf, arf," is the odd reply. The middle aged gryphon has as much to learn about being human as Cloud.

Talon pushes Shadow a little further down the short hall as he closes Cloud's door.

Lev usually gets the hint they want to be alone and returns to the cabin he shares with Firn but not tonight. After helping Cloud frost another batch of cupcakes he'd stoked the fire as she got ready for bed. Now he alternates between lurking around the kitchenette and putting his big booted feet up on the coffee table while several more cupcakes disappear.

"Soar says Cloud did well testing her wings this evening," Lev says.

So that's it.

In spite of Lev's assertion they're safe in the cabins, Talon and Soar are impatient to get everyone under Shadow's protective magic. Cloud's story of bleeding on the eyrie doorstep and promising her loyalty will come to pass only after Shadow claims her rule by doing the same thing.

Cloud's stitches are out and much of her mobility has been restored after Torrent's terrible attack, so there's really no reason to stick around any longer other than to feel near Terry. There's a whole other side of her brother to get to know.

"I suppose," Shadow answers.

"I have news as well," Lev continues.

Talon turns away before resting his chin on top of Shadow's head to avoid her look. He's heard the news already.

"The Jasper Eyrie has gone silent. Word is Torrent has returned."

"We can only hope alone," Shadow wishes out loud. There are so many kind gryphons in Jasper and Torrent could be sick enough to bring the remains of his rogue army with him.

"As I've explained," Lev says as his boots thump the table

top. "Swift's murder is a matter settled by his eyrie. The other allegations against him will be taken before the grand council but they will be hesitant to destroy the Jasper Eyrie because of his actions. Our priority is getting our gryphons home. Cloud feels well enough to make the flight so we check out tomorrow and head to the transition house. Feather is not fit to fly so we will take her in a litter."

"Yes, sire," Shadow concedes. Her sire is right, of course.

Feather is able to shuffle around the cabin she shares with her caregiver, Dove, and is grateful for her welcome into Shadow's eyrie. Dove believes it will be months before she's flying again. Daily treatments of Dove's magic steadily repair her spinal damage and calm the raging neurons and seizures from her head injury.

Tundra, the big gryphon from Welch Peak now bears the mark of Shadow's guard and when not assigned above with Soar and the others, spends his time near Feather. He's also Dove's twin and Firn's son and his long absence infiltrating the rogues on behalf of Sire Lev had been difficult on the family which still feels the absence of its sire.

Talon pulls her chin higher grazing her throat with his teeth. Shadow looks forward to seeing him with his shirt off all the time in the eyrie. Since living in the cabin he's returned to sleeping with his clothes on, barely undressing for sex.

"In the meantime," Lev says. "It's a moonless night. Heavy fog."

"Yes, sire," she says again, running her hands over Talon's denim covered butt and dragging one forward hoping to encourage some interest in the bedroom. Not that Talon ever needs any and tonight is no exception. Shadow feels the prickle of his chest feathers through his shirt before he gets them under control.

It sounds like Lev is finally making an excuse to leave and join the guard patrols aloft but then his heavy sigh derails Shadow's plans.

"A *clever* white gryphon would have no trouble hiding in the trees from a big thug like Talon."

"Really," Shadow whispers as he gets his teeth around the side of her neck. Big tease. She digs a single finger into his ribs. Talon hisses and catches her wrist as he turns away.

"Hunt," Talon says so softly she has to shift her hearing to gryphon sharpness to make it out. "There's nowhere for you to hide, little gryphon. The longer it takes you to surrender the worse it will be for you."

"Oh fuck, Talon," she gasps as she wraps around him, making contact with every inch of her body she can.

"Anyways," Lev says loudly. "I thought I would look around for that copy of *Six Hundred and Seventeen*, help myself to some of Cloud's baking and… babysit for you," he pauses either for effect or because he's not sure of the word.

They don't need him to volunteer twice.

Outside on the unlit porch, Talon is still fussing with his boots by the time Shadow's slid out of her sweats and T. She steps behind and as he leans over she kicks him squarely in the ass, knocking him sprawling.

Three strides later Shadow dives naked from the porch, taking wing before she can land. The salty air picks her up and she tumbles several times as Talon's roar fills the black beach.

"Oh, shit," she gasps as she swoops around behind the cabin. Talon's heavy steps are nearly lost in the crash of the big surf. With her mouth dry with sick fear and heated inside more than she ever imagined, Shadow disappears into the trees.

Sun cleanses the stone opening to Shadow's new eyrie. There's no magic in the act but the eldest common female pouring moonwater around the opening has long been a tradition. Sun is nearly nine hundred and is proud to welcome Shadow as she had Treasure nearly three hundred years before.

Shadow stands alone in the entrance and draws her Dame's small dagger. Lev looks on, chin held high with pride, as Shadow draws it across her palm. The blade is sharp and much to her relief the wound is nearly painless.

"My Sire, my gryphons," she calls loudly so the eyrie residents circling above can hear. As she pauses, the afternoon sunshine breaks through the clouds above, setting her platinum adornment afire and filling the salt-white entry with light. The first lamp ignites followed by the next and into the gentle upward curve of the tunnel. "My blood, my love, my service."

Shadow waits with Lev as her gryphons enter, each bowing and bidding her welcome. Last to enter are Talon, Cloud and the four who bear Feather in the litter.

As everyone waits, Talon and Cloud help Feather to her knees. Before Shadow, Lev and the eyrie's gryphons they bind themselves in blood to their new home.

ELIZABETH MUNRO

Thank you for reading Wingspan. Writing it has been an amazing experience and sharing it with others has made that experience even better. Other readers would love to hear your thoughts on this book (or any others you have enjoyed!) Please take a moment to visit your favourite online retailer or website such as www.goodreads.com or www.shelfari.com and share your thoughts. Your support helps small publishers and independent writers continue to provide great and original stories!

Thank you.

ELIZABETH MUNRO

Skyfall, Taken on the Wing #2

When Cloud receives the news she's been expelled from Master Sky's ranger training program, the last gryphon she expects to find waiting at her den is her old lover Soar. Now she's the only magic royal gryphon with the skills to get inside a corrupt Calgary eyrie and Soar needs her in more ways than one. Cloud has little choice but to accept the mission. Success will get her back in Sky's good books but accepting Soar as her working partner will either heal her broken heart or ruin it completely.

Master Soar walked out of Cloud's life when her departure to the ranger program was inevitable. She was young, motivated and beautiful. Too young to tie herself to a troublemaker like him and as much as it hurt it was better to not hold her back. But when the Calgary eyrie is at the centre of a conspiracy to destroy his own he's forced to play every card he has, including Cloud. When Cloud shuts him out and starts to operate on her own he has no choice but to go in after her, risking the entire mission to get the gryphon he loves out alive.

...coming 2014 (or sooner)

Rovian Descent

Rovian colonist Terra Cossatina had her perfect man, her bodyguard Victor, until she nearly killed him. Given away by her crime boss father to Carl 'the Scar' Tompson in exchange for half of the Southern Dome casinos her new fiancé blackmails her. Carl will kill her secret lover Victor unless she accepts him completely on their wedding night. Refusing to accept her arranged marriage she goes through Carl's friend, her lover Victor, to kill him. Now disowned by her father for destroying his business deal and taking contracts from the scum her family used to snub just to make ends meet, she returns to Victor desperate to put the past behind her...

Handsome and deadly Victor Voss had his perfect woman until she stood next to his best friend to announce their engagement. Victor had no choice but to try and be happy for Carl and his boss' daughter Terra if he's to keep their past a secret. Still healing from Terra's deadly on Carl and her emotional betrayal and on the verge of the biggest deal of his life, Victor has to choose between Terra, the woman he may never forgive and turning her over to his rival in a deal which will put him at the head of her father's crumbling empire...

Set in the twenty-sixth century, humans have lived on Earth's sister planet for hundreds of years. Once called Mars, her new inhabitants quickly rejected Earth's control and renamed their new home Rovi after Rovi Singh, the quiet genius who led their rebellion. After severing ties with Earth the new Rovians set to building a society very much like the one they were ignoring back home; schools, cities, and hospitals and crime...

Excerpt:

Terra quickly stuffed her jacket into her large purse as she took the final turn which put her in the hall to Victor's apartment. If he wasn't home she knew a few other places to look but she guessed it wouldn't take him long to find her. The bribe she'd paid at the airlock got her quietly through and she was quite certain the ill-tempered man who took it would sweeten his mood collecting a few more creds from Victor for announcing her passage.

At his door she pushed her stilettos in with the coat and put the bag down. She pressed the buzzer and stepped back. Without the contents of her jacket pockets and her shoes she was effectively disarmed.

It was nearly a minute before Victor's door opened. The interior of his suite was completely black and Terra slowly raised her hands. She waited, surprisingly calm, for him to speak. His reaction to her could be anything but she expected anger or worse.

"Slowly kick your bag in here, Terra," Victor's low

voice said. The tone he used when trying to push back a challenge without violence. The tone said he'd have no trouble pulling out all the stops if his challenger didn't back down.

Terra kept her eyes down so Victor wouldn't think she was trying to place his position in his dark living room. Her left foot slowly pushed her purse forward and her arms extended to check her balance as her foot went further out. She got a glimpse of his foot as he knocked it aside.

"Inside," he ordered. She knew to move slowly though it didn't much matter with him. When Victor was focused nothing moved faster than he did.

Within a second of the door closing she was up against a wall, her hands up, palms flat on either side of a bright light.

"Keep them open, Princess," he muttered as his hands ran the length of her body checking for concealed weapons then up under her skirt and between her legs. When he checked her long sleeves she caught a glimpse of his dark glasses. As her eyes adjusted to the light his were protected. If she tried anything the light and the glasses would disappear and he'd have the advantage of sight.

Instead Terra assessed the senses he hadn't taken away. Other than their breathing and the wall and floor she touched there was nothing but the smallest hint of a fragrance Victor didn't wear. She could smell his usual scent and the unfamiliar one didn't come from him. She suspected there were more than two people in the apartment.

"Why have you come here," he asked.

Terra pressed her lips together. Asking forgiveness was personal and nobody had known about her and Victor. Except Carl, her fiancé, and he was dead. She wouldn't say a thing unless she was sure they were alone.

"Hm?" he tried again. Victor placed his palm between her shoulders and ran it down her spine as his other rested on her stomach. His stinger, a small device custom fit to his hand would be up against her back. It charged from his energy and he could discharge it causing anything from a bad burn to a hole the size of a fist. Bad news if used on any critical part of the body.

Terra gently shook her head. Even asking to be alone with him could say too much about what they'd been.

"So it's going to be like that," Victor whispered.

"Yeah, just like that," Terra replied. She was sure they weren't alone as the fragrance from the other man in Victor's living room grew stronger then she heard the smallest sound of movement about ten feet behind her. "Just like that."

The stinger on her tailbone electrified her skin as Victor struggled with his control. The thing shouldn't be used by anyone who wasn't in complete command of himself but if she could trust anyone to not vaporize her spine in any mood it was him. His left hand crept higher and she felt the cool smooth tip of a hypo for a split second before it delivered its load into her carotid.

Within a second the smell of strawberries seemed to invade her nose.

"Just like that," Victor whispered.

Terra knew how it was going to go. Victor was going to ask her a few questions and she was going to dream. If she cooperated the dreams would be good. The drug made sure she could only tell the truth, but a lot of things were true even if they weren't answers to his questions. Evasiveness could be terrifying for the consciousness when the subconscious was left in charge.

"Weee're goingggggg to have a taaaaaa..." Victor's voice trailed off in an electronic stutter as his hand stroked her suddenly feathered ass. Then it reached up between her shoulders and stroked her again.

"It's soooo soft Mom," Terra whispered, looking up at her mother's smile as she felt the smooth peregrine feathers on her palm. A good memory to be sure. She was ten and one of the parents had brought the stuffed falcon in for Nature Day. Her father had laughed at the whole idea since people were the only Rovian nature and who the hell would bring a dead bird all the way out here? Mom was as excited as Terra so grumpy

Bruno, Dad's number one security guard, accompanied Mom to school with Terra to see it.

"Everyone had a turn?" Terra looked at the voice and saw old Miss Willis speak. She would pass away before the year was out and Terra still missed her. "The only peregrines left on Earth live in captivity. The very air poisons them and makes their egg shells too thin for their chicks to survive. Their habitats are carefully monitored so the few left can stay healthy."

Just like us, Terra thought. Captives in our domes. Poison outside just like Rovi.

She felt Victor's hand pass down her spine again as the teacher went on about extinction and she wondered if they were going extinct too. Terra reached for her mother's hand for comfort and felt a chill where it should be. When she looked down her mother's hand was grey and boney and Terra's passed right through.

"Give me his NAME!" her father bellowed and for a brief moment Terra saw her parents fighting. Her mother stood face to face with him, his fists at his sides daring her to challenge him any further than she already had. It was the night of the peregrine or maybe another. Young Terra had hidden in the other end of the family apartment and turned on some music to drown it out. Then she was in the hospital, twenty standard years old and Frank was yelling the same thing at her he'd yelled at her mother. Her face stung hard and tears filled her eyes.

"You spoiled yourself!" He went on. "It's bad enough your cheating mother didn't give me a son then you follow in her footsteps with some college boy?"

Frank smacked her again only this time his hand was closed. Her hand was over her cheek and the fist hit near her eye dislocating a finger.

"I'll find out," Frank ranted, his face was almost as purple as Terra's eye felt. "And you better damn well hide it when I find someone to cash you in on."

They were alone in the hospital room and this wasn't

all a dream. It was also a memory. Victor had been away on business for Frank for weeks and Terra had woken up in a puddle of blood. The maid called her an ambulance and within a few hours Frank barged in demanding to know which boy had knocked her up.

It wouldn't have happened on Victor's watch Frank said unaware of the irony that the baby had been Victor's. Supposedly sterile Victor's. After serving two years in a surface labour camp before he turned nineteen Victor's fertility had been all but erased by the poor shielding of the domes and EVA suits. Frank would later order Victor to figure out who hit her for refusing him since she wouldn't say and Frank was too ashamed of his damaged princess to tell Victor the truth. So was Terra.

She looked down through her tears and pain to the mass of blood and feathers between her legs then back at Frank, locked in a birdcage with her. Its shell had been far too thin to protect it and it quivered and cried like a weak newborn, bumping up against her thighs before it stilled. Frank's hand came back one more time and knocked her to the bed.

Terra lay on her side, feeling the soft pressure of a mattress beneath her. Certain her conscious and subconscious were finding their way back together she didn't move. The body didn't respond well to their reintegration and Terra knew if she did any more than breathe during the next ten minutes it could be as bad as a stroke. She relaxed as she became aware of the snug grip around her wrists holding them above her head.

"Good girl," Victor said in front of her.

Terra didn't open her eyes. The bed smelled of him; the taste of his skin and the subtle chocolaty scent of the tobacco he occasionally indulged in. They'd only spent one night in his bed or any bed for that matter; for three years they had seen each other in secret where ever they could until Frank announced her engagement to a man who didn't share Frank's picture of the ideal virginal bride. If she opened her eyes she'd see Victor standing in front of the full wall window providing a blue tinged view of the surface of Rovi. Most apartments didn't have a view. Victor had decorated the place in the rusts and browns of the surface, colours most Rovians avoided.

"So you've set up a bit of insurance to make sure you get home," he said. "And your shoes are in your bag."

She understood why the dream had started out pleasant and turned ugly. Her subconscious wasn't very co-operative. Terra stayed still. The only person she'd seen the drug used on ran for his life as soon as he got his wits about him and died of a massive stroke before he could get to the door.

"You've either caused me a great deal of trouble, Terra," Victor whispered. "Or single handedly brought your father's empire to its knees."

... Coming in 2013

ELIZABETH MUNRO

Deadly Expectations

The Chronicles of Anna Book 1

As a teen Anna Creed discovers she can time travel; a trick she uses to 'jump' from one place to another with no apparent passage of time. All she needs are two wheels, speed and nerves of steel. Now eight years later she's alone and pregnant when her secret power takes control to save her life. Injured and confused Anna finds herself in the arms of Paul Richards, her summer lover and the father of her child.

But Paul has secrets of his own. He's the head of an old conflict weary family and has been Anna's past life lover time and time again, something only he remembers.

ELIZABETH MUNRO

Things come apart for Anna when she starts 'jumping' in her sleep. Both Anna and her sister are in mortal danger from Paul's uncle Damian and a ghost from her past life is driving her to murder. As Anna and Paul's fledgling relationship unravels she takes the final and unforgivable step of attacking him and leaving him behind.

From Northern California to the rainforests of British Columbia Anna gets closer to the truth about Paul's family and the realization that saving Paul and her unborn child may ultimately cost her life.

...on sale now, ebook is FREE